Acclaim for
Someone to Watch Over Me

Virginia Romance Writers Fool for Love Award Winner

"*Someone to Watch Over Me* combines a classic tale of romantic suspense with an ending that took me by surprise. This fast read kept me up late, turning pages, and reluctant to put the book down. Truly romantic and sensual...the perfect balance of peril and passion." — *Wall Street Journal* bestselling author Larissa Reinhart

"Lois Winston is a talented author who never fails to deliver realistic characters, unusual situations, and humor. This book is no exception..." —Amazon reviewer

"...a complicated plot, requiring substantial research. More importantly, her characters are immensely likeable and believable, and the romance is sizzling." — Amazon reviewer

Dori sensed his presence before she saw him. She had expected Mr. York to check in on her, but Mr. York didn't charge the fine hairs on the back of her neck and make them stand at attention. Mr. York, for all his bluster, didn't fill her with a sense of foreboding the way the other man did. Glancing up from the script she was studying in the corner of the television studio, she wasn't surprised to find him assessing her from across the room. A shiver scampered up her spine. She had no idea why this man made her so nervous. She had no idea who he was or his relation to Mr. York. All she knew was that she felt as fearful as cornered prey whenever he came near her.

Books by Lois Winston

Anastasia Pollack Crafting Mystery series
Assault with a Deadly Glue Gun
Death by Killer Mop Doll
Revenge of the Crafty Corpse
Decoupage Can Be Deadly
A Stitch to Die For
Scrapbook of Murder
Drop Dead Ornaments
Handmade Ho-Ho Homicide
A Sew Deadly Cruise
Stitch, Bake, Die!
Guilty as Framed
A Crafty Collage of Crime
Sorry, Knot Sorry

Anastasia Pollack Crafting Mini-Mysteries
Crewel Intentions
Mosaic Mayhem
Patchwork Peril
Crafty Crimes (all 3 novellas in one volume)

Empty Nest Mystery Series
Definitely Dead
Literally Dead

Romantic Suspense
Love, Lies and a Double Shot of Deception
Lost in Manhattan
Someone to Watch Over Me

Romance and Chick Lit
Talk Gertie to Me
Four Uncles and a Wedding
Hooking Mr. Right
Finding Hope

Novellas and Novelettes

Elementary, My Dear Gertie
Moms in Black, A Mom Squad Caper
Once Upon a Romance
Finding Mr. Right

Children's Chapter Book

The Magic Paintbrush

Nonfiction

Top Ten Reasons Your Novel is Rejected
House Unauthorized
Bake, Love, Write
We'd Rather Be Writing

Someone To Watch Over Me

LOIS WINSTON
Writing as Emma Carlyle

Cover design by L. Winston

ISBN-13: 978-1-940795-15-7

"I want to do it because I want to do it. Women must try to do things as men have tried. When they fail, their failure must be but a challenge to others." – Amelia Earhart

DEDICATION

To all the women who persist and persevere.

PROLOGUE

Philadelphia, 2006

"Dasha! More vodka!"

Dasha dropped the pot and scouring pad into the sink, grabbed another bottle of Stoli, and scurried across the kitchen. She stifled a yawn as she squinted through the tobacco-laden haze of the room at the clock over the stove. Another endless night of playing bar wench and scullery maid to her father and his vile cronies stretched out before her. What did they care that she had a calculus exam in less than nine hours?

Sergei Ivanichek slammed the deck of cards onto the table and yanked the bottle from her still sudsy grasp. "Guests first, stupid girl. Where's your manners?" With a shaky hand he reached across the table to refill the three other glasses. The bottle clinked against Borka's glass, spilling a small amount of the clear alcohol onto the plastic tablecloth.

Borka snorted. He stubbed out his cigarette and lit another. "I think Sergei's had too much. Maybe now we can win back some of that money the thief's stolen from us tonight."

Grunting his agreement, Yuri took the bottle from Sergei and handed it back to Dasha. "Pour."

She did as she was told, then wiped up the puddle. After a loud belch, Sergei resumed shuffling, dealing each player several cards. Yuri and Vanya studied their hands, but Borka left his cards on the table, reaching for Dasha instead.

"Lovely," he said, wrapping his large, hairy arm around her waist. "You've grown into a real beauty, Dasha. I remember when you were no bigger than my knee. You'll make a good wife." He lowered his hand and stroked her backside.

Dasha jumped. Borka howled with amusement. Tightening his grasp, he pulled her down onto what little lap he had. The cigarette dangled from the corner of his mouth, ashes dropping onto her. One fat hand stroked her cheek. The hair-coated knuckles of his other hand grazed across her breast.

Dasha stiffened and winced. As much as she wanted to grab the vodka bottle and smash it over his head, she knew better than to cross any of the men sitting around her father's table. So she clenched her fists and bit her tongue.

Borka roared with laughter. "What are you now? Fifteen? Sixteen?"

Instead of answering, Dasha tried to squirm free. Borka's expression grew lecherous. "I may be old, but I'm still strong as a bull." He winked at the other men. "In every way that counts."

Yuri elbowed Vanya in the ribs. "And that's no bull."

The four men yucked it up.

Dasha froze.

"Seventeen," said Sergei, answering for her. He gulped down another shot of vodka.

"Seventeen?" Borka's beady blue eyes grew wide with excitement.

"And the boy?" asked Vanya, motioning across the room to her brother Yusif.

Sergei glanced at his son. "Thirteen," he muttered around his cigarette, but his eyes gleamed.

Dasha knew that look. Her father was as easy to read as a street sign. It was the same look that came over him whenever he made a killing at the track or at the craps tables in Atlantic City. Sergei Ivanichek worshipped a green god with multiple zeros. She exchanged wary glances with her brother. He, too, had seen the glint in his father's eyes.

"I'll take them both," said Borka. His hand slid up Dasha's thigh. "My bed has been cold and empty for too long. Vanya can put the boy to work on the docks." He turned to his second-in-command. "Yes?"

Vanya nodded.

"How much?" asked Sergei.

Borka shrugged. "We'll work the details out tomorrow, my friend. Tonight, we celebrate." He removed the cigarette from his mouth and raised his glass in a toast. The three other men followed suit. "To my new bride!" he said, settling his free hand between Dasha's legs.

All four men downed their vodka in one gulp. Then grabbing the back of Dasha's head, Borka forced his tongue deep into her mouth, muffling her frightened cry. "Ha! You have much to learn, Dasha," he said, breaking the kiss, "and I will enjoy teaching you."

He pushed her from his lap. "Pour another round, girl!"

* * *

Hours later Dasha lay awake in the double bed she shared with her younger sister. Thankfully, Anika had fallen asleep before Borka, Yuri, and Vanya arrived. Out of sight, out of mind. Dasha shuddered. God only knew what fate they might have assigned the frail nine-year-old had she been awake. Sergei resented every penny he shelled out for his children's upkeep. He'd jump at the chance to rid himself of Anika, as well—especially if there were profit in it. The child stirred, snuggling her tiny body closer to her sister.

Every time Dasha closed her eyes, she saw a fat, hairy hand crushing her dreams. Felt a wet, slimy tongue choking the life from her. She stifled a sob. She had plans for her future, and they didn't include being forced to marry a man old enough to be her grandfather. This was America, not Russia. The twenty-first century, not the nineteenth. To everyone except Sergei Ivanichek and his throwback cohorts.

Even though her father had emigrated to America years before she was born, Sergei still held fast to his distant aristocratic roots. Dasha had long ago given up trying to discern truth from prevarication in what spilled from her father's often less-than-sober lips. Was he the descendent of a bastard of the House of Romanoff?

Over the years she'd heard the same claim from half the Russian-American population of Northeast Philadelphia. She found it highly unlikely that Czar Nicholas and his randy relatives had sown their seed from St. Petersburg all the way to Sergei's native Volgograd.

In the next room she heard her father snoring the sleep of a man who had drunk himself into a stupor. After he agreed to sell his son and daughter, Sergei and his friends had partied well into the night. Dasha knew from experience he wouldn't wake until late afternoon.

Across the room she heard her brother rise. The squeaking floorboards echoed his progression from the bed to the closet. "Yusif! What are you doing?" she whispered.

"I'm going to kill that greedy son of a bitch! He's not going to do this to us."

Dasha leaned over and flicked on the bedside lamp. Her brother stood barefoot in the middle of the room, clutching a baseball bat. "No," she said. "Put that down." The time had come to implement her plan.

"Dasha!"

"Get dressed, Yusif."

ONE

New York City
Six Years Later

"No! No! No!" With a sweep of his arm Niles York rid his desk of the four dozen eight-by-ten glossies.

Jake Prentiss sat back on the couch and watched the advertising executive seated across from Niles drop his jaw. His body soon followed as he scurried on all fours to retrieve the scattered photos. "But, sir." The man flattened himself onto his belly to fish several photos from under the massive inlaid desk. "These are top models. Some of the most beautiful women in the world."

"Beautiful, Hornlein? *Beautiful?*"

Hornlein hauled his whining, sorry ass off the floor and panted out a weak, "Yes, sir."

Niles grabbed the photos and waved them in front of Hornlein's face. "If this is your idea of beauty, maybe I need a new agency to represent my companies." He turned to Jake. "Am I being unreasonable? Do you find any of these women remotely pretty, let alone beautiful?"

Jake rose from the sofa and sauntered across the room. He thumbed through the photos Niles offered him. "I suppose if you're into anorexia, silicone, Botox, and peroxide."

"Thank you! I'm glad someone understands." Niles took the photos from Jake and shoved them at Hornlein. "He gets it, and he's not even in the business. Why can't you?"

"I'm certain we can find the right spokesperson for you if you just give us a chance, Mr. York."

"We're set to open the flagship store in less than two months. Your agency's had more than enough time. I want someone signed, sealed, and delivered by the end of next week, or I pull the account. Is that clear?"

"Yes, sir." He tamped the creased photos into a pile and placed them in his briefcase. With the briefcase clutched to his chest, he bobbed his balding head up and down as he backed out of the office. "By the end of next week."

"Moron," muttered Niles. "No wonder I have an ulcer." He strode across the room to a wall of built-in cabinets and pulled a bottle of Scotch from one of the shelves.

"That will help," said Jake.

Niles grunted. Filling two glasses, he handed one to Jake. "Don't play mother. I get enough of that from Beatrice."

Jake tossed back the Scotch in one gulp. "How is the lovable old battle ax?"

Niles choked down his own drink with a grimace. "Feisty as

ever and thankfully off to Palm Beach for the season."

"Miss her already, huh?"

Niles sank into the sofa and propped his feet up on the freeform marble coffee table. "Actually, I'm glad to be rid of her for now. She thinks I'm going to lose my shirt on this one, and you know mother. She doesn't exactly keep her opinions to herself."

"Any chance she's right?"

"I hope not. I think I've got a great concept. I did my homework, Jake. The market research agrees with me. Women today want the convenience of one-stop shopping, but my target consumer also wants selection and quality, not cheap schlock made in China, Pakistan, or Bangladesh. Being on a budget shouldn't have to mean having to settle for second best. That's the whole concept behind N.Y. McStore. The acronym says it all."

"Not-Your-Mother's-Chain-Store."

"Exactly! No housecoats. No tabloids. And definitely nothing that will fall apart after one washing or break as soon as the limited warranty expires. Everything we carry will not only be upscale but affordable, it will be made in America. And bowing to the modern family-oriented career woman who's already dealing with time constraints, we'll be offering all our merchandise not only through retail establishments, but in catalogs and over the Internet." Niles paused, the exuberance draining from his features. "But like any new venture, nothing is guaranteed. Beatrice could be right."

"Then it's a good thing you have a closet full of shirts." Jake eyed his muscular friend. Several inches shorter and at least a dozen pounds heavier than he, Niles still looked like a wide receiver—even if he hadn't set foot onto the Notre Dame gridiron in nearly two decades. "My shirts would never fit you."

Niles snorted. "Some friend you are. Won't even give me the

shirt off your back."

Jake reached for his top button. "Be my guest."

"That's quite all right." He held up a hand. "At least I know where to turn if it comes down to that."

"Any time, buddy. You know that. So tell me, why all this angst over someone to smile at the cameras and cut a few ribbons?"

Niles paced back and forth across the room. "I'm not looking for arm candy. I want a face that will become synonymous with N.Y. McStore but also someone who can identify with its concept. She'll be our spokesperson on TV and radio. Her face will be plastered across billboards and on buses. She'll be at every store opening and online for chats with customers. She has to be someone our customers can relate to, someone who knows what it's like to live within a budget and juggle a career and family responsibilities. I want my shoppers to think of her as a kindred soul."

"And your target market wouldn't associate with a woman who looked like she spent her days doing nothing more than getting her hair and nails done."

"Exactly. So why is that so hard for Hornlein and the rest of those Madison Avenue idiots to understand?"

Jake was about to tell Niles he thought Hornlein was more interested in rubbing shoulders—not to mention various other body parts—with the models he'd suggested, but a light knock on the door cut him short.

"Come in," Niles called, his voice gruff with annoyance.

* * *

From the other side of the door Dori Johnson heard the irritation in Mr. York's voice. She hesitated. The earlier rumblings of dissension emanating from the corporate office had ceased with the departure of one very rattled looking man, but it was obvious that Mr. York was still in one of his infamous moods.

A mere low-level drone in the York empire, Dori had never before come face-to-face with the volatile CEO and therefore, had never been on the receiving end of one of his legendary tirades. She wanted to keep it that way.

Glancing down at the package delivered moments earlier by courier, she wondered if she had made a huge mistake. Although stamped URGENT in large red letters, maybe it wasn't urgent enough for her to be disturbing the owner and chief executive officer. Maybe it could have waited until Mrs. Henshaw returned from her dentist appointment.

And maybe she should have thought of *that* before rapping her knuckles against the solid mahogany door. Now it was too late. She'd committed herself. Taking a deep breath, she turned the brass knob and crossed the threshold into the CEO's office.

"I'm sorry to disturb you, sir, but this just arrived." She held out the envelope without venturing further into the room. "It's marked urgent."

Mr. York, his features set in a stern grimace, turned from the other man in the room and confronted her. For several interminable seconds only the sound of Dori's rapidly beating heart filled her ears and the utter stillness blanketing the office. She stood motionless while Mr. York studied her as though he were sizing her up—or worse yet, undressing her. Dori couldn't be certain which. Neither pleased her.

She silently counted to ten and bit down on her tongue, stifling the acerbic comment that had nearly sprung from her lips. If she didn't keep her mouth firmly clamped, she'd guarantee herself a place on the unemployment line before the day ended.

To divert herself, she hazarded a quick glance at the other man. Dressed in a pair of faded denim jeans, scuffed loafers, and a bulky cream and gray Scandinavian sweater, he at first appeared completely out of place in the well-appointed setting. His body language, however, told otherwise. His long legs stretched out across the coffee table. One arm rested on his thigh. The other draped the back of the leather sofa. Although he hadn't uttered a word, the man exuded an air of self-confidence that bordered on arrogance. He focused his attention on Mr. York.

When he caught Dori staring at him, he trapped her gaze with blue-black eyes as dark as his slightly unkempt, thick head of hair and two-day growth of beard. Dori took a step backwards, swallowing a gasp. Her scalp tingled. Beneath her ribbed turtleneck, gooseflesh rose on her arms. Niles York might be undressing her with his eyes, but she sensed this man was far more dangerous. She had the unsettling feeling that he saw directly into her innermost thoughts.

The corners of his mouth turned up marginally as if he were privy to some private joke, but the smile didn't extend to his eyes, which remained dark and foreboding. Then he cleared his throat, breaking both his grip on Dori and the silence that had wrapped itself around the room.

"Who the hell are you?" barked Mr. York. "Where's Henshaw?"

Stay calm. Don't let him rattle you, and for God's sake, don't be a smart ass. She squared her shoulders and fought back the anger threatening to enter her voice. "Mrs. Henshaw broke a tooth at lunch, sir. She's at the dentist. I work downstairs in Human Resources. I'm just filling in until she returns."

"You work for me?"

Smile, damn it! She pasted a smile across her face and answered. "Yes, sir."

Mr. York continued jabbing his finger in her direction as he turned to the man seated on the sofa. "*This*, Jake. This is what I want. She's perfect."

The man on the sofa—Jake—stood. He crossed the room, his gaze slowly raking up and down her body. "Yes, she is, but I think you might want to rephrase that statement, Niles, before you have this young woman screaming sexual harassment to the EEOC." He turned those piercing near-ebony eyes on her once more. "What's your name?"

"Johnson." The word came out in a choked whisper. "Dori Johnson."

The man nodded. "Well, Johnson Dori Johnson, I think you'd better come sit down. Niles is about to make you an offer you can't refuse."

Still holding firm to the doorknob, Dori glanced over her shoulder. "But the phone—"

"Screw the phone," said Mr. York. "Get in here, and close the door behind you."

All the gossip she'd heard about Niles York didn't come close to preparing Dori for the bizarre situation she'd stumbled into. Suddenly she knew beyond a doubt how Alice felt as she plummeted down the rabbit hole. She stole a furtive glance in the direction of Mr. York's friend Jake. The CEO rattled her, but for some reason this man's very presence raised a host of red flags within her, filling her with an overwhelming urge to flee. Reluctantly, she closed the door and stepped farther into the office.

"Over there," said Mr. York, waving at the black leather sofa.

"Sit down." As she passed in front of him, she offered him the mailer. He snatched it out of her hand and tossed it across the room. "I don't have time for this nonsense." The envelope landed several feet shy of his desk.

Dori jumped. What in the world was going on? She hadn't tumbled down a rabbit hole, she'd stepped into some weird alternate universe!

Jake laughed. "Such tact, Niles." He took hold of Dori's elbow. "Maybe we'd better get you out of the line of fire."

The instant his fingers made contact with her arm, Dori's brain latched onto the romance novel she'd been reading the night before. Jake's touch, although gentlemanly, rocked her in much the same way Lady Bromshire had responded to Lord Farnsworth. And to think she'd actually scoffed when she'd read those passages about waves of searing heat rippling through the heroine's body. She'd never scoff again.

Jake gently nudged her toward the sofa. At first, she couldn't move. Then, when she realized he was staring at her, she pulled her arm from his grasp and willed herself to cover the short distance on her own. With every step she felt the heat of his gaze on her back.

Once seated, Dori forced her attention from Jake to Mr. York. He'd made his way to a row of cabinets on the other side of the room. "Coffee?" he asked her.

"No...no, thank you. Sir."

Mr. York poured two cups of coffee and returned to the seating area. After handing one cup to Jake, he dropped into an overstuffed chair opposite the sofa, crossed his legs, and took a sip of his coffee. Jake seated himself on the sofa next to her.

"How long have you worked for me, Miss Johnson?"

Years ago, Dori had vowed never to let any man control her destiny; yet, although she had no idea what was going on here, she had the strangest sense that her life was about to change. Dramatically.

Perched on the edge of the couch, she studied her questioner. What did he really want? CEOs didn't invite the corporate serfs into the office for tea and crumpets. "Six years," she said, trying to keep the suspicion out of her voice.

"Six years? You don't look old enough."

"I finished school early," she lied, dodging the insinuated question. By law she was under no obligation to divulge her age, but it was apparent that Mr. York expected her to offer the information. Lacing her fingers together on her lap, she fought the urge to flee. Questions about her past made her nervous.

"College graduate?"

"Not yet. I take evening courses."

"In marketing?"

"And computer science."

"Ever do any modeling?"

Modeling? The absurd question took her by surprise. "No, of course not."

"Ever want to?"

Of course she had wanted to. Doesn't every pubescent girl yearn to be the next Heidi Klum or Gisele Bundchen? At various points in her life, she'd also harbored dreams of winning a gold medal in figure skating, walking in space, and being the first woman president—none of which had or would ever occur for obvious reasons. Hardly a leggy beauty, she wobbled on the ice, suffered from claustrophobia, and detested politics. So much for childhood fantasies. "No, not really." A nervous laugh peppered her words.

Mr. York raised an eyebrow. "You find the idea humorous, Miss Johnson?"

"I find it preposterous, Mr. York. I'm not exactly what you'd call model material."

"And why is that?"

Did the man need his eyes examined? "I'm neither tall enough, thin enough, nor glamorous enough," she said, losing the battle to keep her annoyance in check. She watched as Mr. York and Jake exchanged glances. What was the purpose of this cross examination? Before she had a chance to ask, Mr. York changed the subject.

"Let me tell you about my latest business venture, Miss Johnson."

And he did. For half an hour Niles York expounded on his N.Y. McStore concept as if he were selling the idea to a group of investors. He produced architectural renderings, marketing concept art, and demographic studies, tossing papers at her left and right until Dori's head buzzed from an overload of data.

Normally, she would have absorbed such information without trouble. She had a head for facts and figures. What she lacked was a defense for the man sitting beside her. Jake's hawk-like gaze bore into her throughout the CEO's long discourse. Doing her best not to let him rattle her, she tried to concentrate on Mr. York's words. At first, she couldn't fathom why she was the recipient of his long-winded presentation. Finally, it dawned on her.

Niles York confirmed her suspicions with his closing sentence. "I want you for the face and voice of N.Y. McStore, Miss Johnson."

TWO

Dori couldn't believe her ears. She also couldn't begin to consider such an offer. It was impossible. Taking a deep breath, she rose from the couch and stepped around the coffee table. "I'm flattered, Mr. York, but I'm afraid I can't possibly accept."

"What!" York jumped to his feet. "You can't possibly refuse! I'll double your salary."

Dori shook her head, somewhat bemused by his offer. Two times a pittance was still only double a pittance. "I'm sorry."

"Triple!"

The man must think her a fool. Even a low-level catalog model commanded higher fees, but it wasn't the money. "I have family obligations," she said. But that wasn't the real reason, either. Joey and Nikki were certainly old enough to fend for themselves for short periods of time. And there was always Mrs. Menotti, their grandmotherly next-door neighbor who had taken all three of them under her wing. The simple truth was, Dori couldn't risk having her face plastered on signs and billboards across the country.

But Niles York was not a man who accepted defeat. "Take the rest of the day off to think about it," he said. "We'll talk more tomorrow." With a wave of his hand, he dismissed both her and her rejection of his offer.

* * *

"So, what do you think?" Niles rubbed his hands together like a gourmand about to partake of a twelve-course feast. "Who needs Hornlein and his high-priced plastic mannequins?"

"I thought you were looking for someone a bit older," said Jake. "Remember? A woman juggling career and family? Dori Johnson doesn't look like she's much past her teens. No one's going to believe she's married with two point three kids, a house in the suburbs, and a minivan."

"So? I'm entitled to change my mind." Niles's words took on an air of petulance, as if he were trying to convince himself as well as Jake. "It's my company, isn't it?"

"Hey, man. I'm just reminding you of what you told me less than an hour ago."

"She's got a refreshing, wholesome quality to her, Jake. She'll appeal to the women I'm targeting. They'll identify with her. Besides, she's got an honest face."

Jake scowled. "Does she?"

"You spent too many years as an intelligence operative. You see conspiracies in your sleep. Leave them to your techno-thrillers. Dori Johnson is a sweet, innocent kid, not some Third World terrorist."

Jake shrugged. "She's hiding something. My radar isn't that

rusty. When I looked at her, warning bells clanged, and whistles blared."

Niles slapped him on the back. "I think it's because you're still licking your wounds from the last emerald-eyed, strawberry blonde to cross your path."

Jake turned away and stared at the original Georgia O'Keefe painting hanging above the couch. Gwynne Corth had picked him as clean as the bleached bones in the pastel desert landscape. His depleted bank account was reminder enough of the blessedly short but expensive coupling. "This has nothing to do with my former wife," he said through gritted teeth. "Besides, they don't look anything alike."

"Oh?" Niles raised an eyebrow. "Tell you what. Go pull your sleuthing cap out of mothballs and see what kind of dirt you can dig up on my new spokesperson. I'm willing to wager a week in St. Thomas that you won't find anything."

"Your new spokesperson? In case you've forgotten, she turned you down."

Niles acknowledged him with a smile only a man accustomed to winning could possess.

* * *

"I think you're crazy." Joey slammed his mug onto the Formica tabletop. "It's been six years. Nothing's happened. Nothing's going to happen."

Dori stared down into her now cold cup of tea. Maybe her brother was right. As head of the Russian-American Mafia in Philadelphia, Borka's network of connections reached throughout the country. If he'd really wanted to find her, he would have by now.

As for their father, she doubted he missed anything other than the three thousand dollars she'd taken from him—money that by rights belonged to her and her siblings. After his wife's death, Sergei had received monthly Social Security survivor benefits for his three children. On the first of each month, he cashed the check and headed for the track. Sometimes he won; sometimes he lost. Either way, Dori and her sister and brother never benefited from the money.

Still, they'd been lucky, and she saw no reason to push that luck. "You don't know that." She met her brother's stubborn gaze.

"You worry too much."

"I have plenty to worry about. Our new lives aren't exactly legitimate, you know." Dori figured she'd probably broken at least a dozen laws when she created new identities for the three of them, but she had no other choice. Legal methods took time and money, luxuries unavailable to her under the circumstances.

Thankfully, the Internet was a virtual how-to for anyone seeking to disappear. She'd also gained quite a bit of knowledge from years of serving Sergei and his mob cronies. The more vodka they poured down their gullets each night, the more their tongues loosened. These were no ordinary thugs, and this was not Don Corleone's mafia. Borka's genius lay in surrounding himself with high tech soldiers, men who could hack into computers as easily as they maimed and murdered. His crimes were committed both on the streets and in cyberspace.

Little did they suspect Sergei's daughter possessed both a photographic memory and a talent for all things computer related. Even hacking into the Social Security Administration to alter a few records proved easier than she'd expected.

So she'd committed a felony or two or twelve, but she worried less about the long arm of the law and more about the long reach of Borka's tentacles. "For everyone's sake," she told her brother, "yours, Nikki's, and mine—it's best that I keep a low profile."

Joey offered her one of his standard sarcastic smirks. His forehead wrinkled, his mouth skewed, his hazel eyes narrowed into two thin slits. He spit his next words out as an angry accusation that was more statement than question. "So you plan to spend the rest of your life as an anonymous corporate peon?"

"No, of course not. Once I have my degree, I'll be able to get a better job."

He snorted. "And when will that be? Three years? Five years? Ten years? You've already cut back your course load to bare bones because you insist I go to school full time. When I graduate, it will be Nikki's turn. And if you won't let me get a decent job to help out around here, you're sure as hell not going to let her. What about you, Dori? When is it going to be your turn?"

When, indeed? Dori often wondered that herself. When she fled Philadelphia six years earlier, she'd taken her thirteen-year-old brother and nine-year-old sister with her. Life would have been less complicated had she run off by herself, but she didn't regret her decision. She couldn't have left them to suffer the fate she'd escaped. If she had it to do all over again, she'd take the same path. "I don't know when my time will come, Joey, but that's the choice I've made. You and Nikki come first."

Joey jumped to his feet. "Come here." He yanked her off her chair. "I want to show you something." He raced down the hallway of the small apartment, dragging her behind him. At the bathroom he sandwiched her between himself and the sink. Taking hold of her face with both hands, he forced her to look in the mirror. "Take a good look. What do you see?"

Dori scowled, "You and me. Your point?"

"Right. You and me. Dori and Joseph Johnson." Releasing her face, he reached into his back pocket for his wallet and withdrew a tattered photo. "And who's this?" he asked shoving the picture under her nose.

Dori stared at the three faces in the photo, a young child still harboring the remnants of baby fat, a smooth-faced adolescent boy, and a gangly teenager with a mild case of acne. This was the only photograph that remained of the three of them. She'd learned from her Internet research to destroy all photographs before fleeing. That way her father and Borka's men would have no photos to aid them in their hunt.

She glanced back into the mirror. The contrast was startling.

"Look at us," Joey whispered. "We don't look anything like we did six years ago. Dasha, Anika, and Yusif Ivanichek no longer exist. No one is going to recognize you or any of us."

Taking the photo from Joey's hand, Dori held it up next to her reflection. The overly thin teenager with long dishwater braids and a vacant expression was nowhere to be seen in the face that stared back at her—shoulder-length strawberry blonde hair highlighting a creamy complexion and sea green eyes. True, the hair and eyes were compliments of Miss Clairol and Acuvue, but still, if she didn't know better, she'd think the image in the photo was a stranger, not herself six years earlier.

"You can't turn down an opportunity like this, sis. It's a once in a lifetime chance. Think of the possibilities.

She *had* thought about it. She had thought of little else since leaving the office several hours earlier. She had thought of it as she waited for the PATH train. She had thought of it throughout the ride back to Jersey City and her walk from the Journal Square station to the fifth-floor walk-up she shared with Nikki and Joey.

She had thought of it as she paced the four tiny rooms of their apartment, anxiously awaiting Joey's return from class.

And each time she'd dismissed the notion as impossible.

On the outside, Niles York's offer appeared to be a fairy tale come to life. Inside, Dori couldn't shake the specter of an evil ogre lurking in the background, waiting to swoop down and destroy the new life she'd created for herself and her siblings. And that ogre bore a striking resemblance to Boris Borka.

"No, it won't work. The job entails traveling. I can't leave you and Nikki alone."

"Nikki and I can take care of ourselves. It's not like we're kids anymore. Besides, there's always Mrs. Menotti."

The same argument Dori had given herself in Mr. York's office. But that still didn't address the real problem. What if someone *did* recognize her? And told Borka. Using threats against Nikki and Joey, he could blackmail her into marrying him.

Even if he no longer wanted her, Dori knew Borka. She'd overheard enough over the years, eavesdropping on conversations between the Russian crime boss and her father, his right-hand man. Borka would stop at nothing to retaliate for the slight to his ego. She'd done the unthinkable. No one defied Boris Borka and got away with it. Until Dori. Until now. She aimed to keep it that way.

"If you don't take this offer, you'll regret it for the rest of your life." Dori stared at Joey's image in the mirror. His scowl had reappeared with a vengeance. "I won't let you throw away your future for me and Nikki. We'll leave before we'll allow you to do that."

The bottom dropped out of Dori's stomach. *He couldn't mean that!* "Joey, don't. Please. You and Nikki are all I have."

He placed his hands on her shoulders and kissed the top of her head. "And you're all we have, sis, but there comes a time when you have to live your life for yourself and not others. This is your time. Grab it."

She covered his hand with one of hers, not unaware of the role reversal taking place. When had her little brother leaped years ahead of her? When had nineteen-year-old Joey become so wise?

"Did it ever occur to you that Borka might not even be alive anymore?"

Of course! Why hadn't she thought of that. Six years ago, Borka had been an overweight, hard drinking, sixty-year-old chain smoker. If his dubious business affairs hadn't caught up with him by now, surely his health had.

However, she had no way of knowing. Borka insulated himself with enough firewalls, both human and technical, that a Google search of his name never turned up anything more than speculation and rumor. Few people even knew him as Borka, only his trusted cronies. Even fewer knew what he really did for a living.

But the man had to be dead by now, given his lifestyle. Maybe she'd worried all these years for nothing. Maybe she could accept Mr. York's offer without fear of her past catching up with her. "You're sure you wouldn't mind if I took the position?"

"You mean you'll do it?"

She shrugged. Money was always tight. She made little enough to support one person, let alone three. Then there was tuition. Even though she and Joey attended a state school, the bills added up, and she couldn't risk blowing their cover by applying for scholarships or student loans. "It would certainly put an end to our strained finances."

Joey's face broke out in a huge grin. Whooping, he spun her

around, lifting her off her feet in a rib bruising bear hug.

"What's all the shouting about?" Dori heard the front door slam as Nikki called out from the living room.

Joey stuck his head around the doorway and shouted down the hall. "Dori's going to be famous, and we're going to be rich!"

Before that could happen, though, Dori needed some expert advice. Leaving her fate in the hands of Niles York made as much sense as letting the fox guard the hen house. She needed someone who would represent her best interests, not his. After settling down her excited brother and sister and promising them a celebratory treat of pizza with the works for dinner, she headed for the phone.

THREE

A twinge of regret plucked at Jake as he strode into the building that had served as his headquarters for a good part of his adult life. Tucked away in a sprawling office park outside D.C., the unassuming structure belied its true purpose as the home of an elite group of government intelligence officers. No denying that he missed the excitement of the chase, catching the slime of the earth and making them answer for their crimes against his country and its citizens. There was no sound in the world as satisfying as the slam of a cell door locking away society's reprobates.

He stopped at the guard's desk and produced the identification which still allowed him limited access to the inner sanctum. At the time, his boss had refused to accept Jake's decision to bail out, hoping he would come to his senses after a short sabbatical.

"Here," he'd said, tossing the ID back when Jake handed over his top clearance credentials. "Just in case you want to stop by and say hello sometime."

Jake knew his boss was hoping for more than just a hello. Instead of accepting the resignation, he placed him on indefinite leave—a leave which was now entering its second year. During the past twelve months, the ID had merely taken up space in his wallet. Now the laminated piece of plastic would get him past the guard, but that was all. In order to access the restricted files, he'd need his ex-partner Charley's cooperation.

The guard, new since Jake's departure, scrutinized the photo ID, then studied Jake for a long moment. Jake stared back, his face expressionless. He might miss the excitement of his former work, but he certainly didn't miss the bureaucracy that hogtied most government agencies. Finally, the guard waved him through. Jake nodded and headed for the elevator. The man was only doing his job. He couldn't fault him for that.

He also couldn't deny that there was something extremely satisfying about transforming himself into a living legend, albeit a fictional one under the pseudonym of Harrison Kent. On the pages of his novels, no miscreant ever escaped justice through a legal loophole or the maneuverings of a sleazy lawyer. Drake Spaulding, his computer-generated alter ego hero, always got his man. And unlike in real life, it was always the right man.

Jake took a deep breath and forced that thought from his brain. Along with everything else, these corridors held one ghost too many for him. It was that last ghost which had precipitated his decision to leave his former life. The same specter would keep him from ever returning. Some mistakes could never be corrected, and some men should never be placed in a position where they might repeat those mistakes. Jake had learned the hard way that he was one of those men—no matter what anyone else said.

Stepping from the elevator, He headed down the hall to the first office on the right and entered. His former partner, buried behind two computer screens, a stack of books and a mass of open files, grumbled at the interruption without looking up. "Whoever you are, go away. I'm busy."

"Nice to see you, too, Charley."

Charley Davis peered over the top of the monitor. "I don't believe it! The prodigal son returns to the fold." She leaped to her feet, bounded around her desk, and grabbed him in a quick bear hug before holding him at arm's length and scrutinizing him from head to toe. "Well, you don't look like success has turned you into a worthless slug."

"Worthless slug? I'll have you know my latest advance was more than Uncle Sam paid me over the past five years. And I didn't have to risk life and limb for it."

"So where's the challenge, Prentiss? And what the hell are you doing back here?"

Leave it to Charley to zero in on his own mixed feelings about his past and present lives. His former partner had a talent that bordered on mind reading. Not that he was any slouch in that department. Which brought him back to why he was here in the first place. Something about Dori Johnson had nagged at his sixth sense from the moment he laid eyes on her. "I need to do a bit of research."

"As Harrison Kent or Jake Prentiss?"

"Does it matter?"

Charley shrugged. "You're still officially on leave, right?"

"Cut me some slack, Davis. Since when have you ever gone by the book?"

She headed across the cluttered room to the other desk, the one which had been Jake's. "You know, I still can't get over you dumping me," she said, entering an access code into the computer.

"Oh? And have you discussed this with Tony?" Charley stuck her tongue out at him. Jake laughed. Tony and Charley had been married forever and still acted like newlyweds, although both were well past forty.

"We made a good team, you and I, Prentiss. I miss you. When are you going to get this early midlife crisis out of your system and come back to work?" She stood and offered him the chair.

Jake settled himself into the seat. Charley knew a midlife crisis had nothing to do with his leaving. An innocent man had taken his own life because Jake screwed up. No matter what kind of spin his boss and the department put on it, Jake was sentenced to live the rest of his life with Calvin Bigelow's blood on his hands, his death on his conscience. One mistake like that was enough for a lifetime. By leaving, Jake made sure he never made another. "I take it our fearless leader hasn't given you a new partner that meets with your approval?"

Charley grunted. "I've already kicked out half a dozen—all wet-behind-the-ears pups afraid to dirty their hands. They think every crime can be solved in front of a computer screen. Right now, I'm going it alone. Until you come to your senses and return to work."

She shoved a stack of folders into her briefcase, then glanced up and frowned at him. "I know I've said this before, but what happened wasn't your fault, Jake. No one blames you. Besides, if Bigelow was so innocent, why'd he kill himself?" When he didn't respond, she grabbed her coat and purse, and headed for the door. "I haven't seen you, Prentiss. Lock the door behind me."

Jake pushed back from the desk and crossed the room to secure the door. Charley had asked the million-dollar question, the one everyone else in the department had thrown at him countless times in the months after Calvin's death. He didn't know why Bigelow had committed suicide. No one would ever know. The man left no note of explanation, but speculation ran rampant that Calvin Bigelow was hiding a bigger secret, one he feared Jake would eventually uncover.

Jake refused to buy into the theory. The fact remained that he'd pursued an innocent man with what later proved to be bogus evidence. Calvin Bigelow was framed, and Jake had fallen for the bait. At least he'd caught the true perpetrators before he walked away—not that it brought Calvin back. Nothing could bring Calvin back. Or remove the stain of guilt from Jake's hands.

Forcing Calvin once more from his thoughts, Jake spent the next several hours culling through dozens of online records. Having access to files throughout the country, it didn't take him long to discover Dori Johnson's secret. Damn if she wasn't one talented little hacker and forger, but her considerable skills were no match for Jake and a government supercomputer.

Still, it was damn scary that in post-9/11 America a brainy seventeen-year-old kid could break into government computers to access and alter documents with such relative ease. He'd like to know what the hell the guys who were supposed to be keeping the country safe were doing all day?

And now he also understood why she refused Niles's offer. She had too much to lose by accepting it.

Nothing in his search explained why Dori initially fled Philadelphia and changed her identity. There were no outstanding warrants for her arrest. A search of local hospital and police records produced no indications of an abusive home life. Her grades, until the day she dropped out of school and disappeared with her brother and sister, were exemplary.

Frustrated, he drummed a pencil on the desk. Something didn't add up. He shuffled through the stack of printouts, scanning sheet after sheet of information on a woman who'd gone to great lengths to hide what appeared to be a relatively normal life. Why? Where was the missing puzzle piece?

Her escape to a new life had been as complete and thorough as any he'd ever seen orchestrated by the Witness Protection Program. But as far as he could figure, Dori Johnson wasn't part of Witness Protection. If she were, he wouldn't have been able to uncover the forgeries. She and her siblings had run from something. The question was, what? Or who?

He read through the files for a third time, searching for any clue that might yield some answers. "Something's missing," he mumbled. Then it hit him. *Missing.* He quickly leafed through the pile of papers. Not finding what he was searching for, he turned to the computer and once again accessed Philadelphia police records.

You're getting sloppy, Prentiss. Two years ago, you never would have overlooked such crucial information. Jake stared at the column of names scrolling down his screen. Isen. Itzkowitz. Iyer. Jackowski. No Ivanichek. They weren't listed! Their father had never filed a missing person's report on Dasha, Yusif, and Anika Ivanichek. Why?

Staying in the police files, Jake searched for information on Sergei Ivanichek. What he unearthed was enough to make him want to keep Dori Johnson as far from Niles York as possible.

* * *

Sitting in her minuscule cubicle in Human Resources, Dori found it difficult to concentrate on the monotonous data staring back at her from the computer screen. Several floors above her, two men were negotiating her future. At least she hoped they were. There *was* the likelihood that Niles York had unleashed his legendary temper on the representative from the Lincoln Modeling Agency and tossed the man out of his office. There was also the possibility that Mr. York, incensed by her audacious act, might send Dori packing as well.

Not wanting to contemplate the ramifications of joblessness, she shook off the thought and turned her attention back to proofreading the changes in the employees' benefits packages. Hopefully, she'd still possess those benefits this time tomorrow.

The jarring ring of her phone nearly propelled her off her chair and sent her heart plummeting into her stomach. She stared at the telephone through the second ring, her pulse racing. Her fingers trembled as she reached for the receiver, finally lifting it off the cradle in the middle of the third ring. "Ms. Johnson," she said, trying desperately to fight back the case of nerves she heard echoing in her voice.

"You're wanted in Mr. York's office," came the voice Dori recognized as that of Ruthie Henshaw, Mr. York's longtime executive assistant.

"I'm on my way." Dori hung up the phone. As she passed the maze of cubicles filled with her fellow drones, she couldn't help wondering if she were headed for her execution or her coronation. Mrs. Henshaw's calm, business-like tone had given no clue to her fate.

Dori paused at the doorway before exiting the Human Resources Department. Turning, she gazed across the expanse at the frenetic activity. Phones rang; conversations buzzed in the air.

Nails clicked against keyboards, and heels tapped along the terrazzo aisles as her coworkers went about their daily routine. Dori took a deep breath. One way or another she suspected after today she'd no longer be a part of this world. The radical thought both excited her and filled her with dread.

* * *

"You hired her already?" Jake couldn't believe his ears when he arrived at Niles's office early the next morning.

"Signed, sealed, and delivered. Got the contract right here," said Niles, lifting a multipage document from his desk and waving it in the air.

Jake grabbed the papers and scanned them. He wasn't surprised by the contents of the contract, negotiated by a representative from one of New York's top modeling agencies. Dori Johnson was far savvier than her innocent youthfulness indicated. Yesterday's investigation proved that. "I thought you were going to wait until you got my report. Besides, two days ago she turned you down cold. What made her change her mind?"

Niles answered him with a question of his own. "Do you remember the guy who ran the deli near our frat house?"

"Mr. Finkelman? Who could forget a Jewish delicatessen owner at a Catholic university?"

"Yeah, and the priests and nuns devoured his knishes and matzo ball soup. I once asked him why he started his business where he did. Know what he told me?"

Jake raised an eyebrow, not certain what Mr. Finkelman had to do with Dori Johnson, but he rose to the bait. "What did he tell you, Niles?"

"He said in order to get ahead in this world, you need *moxie*."

"*Moxie?*" Jake recognized the term. Loosely translated, it

meant pluck or courage. Brass balls. But he still didn't see where Niles was heading with his anecdote. "So?"

"'You've got *moxie*, Niles,' he once told me. 'I know. It takes *moxie* to recognize *moxie*.'"

"Okay, Niles. You've got *moxie*. We both know that. So what?"

"Dori Johnson has *moxie*, Jake."

Yes, Jake would grant Niles that. Dori Johnson did indeed have *moxie*. Along with a hell of a lot of baggage that could boomerang on Niles York. He reached into his briefcase and withdrew the report he'd stayed up half the night compiling for his friend. "Before you get too excited, you'd better read this."

Jake tossed the report at Niles, then sauntered over to the bar and helped himself to a cup of coffee. "Want one?"

"Something tells me I might need something stronger."

"Probably." He poured two cups, set one on the desk, and carried the other over to the couch, all the while keeping one eye on Niles's deepening frown as he scanned the pages of the report.

"Damn!" Niles pounded both fists on his desk and exhaled a string of expletives. "So what's the bottom line here, Jake?"

"To be honest, I don't know." Leaning forward, Jake propped his elbows on his knees and studied the coffee cup he held between his hands. "She does have *moxie*, though. I'll grant you that."

"Yeah, but I was referring to her bringing in a modeling rep. I figured the other day she was just stalling for time to broker the best deal for herself."

"No. Your offer frightened her. I knew right away she was hiding something. I could see it in her eyes. So, I have to repeat, what changed her mind?"

"Jeez!" Niles threw back his head and stared at the ceiling. "Are you suggesting she's being manipulated by someone?"

"I'm not suggesting anything." Not that he hadn't speculated about the possibility. For Niles's sake, Jake hoped he was wrong. However, the fact was Dori Johnson, daughter of a man with strong ties to the Russian-American mob, fled Philadelphia six years ago and was living in Jersey City, New Jersey under an assumed name.

A chilling thought had crossed Jake's mind when he first discovered Dori's secret. What if the mob had known her whereabouts all along? What if her disappearance was a carefully staged ploy? The last thing Niles needed was a recurrence of his past troubles with the mob.

Early in his career Niles had invested heavily in an Atlantic City casino. As soon as the papers were signed, the Russian-American mob moved in, threatening Niles and his fledgling business unless he agreed to pay protection money. The crime lord had seen Niles as an easy mark, an inexperienced rich kid playing with a large trust fund.

Niles had a few surprises for him. With Jake's help and government connections, he'd participated in a sting that destroyed the man's empire. He was still rotting in jail, but others had risen to take his place, and crime families have long memories. "She could be a plant," said Jake.

Niles shook his head. "Nothing's happened in the six years she's worked here. No labor unrest. No shakedowns. No unexplained accidents. Nothing. Not in any of the divisions.

"She works in Human Resources. She has access to hiring data—a perfect way for the mob to infiltrate if what you're suggesting were true." He eyed his friend. "We both know patience isn't a virtue these guys hold in high esteem. They're not like Al Qaeda. If Dori Johnson were part of their plan for revenge, something would have happened long ago. There's been plenty of opportunity given the expansion we've had over the past few years."

Jake couldn't argue with Niles, but Dori Johnson and her unsavory background sent an electrical charge of skepticism racing through his body. "Look, Niles. If you want my opinion, the last thing you need is another entanglement with the Philly Russkies. Maybe she's safe, but why risk it? Get out of the contract before it's too late."

"I can't do that. I offered this kid a chance to make something of her life. I'm not going to snatch it back before she's even started."

"Are you crazy? Do I have to remind you what happened the last time? These guys play for keeps, pal."

"And so do I. I beat them once with your help. We'll do it again."

"We?" Jake shook his head, holding out his hands as if to ward off some evil spirit that had entered the room. "Now wait just a minute, Niles. I'm out of that line of work, remember? Besides, I have to start researching my next book."

"Don't give me that crap, Jake. You wrote three bestsellers while you were helping bring down a ring of international terrorists. I'm talking about keeping an eye on one young kid. Besides, you can practically write those books in your sleep."

So he didn't write Pulitzer Prize winning prose. He'd be the first to admit it, but Jake didn't care for his friend's jab at his literary skills. The public loved his tales of Drake Spaulding. "Forget it, pal. I'm no babysitter. Hire a rent-a-cop."

"I don't want a rent-a-cop. I want my best friend, the guy who promised always to be there for me whenever I needed him."

Jake jumped to his feet. In three long strides he crossed the room and leaned over the desk, his nose inches from his friend's. "That's playing dirty, Niles."

Niles shrugged. "Whatever works..."

Jake groaned. Niles knew damn well it would work. Jake owed Niles big time. Without his friend's unselfish generosity, Jake would never have had the funds to finish college. Even though he'd repaid the financial debt years ago, contributing the money to a scholarship fund because Niles had refused to accept his checks, the emotional debt would always remain. "Someday you're going to play that trump card one time too many, Niles, and I won't be around to save your sorry ass."

Niles patted Jake's shoulder. His eyes twinkled, and his lips stretched out in a broad grin. "But not today, Jake. Grab your coat."

Jake shook his head and sighed. No, not today. They both knew Jake would gladly swim through a piranha infested river for Niles York. "Where are we going?"

"To meet your newest assignment."

FOUR

Dori sensed his presence before she saw him. She had expected Mr. York to check in on her, but Mr. York didn't charge the fine hairs on the back of her neck and make them stand at attention. Mr. York, for all his bluster, didn't fill her with a sense of foreboding the way the other man did. Glancing up from the script she was studying in the corner of the television studio, she wasn't surprised to find him assessing her from across the room. A shiver scampered up her spine. She had no idea why this man made her so nervous. She had no idea who he was or his relation to Mr. York. All she knew was that she felt as fearful as cornered prey whenever he came near her.

Trying her best to ignore his penetrating gaze, she bent her head and focused on the words in front of her, softly mouthing the fifteen-second spot scheduled to blitz radio and television airwaves in a matter of days. She closed her eyes and repeated the words, committing them to memory. "Hi! I'm Dori. Join me for a new shopping experience. Coming soon—N.Y. McStore, affordable upscale, made in America shopping for the twenty-first century woman. Just a click, a call, or a short drive away. Remember—we're Not-Your-Mother's-Chain-Store."

She repeated the words, still overwhelmed by the circumstances that had thrust her from nobody to a soon-to-be national spokesperson for Niles York's newest baby. Moments after signing on the dotted line yesterday morning, she'd been whisked out of his office and into an alien environment.

The last twenty-four hours had been a whirlwind of fittings, stylings, tapings, and photo shoots that lasted late into the night. Within days her image would beckon from billboards, buses, newspapers, magazines, and television screens. Dori Johnson, the face and voice of N.Y. McStore, would soon be as recognizable to Americans as Tony the Tiger or the Maytag repair man.

Dori Johnson, she reminded herself. Not Dasha Ivanichek. Dasha no longer existed. Joey was right. She looked nothing like Dasha anymore. Her fingers kissed her newly colored and sculpted hair. And thanks to one of New York's top stylists, she looked even less like her than she did two days ago. Pale streaks of blonde now highlighted a sassy new cut that danced in free-falling waves around her head.

She repeated her lines once more, this time with a bit more confidence. Yesterday she had taped variations of the same scripts for radio spots. Today she'd be shooting the television commercials, several of varying lengths, all with basically the same message.

"You *will* smile when you say that, I hope."

Dori's eyes sprang open. Her jaw dropped. She'd been so

consumed with blocking the man from her thoughts that she hadn't sensed him drawing closer.

Before she could gather her wits, Mr. York joined them. "Relax, Jake. The radio spots went off without a hitch yesterday. I'm confident she'll do just as well with the television ads. I can smell success."

Jake eyed Mr. York with a look of skepticism. "Two days ago, you were worried about fulfilling Mother Bea's dire prediction and losing your shirt."

Mr. York nodded. "True, but that was before this young woman walked into my office." He gestured in Dori's direction. "She was the missing piece I needed to pull everything together."

"Hmm." Jake's gaze raked Dori's body from head to toe, then back up again before trapping her in his sights. "Niles is placing a lot of faith in you. Are you capable of shouldering such heady responsibility?"

Dori resented the way this man constantly tried to intimidate her. She'd taken enough of his silent sneers and verbal jabs. How dare he pass judgment on her when he knew nothing about her! She'd shouldered enough responsibility in the past half dozen years to qualify for six lives and a sainthood. Well, maybe not the sainthood, she thought, inwardly grimacing. Still...

Squaring her shoulders, she shot back, "I'm used to shouldering far more responsibility than you could possibly imagine, and since Mr. York has placed his confidence in me, I fail to see where it's any of your concern."

"Bravo!" Mr. York applauded, then slapped the other man on the back. "See, Jake. I told you. *Moxie*! The girl's got *moxie*."

From across the room the assistant director waved his clipboard and called, "We're ready for you now, Ms. Johnson."

"Go." Mr. York stepped aside as Dori slid off the stool. She offered her boss a smile and tossed a glare in the direction of his friend as she passed him.

Mr. York chuckled. "Yes, the two of you are going to make an interesting team."

Dori froze.

FIVE

"What!" Dori spun around to confront the two men.

"Oh, didn't I tell you?" Mr. York's face was a study in innocence. The innocence of a cat with canary feathers sticking out of his mouth.

"Tell me what?"

He draped an arm around the other man's shoulders. "Jake here is in charge of our launch. He'll be traveling the country with you, scheduling your press conferences, coordinating TV and radio appearances, store openings. The whole nine yards. You're a team." He nodded toward Dori, "You're my spokesperson. Jake's the behind-the-scenes guy who makes certain everything runs like clockwork."

"And if it doesn't?" she asked, hazarding a glance at the man in question.

"I fix it," he answered, staring her down, his voice stern and controlled and daring her to question him further.

"Jake can solve any problem that might crop up," said Mr. York, thumping his friend's back. "He's never failed me. And he won't fail you."

"Ms. Johnson, we're waiting!"

Dori glanced over her shoulder at the assistant director. The man scowled at her. "Sometime today?"

"We'll discuss this further after the taping," said Mr. York, shooing her off.

Rattled by the unsettling turn of events, Dori closed her eyes and took a deep breath while a bevy of men and women prattled around her, touching up her makeup and smoothing her hair. Although she hadn't given it much thought—or any thought for that matter—it made sense that a company representative would accompany her on her appearances across the country. She hardly expected Mr. York to slap a pile of airline tickets into her hand and send her on her way. It just never occurred to her that she would be thrust into a twenty-four/seven situation with *that* man.

Why him? Who was he, anyway? Prior to two days ago, Dori had never seen him in the offices, but that hardly meant anything. Niles York Enterprises was a global concern, and up until forty-eight hours ago, Dori had been a mere cog in one of its many wheels.

A woman guided her over to her mark and positioned her, fluffing the cowl of her pale yellow cashmere sweater before leaving. A busy din hummed around her like a hive of worker bees all concentrating on the task at hand. In front of her, the director began shouting out directions. Behind him, shadowed by the bright lights, she saw the murky outline of Niles York and his friend Jake, their expressions unreadable in the darkness.

Above the buzz of commotion, someone shouted, "Quiet!" Then, "McStore Commercial One. Take one."

Dori shrugged off her uneasiness. She had a job to do. She was going to do it and do it well. Jake whoever-he-was be damned. Smiling into the camera, she spoke her lines. Flawlessly.

Unfortunately, the director wasn't happy with the color of one of the props. Then there was a problem with the sound. She flubbed her lines on the third take, and a light blew out on the fourth. She sneezed in the middle of the fifth take. The day dragged on. Nine hours and countless takes later, the director was finally satisfied with the results and called it a day. They'd successfully shot three spots—a fifteen second, thirty second, and forty-five second television commercials.

Thank God I didn't agree to a feature length film.

* * *

"The director says you're a pro. Couldn't believe how quickly you caught on to everything." Mr. York tossed the compliment out across the linen covered table where the three of them sat waiting for their drinks to arrive. He and his friend had remained at the studio throughout the day, Mr. York constantly consulting with the director and his crew, his friend standing off in the shadows. Watching.

Dori offered him a weak smile and mumbled her thanks. All the poise and confidence the director had remarked upon had fled her the moment she was ushered into the small, dimly lit booth with barely a hairsbreadth between herself and Jake What's-his-name.

Prentiss. Jake Prentiss. Mr. York had finally formally introduced the two of them after dropping his nuclear bombshell at the studio. She shifted closer to the stucco wall, managing to claim a second hairsbreadth of space as a buffer. It didn't help. How could she expect to work so closely with this man if she couldn't even sit next to him without every nerve in her body short-circuiting? Even when he wasn't pinning her with that intense gaze of his, she felt his presence.

"Didn't I tell you, Jake?" Mr. York continued. "Did I pick a winner?" His words made her feel like Seabiscuit. Next, he'd be reaching across the table, peeling back her lip to check her teeth!

Dori nervously fingered the napkin on her lap and glanced to her left, wondering, not for the first time, about the dynamics between Mr. York and his friend. Why did a man who ruled over such a vast business empire clamor for approval and validation from a subordinate? If he was a subordinate. Something just didn't add up between those two.

"If you're fishing for compliments, Niles, I'll grant you that Ms. Johnson does seem to have a natural ability in front of the camera." He shifted his body slightly and pinned Dori with those blue-black eyes of his. "Youthful. Fresh. Exuberant." His gaze drifted downward.

Heat flooded Dori's cheeks. Her mouth went dry. Just like in Chapter Eleven when Lord Farnsworth combed his rakish gaze over Lady Bromshire. *Shit!* She'd better switch to reading science fiction. She couldn't afford to start channeling Lady Bromshire.

"And not a drop of plastic," continued Jake. "I'd say you got exactly what you were looking for."

Mr. York slapped the table. "Yes! I knew you'd come around." He grinned first at Jake, then Dori. "And while we're on the subject, I think it's time we all got a little less formal. After all, the two of you are going to be spending a lot of time together. We should all be on a first name basis."

The waitress arrived with their drinks, placing a Scotch and soda in front of each of the men and a white wine in front of her. Mr. York—Niles—lifted his glass in a toast. Dori lowered her head, fingering the stem of her glass.

Niles. This was going to take some getting used to. She could deal with referring to his friend by his given name. After all, she hadn't even known his last name an hour ago. Mr. York—Niles—on the other hand, was a different story. She could just as easily call the queen of England Lizzie if she happened to bump into her at the supermarket. Not that *that* was likely to happen.

"To Jake and Dori," Niles began. Dori's head shot up, her jerking motion rocking her glass and spilling several drops of wine onto the tablecloth. Niles stared at the damp spot for a second before continuing, "two parts of the triumvirate that will spell success for N.Y. McStore."

"You being the third member of this cozy little threesome, I take it?" asked Jake, as he lifted his own glass in response.

"Of course." Niles tapped his glass against Jake's, then turned to her. "Dori?"

Reluctantly, she lifted her own glass. "To your continued success," she responded.

"And yours, my dear." Their glasses clinked. She waited for a moment, expecting Jake to follow suit. When he didn't, she stole a glance at him. His mouth was set in a grim line. Locking eyes with her, he nodded slightly, then brought the tumbler to his lips.

"Shall we order dinner?" asked Niles, apparently oblivious to the slight.

"Dinner?" Dori shook her head. "I'm sorry. I can't. I have to get home. My family is expecting me."

"If your brother and sister are old enough to leave on their own while you travel for Niles, they can certainly prepare dinner for themselves."

Every nerve in Dori's body shot to attention. She had never mentioned Joey and Nikki to either of them. "How—?"

"Don't look so surprised," Jake continued, cutting off her question. "Did you think Niles was going to place the fate of this venture in your hands without first investigating you?"

Investigating? Dori didn't like the sound of that word or the look on the face of the man who had uttered it. His gaze bore into her with an intensity that left little doubt that it was he who had performed the investigation.

But surely, he hadn't uncovered her past. If he had, she wouldn't have been offered a contract. Wouldn't have spent the past two days being preened and photographed. Wouldn't be sitting here now.

Forcing a smile onto her face and calm into her voice, she answered him, adding a nonchalant shrug of her shoulders for added emphasis. "I never really thought about it, but I suppose that does make sense." She didn't trust this man. Ratcheting up her courage a notch, she challenged him. "And I take it you didn't discover I was a coke snorting transvestite?"

Niles chuckled and uttered something about *moxie*, but Jake didn't bat an eye. He leaned closer to her, lowering his head. "I learned nearly all your secrets," he said, his voice a low whisper, his breath kissing her ear.

Dori could almost feel the blood in her veins turning to ice water. She picked up her glass and took a sip of the wine, hoping the rush of alcohol would replace some of the color she knew had drained from her face. He had to be bluffing. "But not all?" she asked, praying he wouldn't drop any further bombshells on her.

"Enough." Jake picked up his menu and scanned it for a moment before reaching into his pocket and pulling out a cell phone. "Why don't you call Joey and Nikki and tell them to order in a pizza with the works." He nodded at Niles. "Compliments of Niles York Enterprises."

* * *

Jake knew he was acting like a real bastard, but for his friend's sake, he needed to find out why Dori Johnson fled Philadelphia six years earlier and whether the shadows of her past still had any control over her. Niles hadn't stopped him, even when they both noticed how pale she'd turned at the mention of his investigation. He took his friend's silence as tacit approval to continue his line of questioning. He took Dori's nervousness as a sign that she had much to hide—how much more than he already knew, only time and his perseverance would tell.

She placed the phone call, then reluctantly accepted the twenty-dollar bill Niles handed her before picking up her own menu. She remained silent as he and Niles discussed the various entrée choices. When the waitress came to take their orders, Dori selected the least expensive item available, a hamburger platter—no appetizer, no soup, no salad. Jake glanced over his menu and caught Niles's grimace of disapproval. Quid pro quo. She hadn't wanted to accept the money for the pizza. This was her way of evening out the equation.

Jake felt like a first-class heel. He also couldn't help but score a notch in her favor on the integrity scale. He knew then and there that if nothing else, Niles needn't worry about Dori Johnson abusing her expense account. The lady may have stolen an identity, but he sensed she wouldn't take a dime she didn't earn.

"I'll have a Caesar salad and the lobster special," he told the waitress, "and so will the lady." He turned to stop Dori's protest before she could utter one. "Niles can afford a pizza. There's no need to deny yourself a nice meal."

She glanced across the table. When Niles inclined his head in agreement, she nodded to the waitress, but she refused to look at Jake.

Niles reached across the table and patted Dori's hand in a somewhat fatherly manner. "Don't get all riled up over Jake. He's overly cautious by nature and only looking out for my best interests. I hope you won't hold his lack of people skills against him." Then he winked.

Dori pulled her hand away and hazarded a glance in his direction. Jake needed to remind himself that whatever secrets she was hiding, she was no government subversive or Third World terrorist. "I'm sorry," he said. "I didn't mean to upset you. The investigation was a standard security check. Nothing more."

So he stretched the truth a little. Okay, more than a little. Hell, he'd just stretched it clear to St. Louis, but he needed to gain her confidence to learn the truth. And he needed to learn the truth to protect Niles from a possible mob threat.

"I understand," she said, but her eyes still held suspicion and doubt.

Although he'd fled his former life after a botched investigation, in all his years of government service Jake had never blown his cover. He was definitely out of practice if a naïve young girl suspected him of ulterior motives. Or was she so naïve?

He reminded himself that he had reason to be suspicious of her. Coincidence rarely factored into intelligence work. Dori Johnson had ties to the Russian-American Mafia, and the Russkies were no friend of Niles York. That was no coincidence. That was fact. Crystal clear fact—as crystal clear as the two large green pools of her eyes.

Jake choked on a swig of Scotch. *Large green pools of her eyes? Damn!* Where the hell had *that* come from?

* * *

After dinner Niles refused to allow Dori to head over to the PATH station for the train back to Jersey City. "It's late. Besides, it looks like rain. Jake can drive you."

He brushed off her protests, claiming the station wasn't a safe place for a single woman at night, and no, she wasn't taking Jake out of his way. Dori knew the first was a lie. She suspected the same of the second statement. The PATH between Manhattan and Jersey City ran jam-packed with commuters at all hours of the day and night. She rarely managed to snag a seat.

And crime was nonexistent unless she counted the harassment from one rather militant and persistent panhandler who often moved between cars and demanded money for the homeless. She suspected any money he received went directly to the nearest liquor store, judging from the stench of his breath.

As for Niles's second statement, Jake didn't look like the Jersey City type. He certainly didn't fit in with the Tumi-toting brokers who'd moved in en masse over the last decade, turning parts of the once dying industrial town into Yuppie Central. She doubted he lived in her ramshackle and as yet, ungentrified neck of the woods, and he definitely wouldn't be driving through her neighborhood on his way to anywhere else.

They'd eaten at a restaurant near the television studio in Astoria. By the time they arrived back in Manhattan from Queens, it was well after ten. Dori had been up since five and had another long day ahead of her tomorrow. She stifled several yawns before one fought its way to the surface.

"Am I boring you?" asked Jake as they headed onto the approach for the Holland Tunnel.

Setting her nerves on edge? Yes. But boring? She doubted Jake Prentiss could be boring if he tried. Even comatose, she imagined his brooding presence encircling and trapping his unsuspecting and unwitting victims. She turned from looking out the passenger window to find those dark hooded eyes of his studying her. For a change. "My day started before the sun rose, and tomorrow is less than seven hours away."

"I had no idea smiling in front of a camera was so tiring."

She wanted to tell him he had no idea about a lot of things, but bit back the comment. She wouldn't stoop to matching his sarcasm with some of her own. Instead, she said, "Neither did I. I have a new respect for fashion models. It might look glamorous from the pages of *Vogue*, but I'm learning looks can be deceiving. It's grueling work." She reached behind and scrunched a muscle in her neck.

"Sore?"

Dori didn't even bother to stifle the next yawn, only politely covered her mouth with her hand. "My aches have aches. I used muscles today I never knew I had." Before she realized what was happening, Jake reached across the console and began massaging her neck. She froze.

"Relax," he said. "This isn't going to loosen those muscles if you tense up."

Relax? With his hands caressing the back of her neck? Right! That would happen about as quickly as the next Ice Age. Her rational side suggested pushing his hand away and mouthing a few choice phrases from the chapter on sexual harassment in the employee handbook.

The problem was, for some irrational reason, she found her traitorous body melting under his touch and wishing he'd apply the same ministrations to every other muscle from her head clear down to her toes. Only she wanted him to pull over to the side of the road and use *both* hands. She closed her eyes, a sigh of contentment escaping from between her lips.

Jake chuckled.

Dori's eyes flew open. Heat rushed to her cheeks. *What the hell was she doing?* She jerked away from his hand, placing as much distance as possible between her body and his, which wasn't much considering the size of the four-seater BMW. Jake returned his hand to the steering wheel. "You don't like me, do you?"

"I could say the same to you."

Rather than the quick retort she expected, silence filled the confines of the car. From the glow of a full moon that kept playing peak-a-boo from behind gathering rain clouds, Dori studied the pensive expression filling his features. Her gaze seized upon his finely chiseled jaw, his aquiline nose, his sexy mouth with its lower lip extended in a thoughtful pout, and despite the best of intentions she found herself wondering what those lips would feel like pressed against hers.

Shit! She couldn't believe the direction her mind was wandering. She was morphing into Lady Bromshire. Either that or exhaustion was causing her to hallucinate. Yes, that was it. Another yawn confirmed her theory. Exhaustion and hallucinations. Nothing a good night's sleep wouldn't cure. Tomorrow she'd see Jake Prentiss for the dangerous man he was. Only now she was more confused than ever as to the kind of danger he posed.

"We didn't get off on the best of footings," he said, breaking into her thoughts.

"An understatement if ever I heard one."

"Think we can start fresh? We are going to be spending a good deal of time together. It would be best for both of us if we buried the hostility."

"I'm not certain I can do that," said Dori. When he scowled at her, she added, "At least not until I know the basis for your animosity toward me. Or do you treat everyone you meet with equal contempt?"

"I told you. I'm only looking out for Niles."

"And I don't buy that. Niles York is a grown man who has built an empire. I find it hard to believe he needs you to babysit him." She took a deep breath. As long as she was laying her cards on the table she might as well go all out and call his bluff. "And I don't believe you're a marketing and public relations executive with the company, either, Mr. Prentiss."

She had expected him to be taken aback by her indictment. Flinch. Sneer. Mouth a snappy retort. Something. Anything. But Jake Prentiss didn't twitch a muscle. In a voice far too calm, he merely asked, "And why is that?"

"Because a PR guy would know what it's like to go through a twelve-hour day of photo shoots and tapings."

"Did I ever say I didn't?"

"You said you had no idea smiling in front of a camera—" but Dori never finished her sentence. He had pulled over to the curb—the curb in front of her apartment building, and she suddenly realized he'd never asked for her address or directions from the tunnel. "Who the hell *are* you?"

SIX

Jake engaged the brake and turned off the engine. With both hands braced on the steering wheel, he stared straight ahead. "Niles and I have been friends since childhood. Good friends." He turned to face her. "He has a lot riding on McStore and needed someone he could trust to handle the startup campaign."

"Niles York Enterprises employs over four thousand people worldwide," she said. "And that's just in corporate. Surely there were marketing and public relations personnel capable of handling things. Why the need for a hired gun?"

"There were other considerations involved."

"What kind of considerations?"

"Nothing I care to discuss with you."

Several caustic retorts sprang to the tip of Dori's tongue, but she clamped her mouth into a tight line and merely glared at him as he opened his car door. "You don't need to get out," she said, swinging her own door open and stepping onto the curb just as the first cold drops of rain began to fall.

"Yes, I do." He slammed his door and followed after her.

Dori marched up the half dozen concrete steps. Jabbing her key into the outer lock, she opened the door of the apartment building, then turned to him. "Thank you for the ride." She stepped across the threshold, but before she could close the door on him, Jake grabbed it and followed her into the lobby. "You can leave now," she said, making no attempt to stifle her annoyance.

Instead, he took her elbow and led her down the hall toward the staircase. "Not until I see you safely into your own apartment."

"Both the building and neighborhood are quite safe." But he looked like he didn't believe her. She watched as he scanned the peeling plaster walls, the cracked linoleum floor, and the large brown water stain that covered nearly a third of the lobby's ceiling.

The censure in his eyes made her seethe. "No, it's not the Plaza, Mr. Prentiss. We have no doorman and no elevator. The pipes rattle, and in the winter the boiler struggles to keep us warm, but my neighbors are good, hardworking people, not muggers and rapists."

"I don't doubt that." He began to follow her up the stairs.

She stopped on the first landing and swung around to confront him. "Maybe you should just come right out and tell me why you don't like me."

"Did I say I didn't like you?"

The man could try the patience of Job! "You didn't have to. Your actions speak volumes."

Jake leaned against the wall, crossing his legs at the ankles and his arms over his chest as though he intended to stay awhile. Or maybe he was digging in for a lengthy battle. "Since when is acting like a gentleman a sign of not liking someone?"

Dori threw her arms up. "You say you want to bury the hatchet, but you continue to treat me as if I'm the enemy. I thought we were supposed to be on the same team. You claim your only concern is your friend's success, but you're doing your best to sabotage him."

"Where the hell do you come off making an accusation like that?"

From half a landing above, Dori heard a door swing open. A moment later a heavyset, elderly woman, her head covered in sponge curlers, leaned over the railing. "What's going on down there?"

"Now see what you've done!" Dori stepped out of the shadows. "It's Dori, Mrs. Calhoun. I'm sorry we disturbed you."

"Dori?"

"Yes."

"Who's that with you, dear? Is he bothering you?"

Dori smirked at Jake before answering her neighbor. "No, everything's fine. You can go back inside."

"You sure? I can call the cops."

"That won't be necessary. My friend didn't realize how late it was and how loud he was speaking. That's all."

"Well, if you're sure..."

"I am."

Mrs. Calhoun shuffled back into her apartment, but Dori caught a glimpse of the elderly woman peeking out at them as she and Jake rounded the floor to the next flight of steps. Knowing Mrs. Calhoun, the woman would stand guard until Dori was safely inside her own apartment and Jake had exited the building.

Jake grabbed her arm as she started to ascend to the third floor.

"Explain that sabotage remark of yours."

Dori pulled her arm out of his grasp, leveling him with a steely glare. "You're undermining Niles by doing your best to make me quit." She fought to keep her voice to a whisper. "In case you've forgotten, I didn't go after this job. Niles York wanted me, and against my better judgment, I agreed."

"Against your better judgment? Why?"

That was none of his business. Since he'd already had her investigated, if he didn't know the answer to that question, she certainly wasn't going to supply him with it. Besides, she now had an additional reason for regretting her decision. Him.

She marched around the corner of the third floor. "The thought of spending the next few months in such close proximity to someone as sullen and confrontational as you, makes me regret my decision."

"Why did you change your mind to begin with?"

"What?" His question caught her off-guard.

"The day you came into Niles's office you were adamant about not wanting the job. You couldn't wait to leave."

Dori shrugged. "I thought the offer was a joke. Besides, I was supposed to be covering the phones for Mrs. Henshaw. I was afraid she'd be angry with me if she returned and found I wasn't at her desk."

"Not a convincing excuse. You were spooked by that offer. Then the next thing I hear, you've signed a contract. Who or what made you change your mind so quickly, Dori?"

"It's personal. Besides, I don't see where it's any of your business one way or the other." She headed for the last set of steps.

"It is if it involves the well-being of Niles York and his company."

Dori stopped short. "Is that what all of this is about?" She spun on her heels and stared at him. "You think someone's paying me off? That I'm involved in some sort of clandestine activity to subvert Mr. York?" She couldn't control the laughter bubbling up inside her. "I don't believe this! Is your life so dull you have to invent absurd conspiracies to entertain yourself?"

Jake braced his hands against the wall, inches from either side of her head. Leaning close—so close that his breath kissed her lips, he whispered, "Humor me, then, Dori. Why'd you change your mind?"

His nearness sobered her at once, the laughter dying as quickly as it had erupted. An intense shudder swept through her body. "I think you already know the answer to that," she said. Without wanting to, she stared, mesmerized by his lips as they moved ever so close to her own.

"Do I?"

Dori twisted her head to the side and averted her eyes to avoid staring at his slightly stubbled jaw, his brooding eyes, and those lips. She didn't want to think about those lips and what they might do to her. He was too close, and that nearness was beginning to do things to her body that she didn't want to feel. Not from him.

She wondered if he was deliberately attempting to rattle her. "You seem to know everything about me already. I have to assume you know that I'm supporting my sister and brother. That it's taken me six years to get through only four semesters of college. That I've put my own education on hold to allow my brother to attend full time." She sucked in a ragged breath. "I have no hidden agenda. I changed my mind for the very reason I originally declined Mr. York's offer. For my family, Mr. Prentiss. Nothing more."

"Jake."

Dori turned back to face him and found his lips even closer than before. One false move and she'd be able to taste the crème brûlée he'd eaten for dessert. She could smell the rich confection on his breath, mingling with the deep roasted scent of espresso.

"What?"

"We're supposed to be on a first name basis. You keep calling me Mr. Prentiss." He let his arms drop to his sides and stepped back, but Dori couldn't move. His gaze continued to trap her against the wall as effectively as his body had.

"Shall we?" he asked, inclining his head toward the remaining steps.

Dori nodded. Forcing one foot in front of the other, she managed to make her way to her apartment door, but she was certain the act was spurred entirely by instinct. Her brain had ceased functioning.

"I'll see you tomorrow," said Jake after she unlocked her door and stepped into the apartment. Not trusting her voice, she nodded once more before closing the door on him.

"Who's the hunk?"

Dori jumped at the question. Spinning around, she found Nikki standing behind her, a half-eaten apple in one hand, a book in the other. "Why aren't you in bed?"

"I was studying. Big chem test tomorrow." She took a bite out of the apple. "Was that Mr. York?"

"Huh?"

"The hunk in the hall. You didn't tell us your boss was so gorgeous. Why didn't you ask him in?"

"That wasn't Mr. York." Dori tossed her purse and keys onto the small table beside the entryway, picked up the day's mail, and began sorting through the stack of bills and junk mail. *Damn, that man had rattled her!*

"So who is he?"

Good question. She glanced up from the unopened electric bill and stared at Nikki. Her sister's eyes were wide with anticipation. "It's not what you think, Nik, so stop drooling. He's just another employee. The publicity guy who's going to be running the launch. Mr. York asked him to drive me home because it was late."

"Did he kiss you?"

"What?"

Nikki cocked her head and offered Dori a sheepish grin. "When you walked in, you looked all dreamy-eyed, like he'd kissed you or something."

"Oh, for God's sake!" Dori tossed the mail onto the coffee table. "He most certainly did *not* kiss me! He doesn't even like me, and I don't like him. So forget it, Nikki. Go to bed."

At any other time, Dori would have accepted her sister's good-natured teasing and played along. Not tonight. Not when moments earlier Jake Prentiss had sent her into a state of shock and unleashed a firestorm of emotions inside her. She needed to be alone, to think and sort through and make some sense of what had happened moments ago on the steps.

"What's going on?" Joey stuck his head out from his own bedroom. "Hey, Dor, you're back pretty late, aren't you? Everything okay?"

"Everything's fine, nothing's going on except Nikki's imagination, and yes, it's late. Go to bed. Both of you. Now!"

As she stormed down the hall to the small bedroom she shared with her sister, she heard Nikki stage whisper to Joey, "Dori's got a boyfriend."

"About time," said Joey.

SEVEN

Jake gripped the steering wheel with both hands and lowered his head trying to make sense out of what had occurred on the stairwell. One moment he's wishing he could wring her neck. The next moment he's drowning in her intoxicating scent, a combination of spicy cinnamon and sweet peaches and cream, fighting a rush of carnal desire unlike any he'd ever experienced. He'd called upon every ounce of self-discipline he possessed to keep from devouring that inviting mouth of hers.

And that was just the beginning of what he wanted to do to her.

He never should have touched her. That neck rub was the worst idea he'd ever had. That's when it started. The moment his fingers made contact with her downy nape, his brain headed south, waking a part of his anatomy that had no business noticing Dori Johnson. Forcing a confrontation inside the building had done little to douse the fire that flared within him. If anything, the verbal sparring only stoked the flame.

It took Herculean strength of will to tear himself from those perfect lips of hers, lips begging to be tasted, whether she'd realized it or not. Thankfully, he'd come to his senses before his testosterone got the better of him.

Shit! Her lips! How ironic! An argument over lips had been the catalyst in his decision to end his marriage three years ago.

Gwynne was a woman obsessed with perfection. What the good Lord had chosen not to give her, she purchased. What he gave her in excess, she paid to have sucked out. All compliments of Jake's American Express platinum card. In the three short years of their marriage, she'd undergone everything from liposuction to rhinoplasty. Breast implants to Botox treatments. All in her quest for the perfect face and figure. And all of it for her. Jake had liked his wife a hell of a lot more before she transformed herself into a *Baywatch* babe. The day Gwynne walked into their apartment with her lips shot full of collagen, was the day he finally decided he'd had enough of his artificial wife and his unsatisfying marriage.

Maybe that was why he was drawn to Dori Johnson's lips. And the rest of her. The woman radiated a natural, wholesome beauty that Jake found intoxicating. And possibly dangerous, he reminded himself. Dori Johnson was as yet an unsolved enigma.

Damn it! The last thing he needed was a complication like Dori Johnson. Even if she posed no threat to Niles, she came with too many questionable entanglements. Jake gritted his teeth and pounded the steering wheel. Damn Niles for throwing him into a situation where Dori Johnson would be in his face nearly twenty-four/seven for the next two months.

* * *

Sleep had done little to settle Dori's nerves over her reaction—or more accurately, unacceptable attraction—to Jake Prentiss. She tossed and turned throughout much of the night, finally falling into a fitful sleep mere hours before the alarm startled her awake. Luckily, she had no photo shoots or tapings on her schedule today, only meetings.

She scowled at the sleep deprived face staring back at her from the bathroom mirror, then yawned. Good thing, too. She doubted there was sufficient makeup in all of New York to transform her into a presentable human being this morning—much less a model.

She reached behind the plastic shower curtain and twisted the spigots, adjusting the temperature until the water was several degrees shy of scalding. Maybe a hot shower would steep the cobwebs from her brain. Stepping over the rim of the chipped, cast-iron tub, she grabbed a loofah and began scrubbing her skin until it tingled—hoping to scrub away a far more insidious tingle that still lingered after seven hours. Jake Prentiss.

Last night that arrogant man had awakened a part of her that she'd successfully kept dormant until now. Damn him! She didn't want to feel that way about *any* man, least of all *him*. There was something about Jake Prentiss that sent warning flares off inside her. But scrubbing wasn't helping. She could rub her skin raw, and it wouldn't remove the memory of his nearness and the erotic feelings he'd stirred up inside her.

The disgust she felt from Borka's fondling had stayed with her for six years, suppressing any desire she might have had to enter into a relationship with anyone. Not that she'd had many opportunities. Her days were filled with work, her nights with school and taking care of Nikki and Joey. Little time remained for a social life. All the better, as far as Dori was concerned. She didn't need a man in her life. Look where it had gotten her mother.

"Hey! Don't steal all the hot water," Nikki called from the other side of the bathroom door, punctuating her words with the pounding of her fist. "I want to wash my hair this morning."

Dori twisted the spigots off and stepped from the tub, reaching for a towel. "Okay," she shouted back, draping the towel around her body. "You can come in." Nikki entered the steamy bathroom, a wave of cold air rushing in with her. Dori shuddered as she slipped her feet into her terry scuffs, then headed down the hall.

"Me first, Nik," yelled Joey, rushing past Dori. "You'll take forever, and I've got an early class."

"So do I," said Nikki, slamming the door on him.

Dori retreated to her bedroom, closing the door behind her as much to shut out her brother's and sister's bickering as for privacy. Now that she was going to be making good money as the McStore spokesperson, maybe she could afford an apartment with two bathrooms. What luxury that would be! Maybe even a small house eventually. College came first, though. For all three of them. Nothing was as important as insuring an education for Joey and Nikki. Then her. After that she'd think about bathrooms.

And other things, she thought, once again forcing Jake Prentiss from her mind.

But that wasn't easy. Especially when she stepped from the apartment building an hour later to find him lounging, arms and ankles crossed, against the side of his fancy black sports car.

"Wow!" said Nikki, close on her heels. "He's even cuter in broad daylight."

Dori shot Nikki a glare before turning her focus back to Jake. Her sister was right. No denying it. Jake Prentiss looked gorgeous this morning. To die for, drool over, straight from the pages of *GQ* gorgeous. He wore a deep olive, double-breasted suit with a tan shirt, complimented by an olive, tan, and black striped silk tie with matching breast pocket hankie. A slight early autumn breeze rippling through his ebony hair, along with his insolent pose, gave him a rakish, Lord Farnsworth quality.

"I'm quite capable of getting to work on my own, Mr. Prentiss," she said as she descended the steps and crossed the sidewalk to confront him.

"Jake," he said, his lips drawing into a thin, straight line.

Dori repeated his name. "Jake."

"From now on you no longer take the PATH."

"What's wrong with the PATH?"

"In a matter of days your picture is going to be plastered all over ads inside those trains, not to mention in the subways and on buses. You're going to be a celebrity, and celebrities don't take public transportation."

"You might want to clue the mayor into that fact. He takes the subway all the time."

"With a contingent of bodyguards, never by himself."

Touché. But she wasn't about to give in—or up. "I doubt celebrities have to haul their dirty clothes down the street to the Laundromat. Will you be doing my laundry for me as well?"

"I'll talk to Niles about getting a washer and dryer for your apartment."

"I didn't mean—" Dori began to sputter, but Jake cut her short.

"No, you're absolutely right," he said, dismissing her protest with a wave of his hand. "I'm certain Niles would not look favorably on Ms. McStore washing her unmentionables in public."

"Cool! How about cable?"

"Nikki!" Dori spun around to confront her sister, but Nikki had eyes only for Jake.

"I'm Nikki Johnson," she said, extending her hand to Jake. "Dori's sister."

"My pleasure." Grasping her hand in both of his, Jake offered Nikki a warm smile. "I see beauty runs in the Johnson family."

"Oh, brother!" Dori rolled her eyes, watching her sister turn to putty in Jake's hands as he transformed from Mr. Aloof and Arrogant to Prince Charming. Funny how he'd never shown that side of his personality to her. All she got from the man were brooding stares and verbal challenges.

And a neck massage that she felt down to her toes. And his warm breath caressing her lips.

Those thoughts sent a surge of heat rushing to her cheeks while another settled between her legs. She grabbed her sister's upper arm and nudged her away from Jake. "Hurry up, Nikki, you'll miss your bus."

"We can drop her off on our way into the city," said Jake, releasing Nikki's hand and turning to open the car door.

"Cool!" Nikki literally bounced into the Beemer. Dori sighed in defeat. Whatever Jake's game plan, he'd already won her little sister over to his side. All he'd have to do now was offer to let her brother get behind the wheel of the BMW, and Joey would quickly follow suit.

EIGHT

Jake wasn't surprised at how quickly Dori grasped the intricacies of the complex structure that would constitute N.Y. McStore. From what his investigation had uncovered, he knew she had an extremely high I.Q. and an incredible knowledge of computers. How else could a seventeen-year-old have pulled off a complete disappearing act for herself and her siblings?

As he sat listening to her ask technical questions that would never have occurred to him, he realized that Dori very likely had managed her sleight-of-hand six years earlier without any outside help. The woman was a genius. But then again, criminal minds often were.

"You really don't need to concern yourself with the technical aspects of the website," Niles said, interrupting a conversation she was having with his systems analyst. "You'll be doing online chats with our customers, not tech support, Dori."

From his vantage point, Jake could see her fight to suppress righteous indignation over Niles's patronizing comment. She sucked in her lower lip and absently fidgeted with a button on her black herringbone blazer, a blazer which her sister had proudly informed him Dori had made, along with the coordinating black wool skirt but not the yellow turtleneck.

Nikki had spent the entire ten-minute ride to her high school regaling him with her sister's many talents while Dori sat stewing beside him. He had no doubt Nikki would be in for a scathing earful this evening.

He was quickly learning that the multitalented Dori Johnson was also a real spitfire, always ready with a biting retort to any injustice, perceived or otherwise. Those sea green eyes of hers spoke volumes, their now-stormy cast unable to hide what her tongue held back.

He watched as she struggled to compose her face into a pleasant, nonthreatening smile, a smile that never made it as far as her eyes. "I don't consider any knowledge useless," she said. "Besides, you never know what someone might ask, and I'd like to be as helpful as possible to all our customers. That is my job, isn't it?"

Score two points for Dori Johnson, thought Jake, glancing over at Niles. He loved his friend dearly, but Jake was afraid Niles York would be a male chauvinist until the day he died.

"Yes, of course. That's all well and good, but you still have to meet with several other departments today before your appointment at Lincoln Modeling." He turned to his computer expert. "Thank you. That will be all."

"Yes, Mr. York." Flipping off the laptop, the man gathered the presentation materials scattered across the large oval conference table and left without so much as a nod to Dori.

This time Dori couldn't quell her displeasure. She scowled at Niles but had the good sense to wait until he was concentrating on a folder of papers in front of him. When Jake offered her what he thought was a commiserating smile, she scowled at him as well.

"Why do I need to meet with a modeling consultant?" she asked. "I thought you wanted someone who wasn't a professional model."

"You asked them to represent you. They have a reputation to maintain. This is their requirement, not mine. I suppose they want to make certain you don't do anything in public that might embarrass them." He glanced up from his papers. "I understand they're overly sensitive after that scandal with the *Victoria's Secret* model last year."

"Embarrass them? How? By picking my nose? I can assure both you *and* Lincoln I won't do anything to embarrass either *their* agency *or* Niles York Enterprises. Didn't I sign a contract stating as much?"

"What about mentioning such a disgusting habit to begin with?"

Score two points for Niles. He smiled when she flushed with embarrassment. Then he turned back to his papers, jotting something on the page in front of him before pushing back his chair and standing. "I have some work to do. Why don't you take Dori to lunch before our next meeting, Jake?"

Without waiting for an answer, he turned his back on them and headed for the door that connected the conference room to his private office.

NINE

At precisely three o'clock Dori, with Jake in tow, was ushered into the offices of former beauty pageant queen turned modeling executive, Almalynne Haines. The Ivana Trump lookalike was dressed from head to toe in a saccharine-sweet shade of pink that coordinated with the office's color scheme. He felt like he'd died and gone to Pepto-Bismol hell. He also suspected Almalynne could go head-to-head with his ex-wife in a fake boobs contest.

Jake glanced at Dori and saw the skepticism in her eyes as she assessed both her surroundings and her instructor. He was reminded once again of why, against his better judgment, he was drawn to her. Natural, down-to-earth Dori Johnson was the complete antithesis of affected women like Gwynne Corth-Prentiss and Almalynne Haines.

Settling into an overstuffed, white leather sofa with a profusion of pink throw pillows, Jake propped his feet on the glass coffee table and leaned back, looking forward to an interesting afternoon. Dori didn't disappoint him.

For three excruciating hours she suffered through a crash course in how to act like a model, or at least Almalynne's and Lincoln Modeling's version of the ideal mannequin. With a combination of drill sergeant precision and the patience of a kindergarten teacher, Almalynne instructed Dori on essential deportment. In a singsong voice dripping with honey-coated Southern charm, she guided Dori through the proper methods of sitting, standing, walking, shaking hands, making eye contact, and speaking.

Dori glided back and forth across the thickly piled pink carpet, performing for Almalynne like an obedient puppy. Throughout the exercises, she maintained the prerequisite smile no matter how many times Almalynne demanded she repeat a task, but the storm in Dori's eyes was growing to Category Five.

The levy broke after Almalynne, standing in the center of the large room, demonstrated the beauty pageant wave. "You've got to be kidding! Not only is that ridiculous, it's demeaning."

Almalynne stepped back, looking as if Dori had slapped her across her face. "I wouldn't joke about something as serious as this!" She turned to him. "This is very important. If she's going to be making public appearances, she has to know how to greet her audiences. We can't have her flailing her arms like some sports jock, can we?"

Dori shot him a don't-you-dare-agree-with-her look, but Jake shrugged the glare off. "I think it would be in everyone's best interest if you learned the wave," he said, keeping all emotion from his voice and a deadpan expression on his face. In truth, he was finding it difficult to contain the enormous guffaw bubbling up inside him. Almalynne Haines was comical enough, but teamed up with Dori as her straight man...well, Jake was beginning to regret he wrote techno-thrillers instead of slapstick comedies. This was prime material.

Dori pasted a smile back on her face, apologized for her outburst, and watched as Almalynne demonstrated the ludicrous wave a second time, but Jake could tell she wanted to strangle someone, and that someone was probably him.

"Now try it with me," said Almalynne. "Ready?" She bent her right arm at the elbow. Holding her forearm upright, she swayed her elbow from left to right, rotated her wrist, and brought her hand first to her throat, then to her lips in an elegant, sweeping gesture. As she performed the pantomime, she sang, "Elbow, elbow, wrist, wrist. Touch your pearls and blow a kiss. Now do it with me."

Dori practiced alongside her, her face frozen in a perfect smile, her words uttered through gritted teeth.

"No, no!" Almalynne released a dramatic sigh. "You're much too stiff, and your movements are jerky. Your arm must flow as if it's gliding along on a gentle breeze. Your body language must convey your pleasure over the adulation the crowd is bestowing on you."

"Whoa!" said Dori. "*Adulation of the crowd?* I think there's been some mix-up here. I'm not preparing for the Miss America pageant. I'm only going to be cutting the ribbons at some store openings."

Right before his eyes Jake watched as the soft-spoken Southern kitten transformed into a bristling she-tiger. Almalynne's face grew tight, her eyes narrowed on Dori as she positioned herself toe-to-toe in front of her. Her soft drawl, transformed into a strident twang, each word punctuated with a perfectly manicured poke to Dori's chest. "I don't care if you're opening an outhouse in Dead Gulch, Wyoming, Miss Johnson. You are a representative of this agency, and you *will* act accordingly. Do I make myself perfectly clear?"

Dori's eyes had gone beyond Category Five. She was about to make Katrina look like a spring drizzle. Jake knew if he didn't step in, she'd either strangle Almalynne Haines or storm out of the office. Maybe both. Either way, Niles would not be pleased.

He jumped to his feet and dragged her to a corner of the room. "Look," he whispered, crushing her body close to his to prevent her from wriggling out of his grasp, "you're right. This is ridiculous. The woman is a friggin' anachronism, but if you want to get this over with, take control of the situation."

She tensed further, her body turning to steel against his, and leveled him with an icy glare. "That's exactly what I was doing before you grabbed me, Jake."

"No." He shook her gently, hissing his words into her ear. "All you're doing is antagonizing her. Master the moronic wave, and we can get out of here. Keep up the hostility, and we'll be here all night."

The fight drained from her. She relaxed her body against his and tilted her head to face him. The storm receded from her eyes until the color was once again a tranquil ocean green. "You're right. I'm sorry."

"Good. Now go touch your pearls and blow me a kiss. Gracefully." Before he realized what he was doing and could stop himself, he lowered his head and planted a gentle kiss on her temple. Dori's head jerked back, her eyes grew wide, and Jake wasn't certain which one of them was shaken more by his sudden, spontaneous action.

* * *

Dori stepped from Jake's arms, the touch of his lips scorching a trail straight to her toes. For a moment she forgot where she was and why she was there. Her entire universe shrank to just her and Jake, their gazes locked. He was the first to recover, the startled look on his face quickly masked by the brooding countenance she was far more used to seeing. He cocked his head in Almalynne's direction. Dori glanced over his shoulder.

Almalynne, her carriage as noble as a queen's, her arms crossed over her raw silk suit—a suit that Dori suspected cost more than her entire wardrobe—glared at them. She raised one perfectly plucked eyebrow at Dori. "Are you ready to continue, Miss Johnson, or will we be forced to charge you with breach of contract?"

Breach of contract? How dare she! Before Dori could give the woman a well-deserved piece of her mind, Jake's arm shot out, his fingers encircling her bicep like a vice. Dori backed down, but she failed to see how she could be in breach of contract for refusing to do some imbecilic wave.

Besides, Lincoln was her rep, not the other way around and as such would be receiving a hefty percentage of her income from Niles York Enterprises, when all they'd done was negotiate her contract and force her to endure three hours of Almalynne Haines and her asinine instruction. "You can let go," she muttered to Jake. "I promise to behave."

When he released her arm, she crossed the room to where Almalynne stood, still glaring. Taking a calming breath, Dori once again plastered a smile on her face and apologized. "I'm sorry, Miss Haines. My outburst was totally uncalled for. It's been a long few days, and I'm still a bit overwhelmed by all of this. If it's all right with you, I'd like to continue."

"Very well," said Almalynne. "Let me see you wave."

Dori spent the next half hour swaying her arm and singing, "Elbow, elbow, wrist, wrist. Touch your pearls and blow a kiss," until she was afraid she'd croon the obnoxious ditty in her sleep. But eventually Almalynne was satisfied that she'd mastered the all-important gesture and finally dismissed her with a warning to present herself according to Lincoln standards. Always.

"Don't ever forget, you are representing Lincoln Modeling as well as N.Y. McStore," she said as Dori and Jake left her office.

"I won't forget," said Dori, flashing her the perfect Lincoln smile.

* * *

Waiting for the elevator, out of earshot of Almalynne and the rest of the Lincoln employees, Dori turned her pent-up frustrations on Jake. "I will *not* do that idiotic wave, and I don't believe Lincoln can sue me for breach of contract. They work for me, not the other way around."

Her piques of rage, when directed toward Almalynne, had made for an interesting afternoon. The modeling executive deserved nothing but derision. Maybe pity, if Jake were in a benevolent mood. Which he wasn't. He couldn't abide women like Almalynne Haines. He had the unfortunate history of having married one.

However, he had a more pressing matter on his mind—the bolt of lightning that had hit the moment his lips touched Dori's temple. The kiss had awakened a certain part of his anatomy that possessed a mind of its own where Dori Johnson was concerned.

A soft ping heralded the arrival of the elevator. The doors

swooshed open, and three leggy blondes, all nearly as tall as Jake's own six-foot frame, exited. From the corner of his eye, he caught the most statuesque of the three offering him an inviting smile, but he barely acknowledged her. His attention was riveted on Dori.

Her eyes closed, she drew in deep breaths of air through her nose, releasing them slowly through her mouth. Calming breaths. He recognized the breathing technique. One. Two. Three. Then she opened her eyes, shuddered slightly, and entered the elevator. He had seen her perform the same ritual several times over the past two days, each time prior to entering an elevator. "I'm sure it's perfectly safe," he said. "They get inspected on a regular basis."

She greeted his statement with a confused expression.

"The elevator," he said, stepping in after her and pushing the button for the ground floor. "You act as if you're afraid of it."

"It's not the elevator." She inhaled sharply as they began their sixty-two story descent.

Then it dawned on him. "You're claustrophobic."

TEN

"Slightly."

Jake remembered all too well how irrational panic could paralyze an otherwise sensible person. His mother had cornered the market on phobias, suffering from the ultimate of them all—phobophobia, the fear of fear. A wave of compassion swept over him. He reached out for her. To his amazement, she allowed him to draw her close. "Close your eyes," he said, stroking her back. "Take deep breaths." His fingers made their way up her spine to her nape. Again. And like last night the soothing ministrations caused the same unsettling effect in him. "Try not to think about it."

"Right." The elevator pinged and lurched to a halt. Dori raised her head to check the digital floor display. When she saw they still had forty floors to travel, she groaned. The doors opened and two linebacker lookalikes entered, consuming half the small compartment. The color drained from her face, her body trembling beneath Jake's arm.

Two floors later a UPS delivery man with a hand truck full of cartons entered. On the next floor a woman with a baby stroller squeezed in, taking what little remained of the available floor space.

Squashed behind her, Jake could no longer see Dori's face, but he felt her shaking and heard the unmistakable gulping breaths of someone about to hyperventilate. "Coming out," he yelled as the elevator stopped on the twelfth floor, and the UPS man exited. The other occupants shifted slightly to their left and right. Grabbing Dori, Jake squeezed them both through the small opening and out the elevator.

He led her to a row of benches lining the wall across the brightly lit hallway. "Don't move," he said, lowering her head between her legs. "Just take slow, deep breaths. I'll be right back."

She cupped her hands over her face and did as he instructed. Obviously, she'd been down this road before. He waited a moment to make certain she'd be all right, then left in search of a restroom.

* * *

Dori wished the floor would open up and swallow her. How embarrassing! Of all times for her pre-elevator ritual to fail her! Didn't she have enough problems where Jake Prentiss was concerned? Now she had to go and have a panic attack in front of him. It was all his fault. She would have been fine if he'd kept his hands to himself. She couldn't believe the fantasy his touch had set off—and in a crowded elevator! What was the matter with her?

"Here. This should help." Jake placed a cool, damp paper towel across the back of her neck. "Feeling better?"

She cocked her head to the side, surprised to see genuine concern in his eyes instead of mockery. She took another deep breath, letting it out slowly. She no longer felt as though someone were squeezing the air from her lungs. "Yes, thank you."

"That happen often?"

"First time." First time in a long time, but he didn't need to know that. She cast a wary glance across the hall. "What floor are we on?"

"Twelve."

"Twelve," she repeated, pushing herself to her feet. "I suppose it's time to get back on the horse."

"Would you rather take the stairs?"

She'd give anything to take the stairs, but Dori knew she'd never conquer her fear of confined places if she gave in to it. "No. I'm fine." She shrugged off the hand he offered her and marched across the hallway to the bank of elevators.

* * *

Jake watched with growing admiration as she pressed the button, then closed her eyes and took her three deep cleansing breaths. Niles was right. The woman certainly possessed an overabundance of *moxie*.

"Would you believe I once wanted to be an astronaut?" she asked, after the elevator doors closed, and the car began its descent. She shook her head and produced a chuckle that sounded more like an ironic snort. "I guess some dreams just aren't meant to be."

The ride this time took them directly to the lobby without any stops. Once they were out of the building and on the street, Dori heaved a huge sigh. "Let's walk for a while," Jake said, taking her arm.

They strolled at a leisurely pace, oblivious to the other

pedestrians rushing past them on the crowded street. Dori showed no signs of anxiety as the frenzy of homeward-bound commuters, fighting to escape the city, bumped and jostled them. "Crowds don't bother you?"

"Not usually."

He wasn't sure he believed her, especially when her arm trembled slightly under his grasp, but with no evidence to the contrary, he changed the topic. "You look like you could use a drink." He steered her toward a small bistro.

"I'm fine. I'd rather just go straight home if you don't mind."

Jake eyed her skeptically. "I do mind, and you're not fine. You're pale as a sheet and still shaking. Don't fight me on this."

A hint of the feisty Dori began to reemerge, along with some of her color. "Mr. Prentiss!"

Ignoring her protest, he yanked open the restaurant door with one hand while his other pulled her along with him. "Jake," he growled into her ear.

"Jake." She spit the word through gritted teeth. "I don't need a drink."

"Well, I do. I've got that damn elbow-elbow, wrist-wrist jingle dancing around in my head, and it's driving me crazy." He rolled his eyes. "That thing could easily replace both Chinese water torture and the rack, not to mention chemical and biological warfare. Blast it over the airwaves twenty-four hours a day, and within a week the country will be reduced to a population of blithering idiots."

Dori grinned, her eyes twinkling with devilment, all signs of her recent trauma vanished. "Don't you dare," he warned her, reaching for her wrist as she cocked her elbow.

"And if I do?"

"I'll lock you in a closet and throw away the key." The moment the words escaped his lips, Jake realized his mistake. The merriment fled Dori's eyes, replaced by a fear that chilled him to the bone. "Hey, I'm sorry. I didn't mean..." *Damn!* He reached out to her, but she stepped back, wedging herself against the small lobby wall.

"Go away," she whimpered.

He moved closer. "Dori."

"Don't touch me." She clenched her fists at her side, her body rigid with rage.

"That's it, isn't it?" Some bastard had locked her in a closet, probably when she was quite young. Probably that no-good father of hers.

She squeezed her eyes closed, and Jake could only assume she was trying to shut out the awful memories triggered by his slip of the tongue. Instead of obeying her command, he swept her into his arms and held her while she fought off both him and the pain. "I'm so sorry," he whispered. He stroked her back and ran his fingers through her hair as she struggled with her personal demons. "So sorry," he repeated over and over.

* * *

What was happening to her? This day had turned into one endless nightmare. Normally, she kept a tight rein on her fears, but twice in less than half an hour she'd lost control in front of Jake. She struggled to keep the tears that stung the back of her eyes from breaking through her tightly squeezed lids. Intellectually she knew why she feared elevators or any small, confined space, but she hadn't thought about the closet in years. Now with one flippant remark, Jake had unleashed the bogey man of her childhood.

She drew in a sharp breath and pushed away from him. Raising her chin, she met his questioning gaze and saw the concern and remorse in his eyes. He couldn't have known how his words would tear at her. "I think I will have that drink."

"Want to talk about it?" he asked after they were seated beside the window at a glass-topped, wrought-iron table with matching chairs.

Dori glanced out at the rush hour traffic. She never spoke of the past to anyone. The most insignificant comment might prove fatal to the carefully constructed life she'd created for herself, Nikki, and Joey. Still, she did owe him some sort of explanation. Besides, she had come to know Jake Prentiss well enough to realize he wouldn't stop prodding until he got some answers.

The waitress arrived with her Chablis and Jake's Scotch and soda. "Ready to order, folks?"

Neither of them had glanced at the menus the maitre d' had handed them. Dori had spent the time staring out the window or at her clasped hands to avoided Jake's penetrating stare.

"Dori?"

She pulled her gaze from her laced fingers to his questioning eyes and nodded. Not up for another confrontation with him, she said, "Why don't you order for both of us?"

"Any specials?" he asked the waitress, without bothering to consult the menu.

"Our special today is shrimp and artichoke hearts with chopped spinach. It's served over a bed of angel hair pasta."

He handed her the menus. "Two of those."

After the waitress left, he reached for Dori's hands. "If I'd known, I never would have made such a callous remark."

"I know." And she did. She'd come to realize that Jake Prentiss, for all his gruff, brooding exterior, was deep down a caring person.

She'd seen it in the way he looked out for Niles. His interaction with Nikki this morning. The way he diffused the situation with Almalynne. And his concern for her in the elevator. She owed him at least some truth.

"When I was little, my mother used to lock us in the closet whenever my father came home drunk. She was afraid he'd hurt us." She paused, biting down on her trembling lower lip. "The way he used to hurt her. Sometimes we'd be in there for hours, sometimes all night, cowering at the sounds of her pleas and screams. Afterwards, it always looked like a tornado had struck. We'd tiptoe around the apartment helping my mother clean up the mess while my father slept off all the vodka he'd consumed earlier."

Jake cursed under his breath. "Why didn't she leave the bastard?"

In retrospect Dori often wondered that herself. She could never reconcile her mother's blind devotion to the man who treated his wife and children like indentured servants. Since both of her parents were products of an archaic world, she could only assume her mother's subservience stemmed from an ingrained and outdated ideology.

"One night," she continued, "when Joey was a toddler, he came home worse than ever. My mother had been sick on and off all winter but had refused to see a doctor. Kept saying it was just a cold." She hesitated for several seconds before continuing. "I don't know exactly what happened, whether he knocked her out or if she passed out during their fight, but that was the last time we saw her alive."

Jake's eyes grew wide. His brief investigation of Sergei Ivanichek had mentioned nothing about any charges filed against him for spousal abuse. "She died?"

In her heart Dori had always blamed her father for her mother's death, although her head knew otherwise. Although Sergei abused his wife and terrorized his children, God had handed her mother the death sentence. "It was cancer. By the time the doctors saw her, there was nothing they could do."

"And you took your mother's place."

Jake jumped to a logical conclusion considering the facts she'd divulged. Logical but erroneous. She shook her head. "No. He never laid a hand on any of us after that. I think in some warped way he loved her very much and blamed himself for her death. I don't think he ever got over it."

"You feel sorry for him?" His words were tinged with surprise.

She shook her head a second time before meeting his gaze. "I feel sorry for all of us."

ELEVEN

Jake watched Dori pick at her food, moving it around on her plate but eating little. She'd survived a rough few hours. Confessing the source of her deep-seated fear couldn't have been easy for her. He admired her for the courage she rallied to face her demons and fight off her panic. Dori Johnson was quickly winning the respect of one very jaded former intelligence officer.

As time passed, Jake found it harder and harder to reconcile the woman before him with the one he'd originally presumed her to be. As yet he'd turned up no proof against her, and even his gut now refused to accept her as a pawn, willing or otherwise, in some scheme of retaliation against Niles. He just wasn't certain he could trust his gut—not when he'd previously been fooled into believing a man's guilt by supposedly irrefutable evidence.

But Dori Johnson was no Calvin Bigelow. Yes, she had her secrets. But when Jake stripped through the many layers that comprised Dori, he found only a caring individual, concerned more for the welfare of others than herself. And that in itself was a conundrum. No underlying deceit had surfaced to explain the great lengths she'd gone to in order to hide her true identity.

Although Sergei had physically abused his wife, Dori had denied her father ever beaten his children after his wife's death. So if she hadn't run away to escape abuse, what had she run from?

On the other hand, maybe she was just a damn fine actress. But if that were the case, Jake had lost every one of his sharply honed intuitive skills, and he refused to believe himself *that* rusty. Or maybe he was. Ever since the Bigelow suicide, Jake no longer trusted his own judgment. He'd been wrong once. He could be wrong again.

It also didn't help that at the moment he wanted to kiss Dori senseless—and then some, a troubling revelation for a man who had all but sworn off women. Nothing like maintaining a professional distance. The more time he spent in Dori's company, the harder Jake struggled to keep his thoughts purely professional. Other than one disastrous mistake, otherwise known as the former Mrs. Jake Prentiss, he'd always operated with his head and not his hormones. Except with Dori, his brain had decided to take a holiday just when he needed his gray matter the most.

Mention of her parents, although painful to her, had offered Jake an opportunity he couldn't pass up. Willing himself back into his investigative persona, he pursued the topic. "When did your father die?"

"Die?"

As he had suspected, his question took her by surprise. He hoped her response might indicate any recent contact with Ivanichek's cohorts. "That is why you're raising your brother and sister by yourself, isn't it?"

He watched as her features hardened, her lips setting into a thin line. She sat up a little straighter in her chair, lifted her chin, and pierced him with an icy gaze. Her words came across equally frosty. "If you don't mind, Jake, I'd rather not discuss my family any further."

She'd drawn a line and let him know he was not to cross it. Now or ever. So much for prying free the information he sought. Jake bowed his head and mumbled an apology to placate her. "I'm sorry. I didn't mean to rouse painful memories for you."

No, he had meant to shake loose her secrets, but either Dori was too savvy for his ploy or too fearful to trust anyone. Her wary expression told him he'd stirred up far more than disturbing memories, but he suspected he'd need a crowbar to force any secrets from her. Dori wasn't about to divulge anything to anyone.

So much for getting to the heart of the matter. He was no closer to the truth, and he was still fixating on branding her with his lips. Only now the fantasy had progressed to include trailing those lips over every naked square inch of her body. Jake knew he was in deep trouble.

* * *

Dori couldn't shake the feeling that Jake knew too much about her, but if that were the case, why didn't he expose her? This new softer, caring side of him rattled her. She preferred the adversarial Jake. At least then she knew to be on her guard. She didn't trust the new Jake, the one who offered comfort, the one who melted her bones and stirred feelings inside her that were best left undisturbed. She had no place in her life for a man—any man, let alone one as dangerous as Jake Prentiss.

She needed to gain control of the situation. Fast. In less than two weeks they began their cross-country sojourn. Just the two of them. Jake and Dori alone together twenty-four hours a day, seven days a week, nonstop throughout much of the next several months. The thought sent a tingle from her head straight down to her toes. Only she couldn't figure out whether the tingle heralded anticipation or signaled a dire warning.

Maybe he was just trying to make an effort to be friendly, but Dori suspected ulterior motives. She wished she knew more about him, but Jake was as closed-mouth about his past as she was about hers. When she questioned him, he mumbled something about being a disillusioned executive, fed up with the rat race and taking some time off. She didn't buy it for a minute.

The only thing she was certain of concerning Jake Prentiss was the turmoil he unleashed within her. And that wasn't good. She vowed to keep a lid on her libido and an emotional distance from the man creating the problem, but he constantly blindsided her, thwarting all efforts. He played dirty. He'd already managed to acquire a willing accomplice in Nikki. She suspected Joey would be next on Jake's conquest list.

* * *

Just as Dori feared, later that evening Jake offered to let Joey get behind the wheel of the BMW. After several trips around the block, the nineteen-year-old Benedict Arnold switched camps.

One rakish grin and a well-directed compliment had already placed starry-eyed Nikki under Jake's spell. Before Dori could mount a counteroffensive, the enemy had taken control of the troops.

TWELVE

Over the course of the next two week, Jake insinuated himself more and more into her life. Dori fought hard to maintain a distance between them but found herself losing the battle—in large part due to the insidious matchmaking shenanigans of a very determined fifteen-year-old and her nineteen-year-old partner in crime.

At the devious duo's insistence, Jake joined them for breakfast every morning and stayed for dinner many nights. Nikki and Joey, the king and queen of zapped meals, had miraculously morphed overnight into from-scratch gourmets.

It took Dori several days to figure out her brother and sister had enlisted the aid of a third traitor, the very talented Mrs. Menotti. Arriving home earlier than expected one evening, Dori caught her sister, casserole in hand, leaving their next-door neighbor's apartment. Dori fumed; Jake chuckled.

"Are you always this easily manipulated?" she asked him the next morning after they'd dropped Nikki off at the high school and Joey at his campus.

"What makes you think I'm being manipulated?"

So that was it! Her sister and brother might think they controlled the cards, but Jake had stacked the deck in his favor. Whatever his scheme, Nikki and Joey had played right into Jake's grand plan. The obvious explanation immediately sprang to Dori's mind. "You still don't trust me, do you?"

"Did I say that?"

"You act it."

"How so?"

"By keeping an eye on me from dawn until late at night. The only time I'm alone is when I step into a restroom, and even then, I have this sneaking suspicion you'd follow if you thought you could get away with it. You act more like a jailer than a business associate, and I resent it." She crossed her arms over her chest and shifted in her seat to stare out the window. Behind her she heard him exhale sharply, a muffled *shit* riding the wave of his breath.

"There's more at stake here than you realize, Dori. I'm only doing my job."

"Yes, protecting Niles's investment. So you've said." She didn't like being thought of as a commodity rather than a person. She'd traded the peace of anonymity for financial security, but she hadn't expected to have to sacrifice her soul in the process—not to mention her heart.

The sobering rogue thought brought her up short, her stomach taking a sudden nosedive. Physical attraction she could understand and explain away. Jake was drop-dead gorgeous, and hormones acted of their own free will. But when had her heart entered into the equation? She refused to accept the disquieting revelation, dismissing it as edginess over an increasingly difficult situation. Dori Johnson gave her heart to no man.

She forced her concentration back to the matter at hand. "However," she continued, fighting to control the wobble in her voice, "sharing three meals a day with you isn't part of my contract with Niles York Enterprises and neither is putting up with the way you encourage my brother and sister."

"Excuse me?"

"You know very well what I mean."

"Consider me obtuse. Humor me with an explanation."

Dori spun in her seat to confront him. "They're trying to get us together."

"Are they?"

"You know damn well what they're up to, Jake, and you're doing nothing to discourage them. If anything, you're encouraging this nonsense. I know you really don't like me, so why are you leading them on? You're using Nikki and Joey, and I don't like it. They're going to get hurt."

Like her. Jake had already inflicted enough pain, intentional or not. Dori could handle her own emotions, but no one messed with her brother and sister, not without answering to her.

Jake cocked one eyebrow but maintained his concentration on the traffic in front of him. "I don't?"

"Don't what?"

"Like you?"

"You know you don't."

He drew his gaze away from the road long enough to spear her with one of his brooding glares. "Did I ever say that?"

"You didn't have to. Besides, we've had this conversation

before."

"Yes, and last time you jumped to the same erroneous conclusion if I remember correctly."

Dori flailed her arms, not an easy task in the small confines of the sports car. "Look. I need some space. Today is Friday. After we finish up this afternoon, I don't want to see you again until we leave for the airport Monday morning. Got it?"

He merely offered her a thoughtful look, leaving her to wonder if he'd agreed to her demand or not, but she quickly lost her train of thought when at the next traffic light, Jake pulled up behind a New Jersey Transit bus, and she found herself face-to-face with a larger-than-life version of herself.

"Nice picture."

Dori stared in disbelief, her hands shooting to her mouth. "Oh, my God!" Suddenly, the full impact of her decision to accept Niles York's offer hit her. Yes, she knew the print and radio campaign kicked off today, but up until this moment the idea of her image blanketing America had seemed distant and surreal. However, the portrait on the rear end of the bus had instantly transformed the surreal into the *very* real. What had she done?

"Don't you like it?"

"It's...it's so big." An incessant honking horn pulled her attention away from the bus and to the mud-spattered red pickup that had pulled up alongside them. Once he had her attention, the driver pointed first to her and then the bus, mouthing, "You?"

Nodding, Dori offered him a weak smile. He tossed her a kiss and a thumb's up, then switched lanes to shoot ahead of them.

"Better get used to it," said Jake. "The blitz has begun." To illustrate his point, he motioned to a billboard mounted on a building to his left. "You're all over the place."

Within minutes the radio concurred when the music on the soft rock station Jake had tuned to broke for commercials. "Hi! I'm Dori. Join me for a new shopping experience. Coming soon— N.Y. McStore, affordable upscale shopping for the twenty-first century woman. Just a click, a call, a short drive away. Remember—we're Not-Your-Mother's-Chain-Store."

Dori groaned. She'd never heard a transmission of her own voice. The broadcast sounded so different from what her ears normally heard, so...sexy!

She refused to believe the world heard her like that. "That's not my voice!" The person on the radio spoke like a cross between the come-hither little girl breathiness of Marilyn Monroe and the throaty sensuality of Lauren Bacall. "I don't sound like that!"

"Well, it's certainly not me."

Dori glared at the radio, but her words pleaded with him. "The technicians enhanced the recording. They must have." She turned to Jake, waiting for confirmation. When none came, she buried her head in her hands, uncertain which bothered her more— images of herself plastered all over the country or the knowledge that every time she opened her mouth, she sounded like she was soliciting sex. "I can't believe this."

"Most women would kill to have a voice that induced male fantasies."

Dori's head shot up. "What!"

"You heard me."

"If you're trying to make me feel better, you're only succeeding in making me angry. I don't appreciate being thought of as a slut."

"Hey! Hold on a minute. When did we leap from sexy to slut?"

She pointed at the radio. "That voice sounded like the voice of a bimbo. I am *not* a bimbo. I can't make public appearances sounding like that. What will people think?"

"That you're a beautiful woman with a voice to match."

"No! They'll be trying to imagine me naked!" She threw her head back against the seat and squeezed her eyes shut. "This is a nightmare. I thought Niles hired me because he wanted someone women would connect with—a working woman on a budget. Isn't that what he wanted? The girl-next-door. Not a sultry siren. Is he deaf? Women won't bond with me. Once they hear my voice, they'll hide their husbands and boyfriends!"

"That's it, Dori! I've had enough." Jake swerved out of traffic and pulled into the empty lot of a boarded-up restaurant. Shifting into park, he yanked up the hand brake, then grabbed her by the shoulders and forced her to look at him. "You are *not* going to get cold feet," he said, his words forcing their way out between tightly drawn lips. "Understand? You have an obligation, and you're going to go through with it. I don't care if you sound like a porno star or Kermit the Frog. You're not bailing. I won't let you do that to Niles. He has too much invested in you."

There it was again. Dori the commodity. She stared into Jake's steely eyes and saw nothing but contempt. For her. If only Nikki and Joey could see this side of the man they hoped would ride off into the sunset with their sister, they'd give up on their foolish matchmaking.

She was part of a business deal, nothing more. Once the launch ended, she'd never see Jake again. He'd go back to his corporate ivory tower and however he made his millions and never give her another thought. As he should. There was nothing between them. Neither of them wanted anything between them. So why did that thought suddenly bother her?

She pulled out of his grasp and sat back in her seat. Staring straight ahead she spoke in a voice devoid of emotion but full of conviction. "You can relax, Jake. I have no intention of breaking my contract with Niles."

"Don't even think about it." Dori turned to glare at him. "What the hell did you think was going to happen?" he continued. "Everything was clearly spelled out. You've known from the very first day how the campaign would unfold."

Intellectually, yes. None of this came as a surprise. But the emotional impact had overwhelmed her. What if Joey were wrong? What if everything she'd worked so hard to achieve—her freedom, her brother's and sister's futures—all came tumbling down because of a picture on a bus? Or a voice over the airwaves?

Jake couldn't possibly understand the turmoil roiling inside her. This wasn't about vanity or stage fright. It wasn't about a sexy voice or a leering truck driver or even overprotective wives and girlfriends. They were excuses because she didn't dare admit the true nature of her fears. Not to him. This was about hiding the past, protecting the present, securing the future. Hers and Nikki's and Joey's. The damage was done. From now on she'd have to be more diligent than ever.

If it weren't already too late.

THIRTEEN

Dori spent the weekend before her trip catching up on the bills, stocking the refrigerator, and second-guessing her decision to leave her brother and sister alone for the next few weeks.

"We'll be fine," Joey repeatedly reassured her. "You worry too much."

"Come on," said Nikki, grabbing Dori's arm and pulling her off the kitchen chair. "Let's go do something fun now that we have lots of money."

Dori scowled at the pile of bills spread across the table. "We're not rolling in cash, Nik. I've only received two paychecks at the new rate so far, and Joey's winter semester tuition is due next week. I also have to pay the utilities and rent before I leave and make sure there's cash for the two of you in case of emergencies."

She studied her sister. "Does your winter coat still fit? I swear you've grown half a foot since last year. And what about your boots? It might snow while I'm gone."

"Jeez, Dori! It's only the end of September. It's not going to snow."

"I won't be back until nearly Thanksgiving. We've had snow in November before."

Nikki rolled her eyes. "My boots fit. Let's go to the movies. Please, Dori? We haven't all been to a movie in ages, and the new Orlando Bloom picture is playing over at Newport Mall."

Dori suppressed the urge to roll her own eyes. She glanced at Joey. From his expression she knew that the prospect of an afternoon of Orlando didn't hold much appeal for him either, but he merely shrugged.

Dori hated the idea of shelling out nearly forty dollars on movie tickets for a film neither of them wanted to see, but Nikki rarely got the chance to do the things that most girls her age took for granted. Her sister accepted their unusual situation without complaining and normally asked for very little.

Nikki continued her cajoling. "Come on, Dori. It's Orlando Bloom! Don't say no, please?"

Dori knew when to give in. And after all, she rationalized, she'd be away from home for several weeks. Nikki deserved a treat before she left. "Okay." She tossed her pen onto the pile of bills. "Just stop whining."

"We can go?" Nikki clasped her hands together and held her breath.

"Yes, we can go. I wouldn't dream of denying you an afternoon with Orlando Bloom. Get your coat."

"You just better not drool all over my popcorn," warned Joey. He yanked on his kid sister's ponytail as she rushed past him.

Five minutes later the three of them hopped onto a bus at the corner—a bus with Dori sprawled along its length as well as on every other placard lining the perimeter of the interior. Within moments she felt the stares of other passengers on her. Settling into a seat, she reached into her purse for her sunglasses and turned her head to stare out the window, but it was too late.

"Hey, Rico, look. We got us a regular celebrity on the bus." Dori ignored the boisterous, intoxicated sounding voice coming from across the aisle and continued facing the window. "Whatsa matter, sweetie? Limo break down?"

"Maybe she gets her kicks slummin'," said a second, equally inebriated voice. "Hey, babe. Lookin' for some action?"

Joey, sitting one row in front of her, jumped to his feet, apparently ready to defend his sister's honor. Dori reached over and grabbed his arm. "Don't. Just ignore them," she whispered.

The two men rose from their seats and sauntered to the middle of the aisle. Dori hazarded a quick glance in their direction and shivered. One stood well over six feet tall. The other was half a head shorter. Both looked as if they spent hours each day pumping iron. Tattoos covered the lengths of their arms; a multitude of piercings adorned their ears and eyebrows. One wore a bandana around his neck, the other a thick metal chain. The insignias on their jackets marked them as gang members.

"You better leave my sister alone," said Nikki. "My brother's got a black belt in karate. He'll wipe the floor with both of you."

"Nikki!" Dori tugged on her sister's sleeve. "Shut up. Don't encourage them." Unfortunately, it was too late.

The bandana bully placed his hand on the back of Nikki's seat and leaned over her. "Is that so, little girl? Well, me and my friend here got us *two* black belts." He tugged on the large brass buckle at his waist, then motioned to the other man. "Right, Pike?"

Pike leered at Nikki. "Yeah. Maybe after we get rid of your brother, we'll show you and your snotty sister a *real* good time."

Dori glanced behind her at the other passengers. None seemed interested in helping them. Some averted their eyes; others leaned forward, appearing eager for the creeps to make good on their threats. She turned her gaze to the bus driver and realized with a mounting sense of dread, that the middle-aged woman, intent on ignoring the commotion behind her, wasn't about to place herself in danger for anyone. Dori was on her own.

The bus slowed to a stop at the next corner. The doors swung open and several more passengers entered. As they maneuvered themselves past the two men blocking the aisle, Dori grabbed Nikki and Joey and bolted for the door. "Run," she yelled, pushing them out in front of her.

The three of them darted across the street and took off down the block. Dori could hear the shouts and heavy footfalls of the two men closing in behind them. Nikki and Joey, several yards ahead of her, dashed across the busy intersection at the end of the block just as the light turned yellow. Deciding her odds were better against oncoming traffic than the two fast-approaching apes, Dori leaped off the curb just as a car turned the corner and screeched to a halt between her and her pursuers.

FOURTEEN

Jake swung open the door and jumped from behind the wheel. Grabbing Dori's arm, he yanked her behind the car. From the corner of his eye, he spotted Nikki and Joey doubling back toward them. "Keep back," he yelled.

Crouching beside Dori, he drew his gun and raised it toward the two advancing men. They froze, bracing themselves against the hood of the car. Jake could tell from the silent message they sent each other that they were assessing their options.

"Go ahead. Try it," he said, taking dead aim at one of them. "I shoot to kill, and I never miss."

The one with the gun pointed squarely at his chest slowly raised his hands. The second followed suit. "Hey, man, we don't want no trouble," he said.

"Doesn't look that way to me, *man*."

Two squad cars, their sirens shrieking, screeched to a halt

behind the BMW. Pistols drawn, four uniformed officers jumped out. "We'll take it from here, sir," one of the officers said.

Jake holstered his gun and watched as the cops cuffed the two, read them their rights, then shoved one into the back of each vehicle.

After they'd sped away, Jake turned to Dori. She sat huddled on the curb, her body pressed against the side of his car. "What the hell were you doing?"

Wide-eyed, her mouth open, she stared at the gun sitting in his shoulder holster. "You have a gun." Her voice shuddered rather than spoke the words.

Yeah, and now he'd have some fast explaining to do. He pulled her to her feet. Explanations he'd rather not divulge—not if he were ever going to get to the truth about her disappearance six years earlier.

"Get in the car, Dori. You, too," he called to Nikki and Joey who were hovering beside Dori. "Let's go."

Dori continued to stare at him, her jaw set in grim determination. "No. You have a gun."

Jake had reached the end of his patience. "And you're damn lucky I do. Now get in the friggin' car. I'm blocking traffic."

A horn honked behind them. Dori jumped.

"Come on, Dor. Maybe we better do what Jake says." Joey wrapped his arm around his sister's shoulders and led her to the passenger side of the BMW. After he'd settled her into the seat, fastened her seatbelt, and closed the door, he returned to the driver's side and climbed into the back seat next to Nikki.

"Jake, you saved us," said Nikki. Her voice dripped with hero worship. "I'll bet the chief of police gives you a medal or plaque or something. They do that, you know."

Jake grunted. He could see the headlines: *Gun wielding author saves thick-headed model.* He squeezed himself behind the wheel and slammed the door shut. Releasing the emergency brake, he shifted into drive and inched back into the line of traffic fighting its way around the car.

"I thought I told you to stay off buses."

Dori sat curled up against the door, her arms wrapped tightly around her stiff body, her face devoid of color. Part of him wanted to grab and shake her until he knocked some sense into that stubborn head of hers. Another part of him wanted to take her in his arms and never let go. She had scared the shit out of him.

"I gave the chauffeur the weekend off," she said, refusing to look at him.

Jake turned to Joey. "Where were you going?"

"The movie theater at Newport Mall. The squirt has a thing for the *Pirates of the Caribbean* dude."

"The one in the eye makeup?" He figured Nikki for better taste, but she was a teenager, after all. No accounting for that strange subset of humanity.

"Not Johnny Depp," said Joey. "The Bloom dude."

Jake swung the car around and headed for the mall. A few minutes later he pulled into the parking garage. At the entrance to the theater, he fished two twenties from his pocket and offered them to Joey. "Your sister and I have some things to discuss. We'll pick you up when the show is over."

Joey hesitated, glancing first at Jake, then his sister. "Dori?"

Dori shot Jake a look that could pierce a foot thick wall of titanium. "Go ahead. Jake and I *definitely* have some things to discuss."

But Joey took only one of the bills. "This is plenty." Even

though he knew it wasn't.

Jake pressed the second bill into his hand. "Popcorn and soda."

"It's still too much," said Joey.

"Buy the super-size."

Joey hesitated, turning again to Dori for guidance.

"Go ahead," she said. "But get a receipt so Jake can add it to his expense account."

When he matched her titanium piercing glare with one of his own, she added, "Under miscellaneous babysitting expenses."

Jake waited until Joey and Nikki bought their tickets and entered the theater before he and Dori headed back to the car and drove off. After several blocks he broke the pervasive silence. "You're damn lucky I followed you."

"I can take care of myself and my family."

"Yeah, you were doing a fine job of it, too."

Dori sprang into attack mode. "Just what *were* you doing following me?"

"My job."

Her eyes widened. "You've been following me all weekend, haven't you?"

He nodded.

"Protecting Niles's investment, huh?"

Jake bit back the scathing words that sprang to his mind. Dori was too independent for her own good. He shuddered to think what might have happened had he taken the weekend off. "Would you rather I let those thugs get their hands on you and Nikki?"

From her change in expression, the question had the desired impact. As his words sank in, Jake watched the fight drain from her features. Her body sank back into the seat. "What have I done?" she whispered.

She looked so young and vulnerable. Jake wanted to scoop her up in his arms and kiss away the worry lines that settled into the corners of her mouth. Instead, he shrugged. "Nothing permanent. No one got hurt. Chances are those two have serious outstanding warrants, and you won't even have to press charges. Forget about it."

"I can't forget about it. My whole life has changed. Don't you see? I've sold my soul for a few pieces of gold. Nothing will ever be the same."

Jake swung the car into the parking area at Liberty State Park.

"Why are we stopping here?"

"Because we don't get many days like this." *And because I need to figure out just what I'm willing to tell you.*

It was one of those brilliant pollution-free early autumn afternoons when the sunlight sparkles like diamonds on the river and the New York skyline glistens like gold and silver against a cloud-free sky. Jake released a latch and pressed a button, lowering the rag top. Then he killed the engine and turned to her. "Life isn't static, Dori. Nothing ever stays the same. Not for long."

She ignored his attempt at philosophy. "I want to know about that gun," she said, pointing to his left shoulder and changing the subject. "And what about the police? How did they get there so quickly? Why didn't they check you out? You're a cop, aren't you?"

As much as he didn't want to explain himself to her, this afternoon's events had created a situation that demanded justification for his actions. He just wished she'd be as forthcoming with him. "The police responded as quickly as they did because I called them when I saw those perverts chasing you."

"You *are* a cop!"

"No, actually I'm a writer."

Dori laughed. "A writer who shoots to kill and never misses?" She crossed her arms over her chest and glared at him. "Tell me another one, Jake."

"I'm telling you the truth, Dori. I *am* a writer." He paused, taking a deep breath. *Now for the hard part.* "I'm also a government agent."

Dori tensed. "What kind of government agent?"

"The kind that can't talk about it."

"I see."

Jake studied her nervous reaction to his admission. Dori chewed on her lower lip. She laced her fingers together, clutched them in her lap, and stared at her hands. "What is it you want from me, Jake?"

"Only to keep you safe."

"Since when do government agents get assigned to protect chain store spokesmodels?"

"Normally they don't."

"Then what are you doing here?"

"I told you. Niles is my best friend, and I owed him a favor."

"So you pulled a few strings and got assigned to bodyguard duty?"

"I'm on an extended leave of absence from my job."

She hazarded a glance in his direction. "That's all?"

"Is there any reason why there should be more?"

She shook her head. "No. No, of course not. Why would you ask that?"

Why indeed? Jake could think of a dozen reasons, none of which he voiced. Instead, he sat back and watched the sailboats skim along the Hudson.

* * *

Jake's admission sent Dori into a tailspin that continued throughout the remainder of the day. Her mind raced through one possibility after another, none of which played out in her favor. She still doubted Jake knew about her, although she found it hard to believe she was capable of outsmarting a government agent.

For six years, she'd held her breath hoping her forged documents would keep her and her siblings hidden from Sergei, Borka, and the rest of the Russian-American Mafia. But a government agent? Surely, if Jake had investigated her, as he'd claimed, he would have discovered her deception.

Was she that good, or was he that inept? Maybe he was on leave because he'd bungled a previous investigation. Then she remembered how he'd come to her rescue earlier that day, and she chuckled in spite of herself. Jake Prentiss just wasn't the bungling type.

That left her back at square one, with Jake knowing about her from the beginning, and that made no sense at all. Not if his main concern was protecting Niles. But protecting Niles from what?

Overwhelmed by frustration and fear of the unknown, Dori slammed down the lid of her new suitcase and locked in her equally new wardrobe, all compliments of N.Y. McStore. As part of a prelaunch test, she'd been instructed to purchase the items off the Internet, which although not yet up and running for consumers, was being tested by various York employees to screen out bugs and glitches.

Tape measure in hand, she'd keyed in her measurements, along with her height, weight, and coloring, at the user-friendly site. When she selected an item, the computer automatically chose the proper size and offered the most appropriate color. It then gave suggestions for a variety of coordinating accessories from shoes and pantyhose to scarves and jewelry. Her purchases arrived within two days of ordering.

To Dori's amazement and pleasure, everything fit perfectly, but just in case it hadn't, Niles had covered that as well. In his quest to make e-commerce and catalog shopping as hassle-free as possible, all McStore purchases came with a prepaid return label. Niles's research found that the biggest reason consumers shied away from virtual shopping was due to the expense of shipping and returns. N.Y. McStore eliminated both costs.

In an attempt to keep from dwelling on weightier matters, Dori turned her attention to the garment bag hanging from a hook on the closet she shared with Nikki. Because her trip entailed visiting locations throughout the country, her luggage contained everything from lightweight cotton dresses to wool suits. October in Orlando bore no relation to October in Oshkosh, and both locations were scheduled stops on her itinerary over the next several weeks. She'd packed both sunscreen and mittens, each available three hundred and sixty-five days a year from N.Y. McStore.

Dori zipped up the garment bag. At least she didn't have to worry about a baggage limit. She and Jake would be traveling in the height of luxury on one of Niles York's corporate jets.

Without provocation, an image of Sergei Ivanichek flashed unbidden before her eyes. Dori cringed. Instead of a father bursting with pride over his oldest daughter's accomplishments, she saw a man consumed with anger and jealousy.

Suddenly, all of her doubts and worries over her deal with Niles diminished. Her own apprehension of Jake, and what he did or didn't know, took a back seat to her fears of her father and his cohorts. She may have broken a few laws six years ago, but in her heart she knew she'd made the right decision.

Dori glanced in the mirror hanging above her bureau and stared at the face so different from the one in Joey's tattered photo. For her sake, as well as her brother's and sister's, she prayed her recent career move wouldn't boomerang on them.

At the sound of the doorbell, she swung her combination briefcase/purse over her shoulder and picked up her carry-on. There was no turning back now.

FIFTEEN

"Never flown before, have you?" asked Jake as the plane taxied down the runway of the small airport in Teterboro, New Jersey.

Dori answered without tearing her gaze from the window. "Is it that obvious?"

"You look like a kid peering into the window of F.A.O. Schwartz at Christmastime."

After learning of Dori's claustrophobia, Jake half expected a panicky, white-knuckled flyer as a traveling companion and had even made certain there was an ample supply of air sickness bags on board before takeoff. Again, Dori surprised him. Not only did the small jet not bother her, but once onboard, she'd expressed interest in seeing the flight cabin.

"Oh!" Dori grabbed her stomach as the plane left the runway and climbed skyward. Jake reached for a bag, but stopped when she began to laugh. "Wow! This is great! It's like a roller coaster!"

He settled back in his seat and enjoyed the view—not of the ground shrinking beneath them but of the childlike expression on the face of the woman beside him. A veteran of more flights than he cared to recall, Jake searched his mind, trying to remember his first plane ride. If at the time the experience had left him with similar feelings of awe, the memories had long since faded.

Jake had flown on York private jets countless times, but his friend's obsession with creature comfort never ceased to amaze him. The Niles York Enterprises fleet consisted of five luxury airplanes. Along with the pilot and copilot, the crew of each plane included a flight attendant far more talented than any of her commercial airline counterparts. Once they'd reached cruising altitude, she began preparing breakfast.

* * *

Dori stared at the tray the flight attendant set before her a short time later. "Somehow, I doubt they serve this on the major airlines."

"Not even in first class," said Jake, taking note of the mimosas and eggs Benedict platters that looked and smelled as good as any served at The Waldorf. He took a bite of his own meal. No, definitely better than The Waldorf. Leave it to Niles.

Dori continued to eat with one eye focused out the window.

"There's not much in the way of scenery at this altitude," he said Jake, mopping up the last of his Hollandaise with a wedge of English muffin.

"But it's beautiful. The clouds look like billowy featherbeds. Perfect for bouncing."

"I wouldn't advice it. Looks can be deceiving."

Dori pulled her gaze from the window and scowled at him. "Some writer. Where's your imagination?"

"I don't need much of one. Truth is stranger than fiction."

"Exactly what is it you write? Dry technical manuals? IRS tax instructions?"

Hardly. But because Jake had begun his literary career while still an intelligence operative, he kept his author persona a closely guarded secret. Only a handful of people knew that Jake Prentiss and Harrison Kent were one and the same. The pseudonymous author, known to his public as an eccentric recluse, made no personal appearances, and his photo remained conspicuously absent from his book jackets. Jake meant to keep it that way. "Not quite but something like that."

Dori turned her attention back to the clouds. "That figures."

After the flight attendant cleared their trays, Jake fished a folder out of the side pocket in his laptop case. "I have our itinerary for the next few weeks. You'd better study it in case you have any questions." They were headed to Atlanta, one of several strategically located distribution points throughout the country.

After a thorough tour of the inner workings of the facility to familiarize her with the maze-like floor plan as well as order taking and shipping procedures, Dori would then take customers on a virtual, interactive visit later that evening. Over the next several weeks, she'd be on hand for the ribbon cutting of each of the first fifteen retail superstores, beginning with the flagship store located in Orlando, where Niles was scheduled to join them Tuesday.

"I've already seen the schedule."

"And?"

"And I'd rather enjoy the clouds right now, if you don't mind."

Annoyed by her attitude, Jake exhaled sharply. "So that's what you're going to talk about on your live chat this evening? Cumulus nimbus? I think that's one item you won't find on the warehouse racks."

"No, but we do carry cloud printed sheets—crib size, twin, double, queen, and king—as well as matching comforters in all sizes *and* coordinating wallpaper."

Jake stared at her in amazement. "How the hell do you know that?"

"It's my job as spokesperson to familiarize myself with the McStore merchandise. I've spent the past few weeks studying the inventory—when I haven't been practicing the beauty pageant wave."

"And you remember all of it?"

"Pretty much. I have a near-photographic memory. However," she added, her eyes twinkling with devilment as she bent her elbow and cocked her wrist, "the wave is still giving me a bit of a problem. I think it's a coordination thing. Maybe I should practice for a while."

"Don't you dare!" Jake grabbed her hand. "It's taken me days to get that damn jingle out of my head." When Dori offered him a sweet "who me?" smile, he groaned. "Nothing like handing ammunition to the opposition," he muttered.

"Oh? And here all this time I thought we were on the same side."

"Only if you swear *never* to utter that rhyme in my presence. Otherwise, consider us mortal enemies."

Dori chewed on her lower lip. Her face took on a thoughtful appearance, as if she were weighing his words. Finally, she spoke. "Swearing's a big-time no-no according to Almalynne."

"Screw Almalynne." H laced his fingers through hers and resting them on his knee. Dori's gaze dropped to their joined hands. "Protection against sneak attacks," he said.

And because it gives me an excuse to touch you. Jake grimaced at the unwelcome thought. Similar ones, all concerning Dori, came more and more frequently of late. He hated himself for allowing his tightly controlled emotions to slip.

"I see." Her fingers trembled slightly as she turned back to the cloud formations, but she made no effort to remove her hand until the captain signaled their final approach into Atlanta.

* * *

A hired car met them at the airport and drove them to a hotel in downtown Atlanta. After checking in and grabbing a quick lunch, they proceeded to the distribution center on the outskirts of the city.

Dick Reichman, the facility manager, a tall, balding middle-aged man with horn-rimmed glasses and a slight paunch, welcomed them at the entrance. Dori barely acknowledged his greeting. Her eyes were focused on a larger-than-life mural of herself, reclining in the "c" of the McStore logo, covering one wall of the lobby.

"Like it?" asked Dick with a sweeping gesture of his arm. He beamed as if he'd painted the logo himself. "Not a bad way to start the workday—being greeted by a beautiful face." He punctuated his last words with a wink in her direction.

Beautiful? She still couldn't get used to that. She'd never thought of herself as anything other than ordinary. Dori managed a weak smile but couldn't swallow back the soft groan that escaped through her tightly pursed lips.

"You knew about this," said Jake. "It shouldn't come as a surprise."

"I just didn't expect it to be so...so...*big!*" Niles had specifically requested this particular image for phase two of the advertising campaign and the company's corporate identity. The same trademark would grace the entryway of each retail store and be featured on everything from shopping bags to sales ads.

Combined with the billboards, the magazine ads, and the television commercials sweeping the country, Dori was getting as much exposure as a presidential candidate during an election year. At this rate, with Niles's backing she could run for office and easily win. She hoped he didn't get any ideas. The ensuing scandal, when her background came to light, would make the Clinton years look like a tea party at a senior citizens home.

Dick ushered them toward the entrance to the warehouse. Dori, relieved to escape the lobby, scanned the interior of the brightly lit room, easily the size of four football fields. She'd expected a huge plant. After all, the five hubs scattered throughout the country would handle shipping for all McStore Internet and catalog sales as well as supply merchandise to the retail stores. But even though she'd seen the architectural renditions for the buildings, she hadn't expected such mind-boggling enormity.

"Most of the downstairs is devoted to inventory and shipping," said Dick. He motioned to a balcony. Filled with endless multicolored cubicles, it ran around the perimeter of the warehouse. "Upstairs the computer operators handle phone orders, track website and catalog sales, and handle customer service."

The balcony reminded Dori of the human relations department at Niles York Enterprises. The downstairs, however, was like nothing she'd ever experienced. Workers, some moving through the aisles on inline skates, pulled stock, sending the items along a maze of conveyor belts to the opposite end of the building where, according to Dick Reichman, other workers scanned, sorted, packed, labeled, and shipped the orders. Dori would have to take his word for it. The warehouse was too vast for her to see to the other end of the building.

The setup, although comprised of the most up-to-date technology, surprised her in its cheeriness. Although spotless, the working environment was far from austere or sterile. In the center of the warehouse stood a large, glass enclosed, two-story atrium which Dori knew from the architectural specs, housed the company cafeteria.

"I've named that The Oasis," said Dick, following her gaze. "The greenery and specially tinted panes block out both the noise and movement from the surrounding warehouse. You step in there for a break or a meal, and you get the feeling you're on vacation."

"No problem getting people to leave and head back to work?" asked Jake.

"With our profit-sharing and incentive plans, I'm hoping that won't be much of a problem, but I'm sure I'll have a slacker or two from time to time. Every company has them." He patted Jake across the shoulder. "Don't worry, good buddy. I know how to deal with them."

Possible future employee difficulties didn't concern Dori. Her attention was focused on a more immediate problem of her own. "Our virtual tour is supposed to last half an hour," she said. "This place is so big that I'd need nearly that much time to walk from one end to the other."

"We've taken that into consideration," said Dick. "Not only for you but for our regular employees."

A skater glided past her, and Dori shook her head. "Thank you, but if I fall flat on my face in cyberspace, I'd prefer doing it figuratively rather than literally."

"Can't skate?" asked Jake, raising an eyebrow in challenge.

"Sure," said Dori. "As well as I wave. Maybe I could work up a routine, complete with words and music." She cocked her wrist. "Want a demonstration?"

Jake snatched her hand. Lacing his fingers through hers, he brought it back down to her side. "I think I'll pass." He turned to the plant manager. "Skates are out."

"Actually, I never considered them in," Dick darted a questioning glance at Dori's and Jake's entwined hands. "Only our youngest, most agile employees skate. The little lady will travel in style like the rest of us—by golf cart."

Dori considered the comment an insult, but she held her tongue, too addled by the surge of heat produced by Jake's touch. "You can let go now," she whispered as they followed Dick toward one of the electric-powered vehicles.

"Can I trust you?"

"I'm beginning to wonder if I can trust you."

She stepped into the cart. Did the man have any idea how much he rattled her each time they made physical contact? She hoped not. She'd spent the better part of the flight down to Atlanta trying to dismiss the searing need insinuating itself into every cell of her body. If holding hands with Jake Prentiss produced such fire, she couldn't begin to imagine what one of his kisses might do to her.

To make matters worse, despite his heavy-handed tactics and her suspicions of him, part of her—the illogical part ruled by hormones she had tried hard to suppress—was increasingly eager to find out. Meanwhile, her pragmatic side was gearing up to run for the hills.

N.Y. McStore catalogs had been shipped to arrive in homes across the country Saturday. NYMcStore.com had gone online for the first time Saturday evening. By the time Jake and Dori arrived at the hub, the warehouse had been in full swing for only a day and a half.

"Everything working out so far?" asked Jake. "No last-minute glitches?"

"Not a one," said Dick. "My employees are operating with the ease and efficiency of a team that's worked together for years."

The plant manager continued his self-congratulations as he conducted his tour. Between his verbosity, the vastness of the facility, and Dori's endless questions, one shift of the round-the-clock plant finished for the day and the second arrived before the tour ended.

"Flawless transition," noted Dick, nodding toward a group of employees as they headed out the door. "And this is only our second full day."

"Very impressive," said Jake, "but then again, I guess that's why Niles lured you away from FedEx."

Dick looked surprised. "You know about that?"

"I know everything," said Jake, casting a quick glance toward Dori.

Dori held Jake's gaze as she spoke to Dick. "He just thinks he knows everything, Mr. Reichman."

Jake's brows knit together, his face taking on that brooding look he leveled at her from time to time. Clearing his throat, he glanced at his watch. "We might as well have dinner here," he said. "The tech crew is due to arrive soon to set up for the virtual tour and online chat."

"I think you'll find our cafeteria's fare as tasty as any you might find in the finer restaurants of Atlanta," said Dick. He swung the golf cart around and headed back to the center of the facility.

The interior of the cafeteria reminded Dori of photos she'd seen of tropical resorts. A circular buffet stood in the center with tables and chairs scattered around the inner perimeter of the atrium. Small groups of employees sat eating and chatting throughout the room. In the background a New Age recording of rushing water and singing birds drifted on a climate-controlled soft breeze. "Where is the food prepared?" she asked, filling her tray with a large Cobb salad, a slice of still-warm French bread, and a cup of coffee. "I didn't see a kitchen on our tour."

"Downstairs," said Dick.

"Downstairs?" Dori tried to remember a below-ground level on the drawings Niles had shown her.

"That part of the building wouldn't interest you," said Dick, leading them to a table. "It's just the kitchen, the physical plant, a dispensary, and the mainframe system." He laughed. "We hide the techies down there away from the rest of the employees. We also have a daycare center, but that's located in a separate building."

"The mainframe is housed here? For the entire operation?" Dori's voice conveyed her excitement. "Do we have time to see it?"

"You'd find it boring," said Dick. "Just a bunch of computers and geeks writing code."

"Dori's kind of people," said Jake.

"What's that supposed to mean?" she asked, afraid she already knew the answer. Jake repeatedly dropped hints that he knew more about her than he was letting on, and that continued to worry her. She also didn't care for the patronizing way Dick Reichman was treating her. At any moment she expected him to reach out and pat her on the head.

Jake's face remained expressionless. Ignoring her question, he continued speaking to Dick. "We don't have time now, but how about after the tour and chat?"

Dick shrugged. "To each his own. Me? I give those guys wide berth. They speak in code just to confuse the rest of us. They're supposed to maintain the website, make sure the systems keep running smoothly, and prevent us from getting zapped by hackers.

"Frankly, I think they've got us all bamboozled. Remember the Y2K scare? How New Year's Eve came and went without a problem? In my opinion the whole thing was a hoax perpetrated by geeks to insure themselves some well-paying consulting work."

He turned to a young man sitting alone at the table next to them. "Isn't that so, Paul?"

At the sound of his name, the man, who appeared not much older than Dori, lifted his nose from the book he was reading. "Sir?"

"I was explaining your function to our guests. That you and your computer buddies spend your time downstairs shooting up space aliens while the rest of us work our tails off up here."

Paul shrugged as if this weren't the first time he'd heard Dick's complaint. He offered his boss a tight smile that didn't extend to his eyes. "Guess you finally caught on to us, Mr. Reichman." Then he glanced across the table, settling his gaze on Dori. "You're the model. The one plastered all over the front wall and everything."

She wasn't crazy about his point of reference, but she also didn't care for the way Dick Reichman had spoken to the man. The plant manager rubbed her the wrong way. Although he projected affability, she found him patronizing. From the little she'd observed, Dick Reichman struck her as a man used to grabbing credit. She had a sneaking suspicion that in the case of failures, he'd be equally swift at assigning blame rather than accepting responsibility himself.

Dori reached over and offered her hand to Paul. "That's right. Dori Johnson."

With his spiked hair, pierced eyebrow, white short-sleeve dress shirt, and Looney Tunes tie, the man looked part punk, part nerd. He hesitated for a moment. Then he took her hand in his, quickly extracting it after a brief, but surprisingly firm, shake. "Josh Paul," he mumbled.

Undeterred by his lack of social graces, Dori pressed on. "What are you reading?"

"Something you wouldn't understand." He turned back to his page.

Great! Another male chauvinist. "Really?" So much for offering a hand of friendship.

Dori had come up against his type before and wasn't about to be dismissed solely on her lack of a Y chromosome. She'd spent a lifetime dealing with sexism, first from her father and his immigrant cronies, then from many of the male college students who filled the classrooms of the technical courses she took. Most recently, she'd added Niles York to her list of men in need of reeducation. Now she could add Dick Reichman and Josh Paul.

Dori glanced over her shoulder at Jake, still not sure on which side of the fence he fell. Although condescending at times, she often sensed a grudging admiration directed toward her. Whether the *grudging* was due to inherent chauvinism or just plain ego, she hadn't yet decided.

Reaching across the narrow space that separated the two tables, she picked up Josh's book. Someone needed to teach him and Dick a lesson, and as the sole defender of her sex at the moment, the task fell to her. "*Complete XML*?" She shrugged, tossing the book back to him. "Frankly, I find Royerson's *XML Master Reference* far more comprehensive as a resource guide to building e-commerce applications."

"Well, I'll be damned!" Dick snorted. "A computer geek model."

Josh's eyes grew wide with a combination of surprise and confusion. His face flushed a bright crimson. "Excuse me," he said, quickly gathering up his book and coffee cup. He rose to leave, then turned back to Dori. "Do you mind if I ask you something?"

"Of course not."

"If you're so smart, why are you using your body instead of your brains to earn a living?"

His question caught her off guard. She *was* using her brains, but she resented Josh placing her in a defensive position. Her choice was none of his business. He stared at her for another moment, but when she didn't answer, he shook his head, frowned, then strode from the atrium.

"Punk," muttered Dick to Paul's departing back. "I'll have to keep an eye on him. I don't tolerate troublemakers in my plant."

The comment forced Dori from her contemplation. "He asked a valid question. Maybe a bit too bluntly for a total stranger, but I don't see how that makes him a troublemaker."

"He was out of line," said Dick. "I'll make sure he gets a reprimand from his supervisor."

Dori was horrified by Dick's over-reaction to Josh Paul's question. "I'd rather you didn't. I don't want to get anyone in trouble."

"I know how to handle my employees, Miss Johnson. You do your job; I'll do mine."

His tone upset her even further, but a page from the P.A. system alerting them to the arrival of the tech crew, kept her from pursuing the subject.

"Show time," said Dick. Slapping his hands on the table, he rose. Like a chameleon changing color, his belligerent demeanor of a moment ago disappeared, revealing the jocular side of his personality.

Dick's words, delivered more like a carnival barker than a plant manager, sent a nervous shiver racing up Dori's spine. All thoughts of Josh Paul fled as she wrestled with a massive case of stage fright.

She offered Dick and Jake a weak smile as she rose from her seat. Could she pull this off? The next thirty minutes would determine whether Niles York had created a brilliant marketing strategy for the newest baby in his empire or given birth to a resounding dud of an idea.

And it all depended on her. Forcing one foot in front of the other, she headed for the cafeteria exit to meet her destiny—either America's newest *personality* or the star freak of a billion-dollar sideshow.

SIXTEEN

Throughout the next half hour, Dori came to a startling conclusion: she *really* enjoyed her new position. Relying on the information she absorbed during Dick Reichman's earlier tour, she proceeded to give one of her own to the tens of thousands of prospective shoppers logged on to meet her. She introduced them to various McStore personnel and answered the questions they posted to the computer screen housed in the high-tech golf cart.

"I'd like you to meet Laurie Baskin," she told her audience, gesturing up toward the balcony. A round-faced woman with a wide smile leaned over the railing and waved. "Laurie is but one of several hundred highly trained customer service representatives who will be available twenty-four hours a day, seven days a week to handle questions concerning your orders.

In addition, you can contact me directly with any other questions or concerns by clicking on the *Ask Dori* button at the top right of our homepage. If I don't have the answer, I'll find someone for you who does."

A query flashed across her monitor. "Jean from El Paso wants to know what kind of questions I'll answer." Dori paused for a moment. She'd voiced her concern over this aspect of her job to Niles, but he'd dismissed her anxiety, insisting she maintain a high profile and ready accessibility to McStore shoppers.

Other retailers employed celebrity spokespersons far removed from the average middle-class consumer. No one really expected to bump into Beyonce at Walmart. Niles wanted his customers to understand that Dori was one of them. And the best way for him to get that message across was to have Dori personally interact with them.

Dori smiled into the camera. "Well, Jean, certainly not a question better suited for Dr. Phil or Dear Abby, but I can help you coordinate a room on a budget, assist you in finding the perfect birthday present for your favorite aunt, or offer accessory suggestions to get the most diversity out of that classic black linen suit we sell for only a hundred and twenty-nine dollars on page fifty-two of our catalog."

Out of the corner of one eye she noticed Dick Reichman reach across a counter and grab a McStore catalog. After quickly thumbing through the pages, he held the large book up to Jake and pointed to a spot on the page. Then he scowled at her.

As soon as the virtual tour ended, Dick approached her. "Did you rehearse that line about the black suit in the catalog?"

Dori shook her head. "No, it just came to me as I was speaking, but I did order that suit during the web test last week."

"And you just happened to remember the page number and price?"

"I have a head for numbers."

Jake cleared his throat, but Dori chose to ignore him. She knew if she glanced his way, she'd find him smirking at her. She wished she could level out the playing field, know what he knew or *thought* he knew about her. This advantage of his, perceived or otherwise, left her with a decided disadvantage. Jake played dirty. And that wasn't fair—especially when he kept short-circuiting her internal chemistry.

More and more she wished she could come clean—with Jake and everyone. She hated having to watch every word she spoke. Hated the necessity of constantly looking over her shoulder, worried that someone from her past might recognize her. But she'd committed a crime, and as much as she detested living a lie, getting caught and going to jail scared her enough to keep her from confessing.

Worried over what might happen to her if caught and prosecuted for forgery, she'd accessed the government criminal codes on the Internet. The punishment for her offenses was a fine or imprisonment—up to fifteen years—or both. Every so often, she read in the news of someone arrested and sentenced for fraud. Federal prosecutors took such crimes seriously. Very seriously.

And then there was the money she'd stolen from her father. No matter how she rationalized that the three thousand dollars rightfully belonged to her, Nikki, and Joey—it was but a small percentage of the Social Security benefits Sergei had collected in his children's names and spent on himself since his wife's death— she still took the money without her father's knowledge or permission.

Some of that money had enabled her to purchase the computer equipment she used to create their new identities. Dori worried that an overly zealous, ambitious prosecutor might use that information to insure her the maximum prison sentence.

"You should have checked with me first," said Dick, jolting her back to the present.

His annoyance puzzled her. "Why?"

"If you take it upon yourself to hawk a specific item, and I don't have enough in stock, I wind up with egg on my face. Next time, check first."

"How can we not have enough in stock? That's incongruous with the entire McStore philosophy."

"Except when the McStore spokesperson prattles on about one specific item to tens of thousands of customers at once. Even on The Home Shopping Network viewers are advised of the available of inventory."

Dori hadn't thought about that. Her off-the-cuff remark could result in a barrage of orders. Within minutes they might sell out of certain sizes. "I'm sorry."

"Sorry doesn't solve the problem."

"Look," said Jake. "Let's not overreact." But before he said anything further, his cell phone rang. He reached into his pocket and removed the phone.

"Prentiss here." He listened for a moment, then held the phone out to Dori. "Niles. For you."

Dori had expected a call from her boss, knowing he'd be watching her debut presentation. Niles had wanted to be at the distribution center with them this evening, but other business obligations kept him away. Worried that he might react as Dick had, she glanced at Jake as she placed the phone to her ear. His unreadable expression gave her no clue to Niles's mood. "Hello, Niles."

"Wonderful first outing, Dori."

She allowed herself a sigh of relief and a quick glance toward the plant manager. "Thank you, sir, but Dick expressed concern over my remark about the black suit. He feels we may get more orders than he can fill."

"Nonsense. Dick Reichman worries too much. I loved the way you tossed in that remark about the suit and even mentioned the price and page number. I'm thinking we should do some online merchandise promotions like that each week."

"Weekly online merchandise promotions?" repeated Dori for Dick's benefit, tossing him a sweet smile. "That sounds like a wonderful idea, Niles."

"Good. We'll flesh it out over dinner tomorrow. By the way, I'm looking at the numbers right now. Orders have already jumped twenty percent in the last few minutes since your tour ended."

"Those could be customers who were planning to order anyway and just wanted to wait until I finished the tour."

"No, my dear. Those are no longer customers. They now consider themselves your friends, and they're buying from us because of you."

"That's a pretty big leap, Niles."

"Is it? Go access the Customer Comments page on the site."

Dori walked over to the golf cart and clicked on the *Tell Us How You Like Us* button. For several minutes she scrolled down dozens of messages about her just ended cyber-tour. Niles was right. Strangers from Eureka, California to Portland, Maine now considered her their newest best friend.

Such a friendly, honest young lady, wrote one woman who signed herself Granny G from Wichita.

I'm so happy to have met her. I feel I've known her all my life, from Miss Mabel in Berne, Indiana.

Why would I want to shop anywhere else when I can shop with Dori? asked Leona R. from Nashville.

"All of these in the last five minutes?" she asked, scanning page after page of messages that read more like personal inscriptions in a high school yearbook than customer comments.

Dori has the kind of smile that lights up the dark corners of my mind, A. Friend.

"And most of them placed orders," said Niles. "Nice work, Dori. I've got to run. I'll see you and Jake tomorrow in Orlando." He disconnected before she could say anything further.

"Looks like you're developing quite a fan club," said Jake, coming up from behind her to read over her shoulder.

"I suppose." She frowned at the monitor, still fixating over the hidden anguish she read between the lines of the last message.

"What's wrong? You were a big success. You should be on Cloud Nine."

"Just something Niles said."

"What?"

She motioned to the screen. "Some of these messages are so personal. Too personal. After thirty minutes these people think of me as a long-lost relative. Even though they know nothing about me. Read this." She pointed to the message from A. Friend. "*Dori has the kind of smile that lights up the dark corners of my mind.* Don't you find that sad?"

"*All the lonely people, where do they all come from?*"

"Exactly," she said, recognizing the old Beatles' lyric.

"I take it Niles didn't mind the plug?" asked Dick, his words tight and clipped.

Dori sensed Dick was battling to control his annoyance at being countermanded by Niles, especially in front of her. "He loved it," she said, trying not to gloat. "Wants more of them, in fact."

Dick shrugged. "He's the boss." But he looked far from happy.

"Yes." Hoping to placate him, she added, "I'll mention your idea of keeping track of the inventory during a pitch, though. It makes sense."

Then she turned her attention back to Jake and the computer screen where she continued to scroll down the comments. "This is so sad. These people need to get a life."

"Don't try to overanalyze those messages," said Dick. "These people aren't New Yorkers. You'll find as you tour the country, most people are very friendly. They believe in good manners— especially Southerners and Midwesterners. What you're seeing in those e-mails is nothing more than good, old-fashioned thank-you notes."

"Are you implying Jake and I are guilty of New York cynicism?"

"All I'm saying is maybe you shouldn't jump to any conclusions just yet. Middle America is different from the people you're used to in the Big Apple. That's all."

In her limited experience people were pretty much the same no matter where they lived—not that Philadelphia and Jersey City gave her much of a basis for comparison.

"Are they?" she asked Jake.

Instead of answering, he glanced at his watch. "I think if you want that tour of the underground, we'd better get started. It's getting late, and we have an early flight tomorrow morning."

"Elevator's right this way," said Dick, motioning them to

follow him.

SEVENTEEN

Jake engaged Dick in conversation as they waited for the elevator, distracting the plant manager from noticing Dori's breathing ritual. "You okay?" he whispered after the doors closed behind them.

Dori nodded. "I'm fine." But her words did little to hide her pallor or the slight tremble in her voice.

The freight elevator, although oversized, felt confining even to Jake. Heavy gray mover's padding hung from the walls. An overhead fixture gave off a dim, muted light. The air smelled stale.

"One of the few things not working up to spec," said Dick, pointing toward the ceiling. "The ventilation guys can't seem to get the air-conditioning to function properly in this thing. Either it blasts an arctic gale or spews tropic-like heat." He scowled at the hole in the ceiling. "Nothing's coming out now. I'm beginning to think the problem lies more with the ventilation engineers than the equipment. It shouldn't take this long to nail down a simple air-conditioning problem and correct it."

"Is this the only elevator?" asked Jake.

Dick nodded. "The lower level covers only a small fraction of the main floor. One's sufficient, but we needed it large enough to handle moving equipment down to the computer room."

Jake studied the space. "What about machinery for the kitchen and physical plant? You can't fit a replacement boiler in here. Or even an industrial size stove."

"The site is sloped. There's outside entry to the kitchen and physical plant, plus stairs from within, but the computer section is limited to specific personnel. Key card access only, either by this elevator or a set of stairs across the way."

The elevator glided to a halt, the doors opening onto a brightly lit lobby. Directly across from the elevator, a set of oversized double doors provided entry to a large, glass enclosed room.

"Welcome to Geek City," said Dick. He inserted a plastic key card into a slot, then ushered them inside once the doors automatically opened.

A tall African American man, sporting a closely cropped head of near-white hair and a friendly smile, approached them. "Ignore everything Dick's told you about us. Every word is a pack of lies."

"Meet Alva Hewitt," said Dick. "Head geek but basically an okay guy. Al keeps the other geeks from driving me crazy. I suppose you already recognize Miss Johnson," he said, motioning to Dori, "and this is Jake Prentiss, who I'm told is a mere heartbeat away from our illustrious leader."

Al shook hands with both Jake and Dori. "We monitored your tour from down here, Miss Johnson. Great job."

"Thank you, Mr. Hewitt, but please call me Dori."

"And I'm Al."

"Our new spokesperson has a major flaw," said Dick. "She likes computers and requested a tour of this godforsaken area."

"I'd be happy to oblige," said Al.

"Great." Dick turned to Jake. "I leave you two in good hands—or at least the best pair of hands down here. I'm going to track down those ventilation guys. They'd better have a good excuse for that elevator." He glanced around the computer room. "At least they're not down here playing computer games with the programmers."

Al chuckled. "You know, it's getting harder and harder to fool you into thinking we work down here, Reichman."

"Is that what you call it?"

Al turned to Dori and Jake. "We make allowances for him," he said, motioning to the departing plant manager.

Jake frowned. "That's very understanding of you."

"All bark, little bite. Besides, can you blame him? We geeks, as he refers to us, wield considerable power. With a click of a mouse any one of us could create major chaos. That's got to worry a man responsible for the daily workings of such an enormous endeavor."

"I suppose." But some of Dick Reichman's attitudes rubbed Jake the wrong way. He made a mental note to apprise Niles of the way his handpicked plant manager interacted with some of his personnel.

Jake hung back as Al Hewitt guided Dori through the computer operations. She spent considerable time speaking with various programmers, asking astute questions, and occasionally offering her own suggestions and observations on a variety of technical subjects.

When they approached the workstation of the man from the

cafeteria, Dori stopped to speak to him. "I want to apologize for what happened earlier. I'm afraid I came across as arrogant. I only wanted to suggest a different book, one I've found more comprehensive than the one you were reading."

"You know Paul?" asked Al. His face mirrored the surprise in his voice.

"We met earlier," said Dori, "under less than auspicious circumstances, I'm afraid."

Josh Paul studied Dori for a moment before speaking. "Forget it." He waved his left hand dismissively while his right hand continued to peck at his keyboard. "So, where'd you learn programming?"

"I taught myself."

"Hmm. So you don't have a degree? Still doesn't explain why you're wiggling your buns for a living."

Dori's eyes reflected first hurt, then anger over the statement. Jake glared at Paul. The programmer ignored him, turning his attention back to his monitor.

"Why don't we go check out the mainframe?" Al suggested. Once they were out of earshot, he apologized. "Sorry about that. Sometimes I think when the good Lord handed out people skills, Paul had his nose buried in a tech manual and forgot to stand in line."

"Why hire someone like that in the first place?" asked Jake.

"Because he's a real whiz kid. We encountered some major problems in the development and startup of this baby. Technical glitches that had the rest of us baffled. Paul solved them as if they were kindergarten puzzles. He's just one of those guys more comfortable around computers than people."

Dori glanced back at Josh Paul. His fingers flying across the keyboard, he stared at his computer screen, oblivious to the rest of the room and probably the world.

* * *

When the tour ended, Al walked them back to the elevator. "Nice meeting you." He shook Dori's hand, then Jake's. "Come back to visit any time."

"Would you rather take the stairs?" asked Jake after Al reentered the computer area. "This elevator is pretty oppressive."

Dori shook her head as she inhaled a calming breath, then slowly exhaled. "No. I refuse to allow irrational fear to rule me."

Jake admired her pluck. The elevator doors opened, and she stepped inside, her jaw set, her body rigid but determined.

"Long day." He stifled a yawn as he pushed the button for the first floor. The car began its ascent.

"I'm sorry," said Dori after taking another deep breath. "I didn't realize—"

The elevator lurched, cutting off her sentence. The sudden jolt lifted her into the air, hurling her into Jake's chest and stealing the air from her lungs with one terrifying scream. A second violent convulsion knocked them both to the floor, leaving Dori flat on her back, pinned under Jake.

"Don't move," he said, wrapping his arms around her as the car shuddered, then groaned before coming to a stop. A moment later they were plunged into darkness.

Panic held Dori hostage. Its fingers tightened around her throat, closing off her airway. Gasping, she struggled to suck oxygen into her lungs.

"Are you hurt?" asked Jake, carefully shifting his weight off her.

Unable to force out any words, she shook her head, even though the darkness was too pervasive for him to see her. "N...no," she finally managed. "I don't...don't th...think so."

"Deep breaths," he reminded her. He sat up and drew her along with him. "Slow deep breaths, Dori."

She forced herself to comply, one ragged breath after another, as she held onto Jake. "We're trapped," she whimpered, hating her fear and weakness but powerless to control it.

"Hang on." He drew her closer, stroking her back. "They'll have us out of here in no time." A moment later he dropped his arms from around her and pushed himself to his feet.

"Don't!" she cried clinging to his leg.

"I'm just going to grab the emergency phone." She loosened her grip and wrapped her arms around her up-drawn knees as she listened to Jake feel for the control panel. "Got it," he said. Then a moment later, "Damn!"

"What?"

"The phone's dead."

Bile churned in Dori's stomach. She lowered her head onto her knees and took another drag of the stagnant air.

"I can't get a signal on the cell phone," said Jake. "Too much metal around us." A moment later she heard him emit a loud, deep grunt, then a groan.

"Jake!" Panic froze the word in midair.

"I'm all right. I tried to pry the door open."

"Jake, I'm scared. What if a cable snaps? Who'll take care of Nikki and Joey?"

A moment later he was on the floor beside her, his arms wrapped around her shoulders. "The cable isn't going to break, and even if it did, we're only half a flight above ground. We're going to be fine, Dori. They know we're here. We'll be out in no time. Try to relax."

Relax! When her worst nightmare had come to life? She shuddered beneath his arms. "I can't."

"Yes, you can." He shifted position until he sat behind her. Drawing her up against his chest, he began massaging her neck and shoulders.

Dori hugged her torso and moaned. "I thought if I forced myself enough times, I'd conquer my fear."

"Close your eyes," he whispered into her ear. His fingers made their way up her scalp. "Listen to the water lapping the shore."

"W...water? What are you talking about?"

"Shh. Feel the sun warming your skin."

Sun? Had he lost his mind? They were trapped in a pitch-black elevator!

"The gentle salty breeze blowing through your hair."

Dori shuddered through another ragged breath. No salt. No breeze. Almost no air. Her throat constricted on an hysterical whimper, and she forced her words around the rock-hard lump that pressed against her vocal cords. "You're crazy, Jake Prentiss."

His fingers made lazy circles against her temples. He chuckled. "Now who has no imagination? I'm stretched out on a beach in Maui. If you want to stay stuck in this elevator, be my guest, but I've got to tell you, Dori, it's a perfect day in Hawaii."

Tears stung her eyes. She blinked, sending one trickling down her cheek. He was doing this for her. Not because he was crazy. Not to tease her. Not to make fun of her fear but to help her survive it. Slowly, some of her tension drained away.

She took a deeper breath, this one more controlled and less ragged. "Jake?"

"Hmm?"

"What about sharks?"

He wrapped his long, muscular legs around her. "None around, and the water's like a bathtub. Want to go for a dip?"

"Are we wearing bathing suits?"

"No way." He wove his fingers through her hair, his lips skimming her ear. "This is a very private beach."

Dori shuddered in his arms, no longer from panic but the aching hunger Jake had released within her. All thoughts of the elevator, her anxiety, their predicament fell away. Her head filled with the sensations of Jake, his touch caressing every inch of her, flooding her body with wave after searing wave of torrid heat.

He shifted his legs and turned her toward him.

And then he kissed her.

The world as Dori knew it shattered around her. In a blinding instant of clarity, she realized nothing would ever again be the same. Not for her, not for Jake. His kiss, deep and erotic, bared his soul as his words had refused to do, proclaiming a need and hunger beyond any form of communication other than the most ancient and primal.

And carnal. God, how carnal! Dori's insides shuddered from the forces he unleashed in her. Potent, aching, wanton forces she'd never believed possible. Not for her. They frightened her. And empowered her.

His lips, firm and decisive, captured her heart. His tongue plundered her soul. Dori gave herself to him and in so doing, discovered a freedom of spirit and overwhelming joy unlike any she'd ever experienced. Years of fear and heartache melted away like snow on a warm spring day. She floated above herself, watching her life blossom in a profusion of riotous color, Jake's kisses transforming her black and white world into a Technicolor universe.

* * *

The moment his lips claimed her, all reason deserted Jake. For weeks he'd denied his attraction to Dori, an attraction which struck him like a nuclear missile the moment she'd walked into Niles's office.

He'd hidden his growing hunger for her behind skepticism and suspicion, sarcasm and ridicule. He'd rejected his lust as lunacy and an adolescent urge easily quelled with a good dose of logic and a masochistic cold shower. Time after time, he'd reminded himself that the woman in his arms, the woman who tasted like peaches and cream and honey, had broken the law. She could very well be part of a plot to destroy his friend and all that Niles had built.

But with each passing day Jake believed that less and less. Because he wanted to. Needed to. The more he fought to deny his need for her, the stronger that need grew until she possessed him day and night like some obsessive sorceress who'd woven an insidious spell around him.

He cupped one hand around her breast, the other over her bottom, drawing her even closer, then rolled on top of her. Her heart raced against his chest; his need, hard and hot, throbbed against her belly. Lowering his head, he captured one of her nipples, sucking through the thin layer of her silky blouse. His fingers fumbled with a button and then another. Drawing back the damp fabric, his tongue skimming across the textured lace of her bra.

He was out of control, and damn her, Dori wasn't helping the situation. If anything, she was making it worse. Much worse. She arched her back, and with a husky moan, offered more of herself to him. Her hands clutched at his back, clinging to him as if afraid he might stop. Might leave before he quelled the blazing inferno consuming them both. Fat chance. If someone didn't get those damn doors open soon, he'd take her right there on the elevator floor.

And then he'd take her again.

The pulse alongside Jake's temples pounded in cadence to the throbbing below his belt, growing faster. Louder. More insistent. Pounding. Pounding. Echoing within the dark compartment.

"Jake! Dori! Are you two all right?"

EIGHTEEN

Dick's words were like a bucket of ice water thrown over them. Dori froze in his arms. The pounding continued, not from inside his head but from the other side of the elevator doors.

"The cavalry's here." He rolled to his side and knelt beside her. "We're okay," he yelled toward the closed door.

"We'll have you out in a minute. Stand back from the doors."

Jake helped Dori into a sitting position and cradled her in his arms. He wasn't quite sure whether either of them really wanted to be rescued. At least not just yet.

"To be continued," he whispered against her lips.

A moment later someone levered a crowbar between the doors, prying them apart. The compartment flooded with light. Dori drew her knees up to her chest and lowered her head. Jake blinked back the assault to his eyes, then rose to face their rescuers.

"Sonofabitch!" Dick stuck his head into the opening and

looked down at them. "You look pretty battered. I'll call for an ambulance."

Jake glanced down at himself. He looked like he'd gone several rounds with Mike Tyson—his suit rumpled beyond recognition, his shirttails hanging out of his waistband, his tie askew.

He ran his fingers through his disheveled hair and rubbed the five o'clock shadow covering his jaw. "No," he said, tucking his shirt back into his waistband. "We're just rattled and a bit bruised. Nothing a hot soak in a tub and a good night's sleep won't cure."

Swiping at his brow, Dick acknowledged Jake with a worrisome nod, then proceeded to vent his anger on a nervous looking man bending beside him. "Damn it, Rossnauer, what the fuck did that incompetent crew of yours do to the elevator? You were supposed to fix the air system, not turn the thing into a goddamn deathtrap!"

Rossnauer jumped up and backed away. "This isn't my fault!"

Dick rose. From Jake's vantage point he could no longer see their faces, but he did see Dick jab a finger into Rossnauer's chest. "Oh, yeah? Show me someone else who was working on this elevator for the past two days. You could've killed them!"

"Don't touch me! You've had it in for me since day one, Reichman, and I'm not going to stand for it any longer. Get off my back, or I'll have the fucking union on yours!"

"Knock it off!" yelled Jake. "Settle your labor problems some other time, Reichman. Get a ladder and get us the hell out of here. Now!"

Dick kneeled back down and said, "I sent someone for a ladder. We'll have you out of there in a minute or two." Then his gaze landed on Dori, and he muttered another barrage of curses. "Is she okay?"

Jake followed Dick's glance. Dori hadn't said a word. She'd drawn herself into a tight ball, her back toward the open doors. "Dori?" he asked.

"I'm fine." She nodded but refused to face either of them.

Reichman turned and yelled to Rossnauer, "Find out what's holding up that ladder."

Jake crossed the compartment and kneeled in front of Dori. He lifted her chin with the tips of his fingers. The moment their eyes met, he understood. He drew his index finger across her kiss-swollen, trembling bottom lip, then along her jaw, where she wore the evidence of his stubbled chin. She looked erotic as hell. And completely mortified.

She hugged her arms around her breasts, drawing his attention to the damage he'd inflicted elsewhere. No matter how she held herself, she couldn't hide the dark, damp circles outlining her still hard nipples. Jake shrugged out of his jacket and slipped it around her shoulders. Drawing the lapels up around her neck, he helped her to her feet. "No one will know," he whispered.

Two men lowered a ladder down the opening. Jake guided Dori toward it, her head remaining lowered.

"She doesn't look so good," observed Dick. I really think we need to get her to a doctor."

"No!" Dori's forceful refusal startled the men gathered around the opening. She clutched Jake's jacket tighter around her torso. "I'm fine. I just want to go back to the hotel." She raised her head and cast pleading eyes toward Jake. "Please, no hospital."

"No hospital," he promised.

* * *

Why you? thought Dori as she stole a glance toward Jake during their silent trip back into Atlanta. *You scare me, Jake Prentiss.*

You're hiding something from me, something I sense could destroy everything I've worked so hard to achieve. For myself. For Nikki. For Joey. Why couldn't I fall for someone safe?

However much she wished otherwise, Dori suspected Jake's feelings for her centered entirely around sex. Pure and simple. Nothing more. He'd uttered no words of love. Made no promises of forever. Or even tomorrow. Why couldn't it be that simple for her? Why did she have to lose her heart to this brooding, secretive man? And much to her chagrin and against her better judgment, she *had* lost her heart. No argument to the contrary could change what she now knew for truth.

Her head told her she should stop this insanity before it went any further—before he pulverized her soul to a fine powder and scattered it to the wind. So why did every cell in her body continue to scream out for his touch? Why was the ache between her legs so intense that she'd sell that same soul for the relief she knew only Jake could provide?

As if reading her mind, he reached over and caressed her thigh. The shiver that coursed like quicksilver through her body drove away all rational thought. She wanted him as much as he wanted her. She'd deal with the ramifications of that need tomorrow. Tonight, she'd give herself over to the hedonistic pleasures he promised. And she'd savor every precious, fleeting moment.

* * *

"Are you hungry?" he asked when they arrived back at the hotel and walked past one of the lobby restaurants.

Dori shook her head. "Are you?"

Jake laced his fingers through hers and drew her hand to his lips, planting a gentle kiss on the tips of her fingers. "Not for anything they serve there."

Tingling anticipation raced up and down her spine. She'd shivered and quivered quite a bit since meeting Jake Prentiss, she realized, fantasizing about that ultimate shudder they were heading toward, the one they'd experience together. Spectacular, she decided. Mind-boggling, over-the-edge sensational. She had no doubt. Every romantic movie she'd ever seen, every romance novel she'd ever read flashed before her mind. Tonight, she'd experience that pleasure for herself.

"Did I cure you?" he whispered in her ear as they joined half a dozen others entering the elevator.

"Cure me?"

"You didn't take any calming breaths."

No, she hadn't. With her mind and body centered completely on the coming event, she hadn't even been aware of stepping into the crowded elevator. "Maybe I was going about tackling this phobia all wrong."

He draped his arms around her shoulders and drew her up against his chest, an extremely large, firm part of his anatomy pressing against her bottom. "In that case, I hope you have others I can help with. I'm looking forward to a very long night."

The position of their bodies left little question as to the meaning behind his words. Dori felt her cheeks ignite, and once again her body trembled beneath his arms—and continued to tremble as they made their way from the elevator down the hall to their rooms.

Niles's travel planner had booked them into a suite on the concierge level—two bedrooms on either end of a large living room. "Your place or mine?" asked Jake, swinging open the door.

Dori hesitated, lowering her head to hide her blush. "Jake,...I..."

He placed his hands on either side of her face and lifted her chin until their eyes met. His were smoky with lust. His voice, when he spoke, strained with a huskiness she' never heard. "If you're going to change your mind, Dori, do it now because I don't think I'm going to be able to stop once I get started." He bent his head, brushing his lips across hers as he continued to speak. "If I don't bury myself inside you soon, I'm going to go crazy. I've never wanted a woman more than I want you right now."

And she had never wanted a man as much as she wanted him. "I'm not changing my mind."

Jake released a deep sigh. "God, I'm glad to hear that." He slipped the jacket from her shoulders and tossed it on a chair. Lifting her into his arms, he carried her across the living room and into his bedroom in a half dozen long strides. "This one's closer," he said, lowering her onto the already turned down bed.

He sat down beside her, his penetrating gaze slowly roving her body. Her limbs refused to move. Her heart sped up from the intensity of his scrutiny, as though she were a chess board and he a grand master contemplating the quickest route to checkmate. She wished she could read his mind and yet, at the same time was glad she couldn't.

He reached over and fingered a still damp spot on her blouse, the tips of his fingers brushing lightly across her nipple. The sensation swelled her breast and further tightened the puckered nub. Dori inhaled sharply, the sudden rush of air stinging her already dry throat.

Jake lifted his head and trapped her with those midnight eyes of his. One thing and one thing only was on the mind of the formerly unreadable Jake Prentiss.

Without taking his eyes from her face, he deftly unbuttoned her blouse and unfastened her skirt. Each time his fingers made contact with her flesh an involuntary shudder coursed through her, her breathing quickened, and her pulse accelerated.

None of it went unnoticed by Jake. He teased her to a fevered pitch without ever laying more than his fingertips on her. By the time he stripped her of all her clothing, she wanted to scream with delirium and jump out of her skin. Or jump his bones. His satisfied smirk told her he knew exactly what he was doing to her and that he was enjoying every minute of her torture.

* * *

Once he had her completely undressed, Jake allowed his gaze to roam her body, but he kept his hands firmly planted on the mattress, forcing himself to go slowly. Even if it killed him. "You're beautiful," he murmured, finally lifting one hand to explore with touch what his eyes had already consumed. He began with the sculpted hollow of her throat, his fingers caressing each curve and recess as they danced across her breasts, her belly, her thighs.

Dori arched her back.

"More?" he asked.

"Please!"

His second hand joined his first, and his touch deepened, now kneading the flesh he had previously only caressed with a featherweight touch. She moaned, deep and low and needy, her body writhing beneath his hands. "Are you on fire yet?" he asked, cupping a hand between her legs.

"Yes!" Her answer traveled on a gasp from her lips to his ears.

Jake stood. Kicking off his shoes, he quickly stripped off his own clothes, tossing them to the floor. Then he yanked open the nightstand drawer and found one of the foil packets he'd placed there earlier. Noticing Dori's startled expression, he grinned sheepishly. "A gentleman always travels with protection."

She said nothing, just continued to stare wide-eyed at his shaft as if she'd never seen an aroused man before. And damn if he wasn't more excited than he'd ever been. As much as Jake had hoped to prolong foreplay, he was only human.

When Dori's tongue darted out to moisten her parched lips, any thoughts other than burying himself deep inside her, fled. He bent down to capture her lips. Straddling her body, he simultaneously plunged his tongue deep within her mouth and his shaft even deeper within her body.

Her strangled cry rocked him.

Jake pulled back, shocked by the realization of what had just occurred. "Why didn't you tell me?" His voice sounding harsh even to his own ears. Her lower lip trembled. Her eyes remained squeezed shut, the lashes damp with unshed tears. When she didn't answer, he yelled at her, "Damn it, Dori! Open your eyes. Look at me!"

Her lids fluttered open, but she averted her gaze, talking into the hand she clamped over her mouth. "I was afraid you wouldn't want me if you knew."

Not want her! How could she think such a thing? Jake swung his legs over the side of the bed and sat up. His elbows on his knees, he buried his hands in his hair and cursed under his breath. After uttering every expletive in his vocabulary at least twice, he stalked off to the bathroom, slamming the door behind him. The juvenile release of anger didn't help. He felt like slamming his head against the wall.

Jake never hated anyone or anything as much as he hated himself at that moment. He braced his body against the sink and stared at his reflection in the mirror, continuing to hurl curses at the insensitive bastard who stared back at him.

Surely, there'd been signs. Why hadn't he noticed them? Pulling his hands through his hair, he wracked his brain in search of the clues he'd missed. He was a man trained to pick up the most insignificant detail, but once again he'd failed. Dori's virginal status hardly qualified as insignificant, yet he'd missed it completely.

Or had he? Even as he repeatedly asked himself that question, he knew he hadn't overlooked anything. The signs were there all along. He'd chosen to ignore them. Everything about Dori shouted innocence. Everything. Even if she'd committed a felony.

Jake threw his head back and groaned as the unwanted thought forced its way into his head. There was no denying that Dori had falsified records and illegally changed her identity as well as Nikki's and Joey's. Two years ago, he would have alerted the federal prosecutors the moment he'd discovered her crime.

But that was two years ago—back when his entire life centered around an unquestioning code of black and white, good and evil, right and wrong. Back when he based a man's guilt or innocence on the evidence at hand and looked no further. And now everyday he lived with the ramifications of that rigid ethic.

Maybe Dori had no idea of the magnitude of her crimes. His heart convinced him she'd acted out of desperation and self-preservation, not deceit and certainly not to cover up a more serious offense. Nothing he'd uncovered led to such a conclusion. But that in itself was part of the problem. Nothing he'd uncovered led to *any* explanation for her actions. His head be damned. The evidence be damned. Dori might have incredible computer talents, but she was incapable of ulterior motives.

Sweet, innocent Dori was no more involved with the Russkie

mob than he was. She was too loving. Too trusting. Whatever her reason for fleeing Philadelphia, Jake swore he'd do everything in his power to help her—if she'd ever let him near her again. And right now, after the insensitive way he'd forced himself on her, that was a very big if.

* * *

Dori curled up into a tight ball and fought a losing battle to keep the tears from flowing down her cheeks. Feelings of inadequacy consumed her. When she closed her eyes, a vision of Jake, his face contorted, his lips spewing words of accusation, assaulted her. The night had taken a dreadful turn. Jake no longer wanted her. He'd fled in disgust, and it was all her fault. She was a miserable failure as a lover.

Where were the rockets and roller coasters she'd read about, the bells and whistles and blinding white lights experienced by Lady Bromshire and countless other romance heroines? It had been over before it began, and she'd experienced none of the wonderful things she'd expected. It wasn't Jake's fault. He seemed to know exactly what he was doing. The blame lay with her, and she knew why.

Without a mother's guidance, she'd acquired her knowledge of puberty from more physically mature school friends discussing the period not found at the end of a sentence. At least she'd learned enough not to freak when she began bleeding shortly after her twelfth birthday. An eighth-grade mandatory health class filled in the holes on the physical aspects of sex, stressing STD's and teen pregnancy and avoiding any mention of pleasure. Lady Bromshire and her romance counterparts supplied that information.

Her personal experience had never gone any further than some minor petting. Sergei had forbidden her to date, and once she ran away, her responsibilities to Nikki and Joey severely limited her social life. Besides, every time a date touched her, she experienced flashbacks to the night Borka's fat hairy hand crawled up her thigh. Each time, the ugly recollection succeeded in dousing any flames of passion in her.

Before Jake, no man had ever made her forget Borka. But although his touch erased the memory of the big Russian's assault, her body somehow remembered and refused to let her relax enough to enjoy what other women took for granted. From the reading she'd done, she expected a certain amount of pain at the beginning. She'd braced herself against it. Maybe too much. She'd tensed at the last moment. Cried out from a pain greater than she'd anticipated. She'd turned Jake off. But the physical pain had only lasted a few seconds. The pain now tearing her heart apart grew more severe with each passing minute.

Dori had no idea what Jake was doing in the bathroom or how long he intended to stay in there, but she couldn't bear to face him once he returned. Gathering up her clothes, she tiptoed from his room.

With her face buried in her pillow to muffle her sobs, she didn't hear him enter her bedroom a few minutes later. Jake sat down on the edge of the bed and ran his fingers through her hair. His tentative touch only deepened the ache and emptiness consuming her.

"I'm so sorry for hurting you," he said, his voice choked with emotion. "It shouldn't have been this way, sweetheart. Not your first time."

She didn't understand why he was apologizing to her. This was her fault, not his. She was the one with the sexual hangup—thanks to Borka and her inability to put the past behind her.

"Let me make things right for you. Please."

* * *

Dori lifted her head off the pillow. Sniffing back a sob, she shifted her body to one side and look at him over her shoulder. Her cheeks shone from a thin glaze of dampness. The pain and confusion clouding her eyes pierced Jake in the gut. "Make things right?"

Jake sighed. He had no power to wave a magic wand and erase the last half hour, but he could replace her pain with pleasure. A pleasure unlike any she'd ever experienced. If she'd only give him the chance. He drew a corner of the sheet up over her shoulder and wiped away the tears staining her face. "Trust me." He bent to brush her lips with his. "The night's going to get a whole lot better from here on. We just need to finish what we started."

Dori's brow wrinkled. Puzzlement settled into her eyes and mouth. "Finish?"

Jake pulled his head back and studied her. Could she possibly be that innocent? But he saw the answer to that question in her eyes and somehow that made him feel better. If that was all she expected from the sex act, he was about to take her on the trip of her life. He scooped her into his arms.

She shuddered against his bare chest. "I'm afraid I'm not very good at this."

Jake fought to stifle a laugh but failed miserably. "Maybe I should be the judge of that."

She released a ragged sigh and snuggled closer against him, her fingers tentatively weaving through the hairs of his chest. "You're not angry with me?"

"I'm angry with myself."

"Why?"

"For being an insensitive caveman. I should have realized."

"How?"

"I just should have. You started to tell me earlier, didn't you? When we first came back to the hotel."

She nodded. "You didn't want to talk."

"I'm a guy, sweetheart. Sometimes our brains head south." He held her in his arms and gently rocked her, stroking one palm across her back while the fingers of his other hand kneaded the muscles in her neck. "Will you come back to bed with me?"

"Only if you promise to make love to me."

"With pleasure."

Once Jake had her back in his bed, he kept his promise. In spades. Throughout the night he made love to her like he'd never loved any other woman. Afterwards, somewhere between the last vestiges of night and the early light of dawn, just as he drifted into a deep sleep, Jake was struck by a thunderous realization—this was a hell of a lot more than just sex.

NINETEEN

Dori woke with a start. Her heart pounding, her mind disoriented, she gazed at the man sleeping peacefully beside her, his leg draped over her thighs. Jake. The memories of the last several hours came flooding back to her, momentarily chasing away the nightmare that awakened her.

Nothing could have prepared her for the pleasures Jake had given her. He'd introduced her to the wonders of her own body. And his. And she'd reveled in the sensuousness of it all. Like an addict her body craved his touch, never wanting him to stop once he began. For the first time in her life, she felt free—free of the worry, free of the guilt—for those few precious hours she'd given herself over to him.

Dori snuggled closer to Jake and closed her eyes, wanting to relive those hours, but the nightmare came crashing back with a vengeance. She took several deep breaths, attempting to clear her head, but instead of dissipating, the images grew sharper. Hovering at the recesses of her brain, the disturbing visions forced their way to the front of her mind and replayed in her wakeful state.

The pictures trapped her like an insect in a web. The more she fought to free herself, the more tangled she became. Finally, inextricably snared and unable to move or call for help, she watched in horror as her nemesis approached. Dori choked back a sob and clutched Jake's arm. *Oh, Jake. What am I going to do now?*

Beside her, Jake stirred, reaching out for her in his sleep. Dori sought the comfort of his hard body. With the best of intentions, she'd managed to entangle herself in a nightmare of her own making. Somehow, she had to figure out a way to cut through the web of deceit she'd spun around her life and straighten out the mess. Sooner or later, no matter how Joey tried to convince her otherwise, the truth was going to catch up with them, and their carefully constructed lives would crumble at their feet.

The lies were eating her alive. Her mind turned to stories she'd seen on the news, and she saw the faces of the men and women who now languished in jail cells for offenses similar to her own. In her dream she'd seen herself behind bars, desperately pleading for release. Release from prison. Release from the lies. She saw Jake standing on the other side of the cell, shaking his head, then turning and walking away. As he faded into the mist, she heard him say, "I'm sorry, Dori. I was only doing my job."

As much as she wanted to tell Jake the truth, she first had to find out how that truth would affect her and Nikki and Joey. Jake still hadn't revealed any more of his past to her, but he carried a gun, and he knew how to use it. He'd told her he was on an extended leave of absence from a government position. Logic convinced her that profession involved law enforcement. Whether FBI, CIA, or ATF, it didn't matter. She could hardly confess her secrets to an officer of the law. Jail was just not an option.

Dori could think of only one person she might be able to trust to guide her out of the miasma of deception she'd created. She only hoped she could still count on him. *Once* she found him. *If* she could find him. For most of the remainder of the night she lay awake formulating a plan of action.

TWENTY

He sat at the end of the bar tossing back shots, his anger mounting with each burning swallow and every passing hour. If the bitch thought she could get away with what she'd done, she had another think coming. He knew where to find her, and he was going to make her pay. He'd make them all pay. "Hey," he yelled to the brassy-haired bartender, "hit me."

She scowled at him as she reached under the counter. Producing a half empty bottle of rock gut, she refilled his glass. "You've been here all night. Maybe this should be your last shot."

With one hand he grabbed the bottle from her. With his other he slapped a twenty onto the bar. "I'll be the judge of that. Leave the bottle."

With a shrug she pocketed the money and headed over to another customer. "What do I care if you pickle your liver? It's your funeral."

He snorted. "Not tonight, babe." But it was sure as hell going to be someone's funeral and damn soon. The bitch was going to get hers. They all would. No one screwed with him and got away with it. No one.

TWENTY-ONE

From years of conditioning, Jake woke, as usual, at dawn. For several minutes he lay watching Dori sleep beside him. Her tousled hair fanned out across the pillow in a lacy pattern of waves. A weak frown played across her slightly parted lips. The sheet had slipped below her shoulders, revealing the tops of two perfectly shaped breasts that rose and fell in a soft rhythm as she breathed. Jake reached out and skimmed his fingers across their milky white smoothness, remembering their sweet taste and how they had responded to his touch. How Dori had responded to him, giving herself so freely. Trusting him with the most precious of gifts.

He had lost count of how many times they made love last night. Certainly, he'd defied the laws of male physiognomy. And still he wanted her. He laughed at his own foolishness in thinking one night with Dori could purge his need for her from his system. Last night had only increased the itch, not abated it. She'd become an addictive drug, invading his body, his mind, his soul. He couldn't get enough of her, and for a man who'd always prided himself on keeping a tight rein on his emotions, that frightened Jake more than he wanted to admit.

He pulled a blanket up around her and forced himself from the bed. In all likelihood, she'd be sore as hell this morning. After a gentle re-beginning their lovemaking had grown intense. Forceful. Even desperate at times.

Jake glanced at the digital display of the clock-radio on the nightstand. Four hours from now Dori would cut the ribbon at the opening of the McStore flagship in Orlando. The last thing she needed before starting her hectic day was another round with him. For her sake, he reluctantly dragged himself from bed and headed for the shower.

Somehow, he had to figure out just what he was going to do about Dori—other than continue to make love to her—and he needed a clear head for that. The last thing he'd wanted was to fall for another woman—any woman, let alone one with a dubious past and a truckload of secrets, but it was too late. He'd fallen and fallen hard.

Last night he'd convinced himself of her innocence, rationalizing away the forgery of false identities. In the light of day he realized his emotions had clouded his judgment. Courts of law didn't recognize a man's heart. If he were to help Dori, he'd have to operate with a clear head and that meant rooting out her secrets. Except Jake found himself not wanting to know the full extent of those secrets. He already knew more than he was comfortable knowing about Dori's past. Although technically on an extended leave of absence, he was a man sworn to uphold the law, but Jake knew he'd break every law on the books to protect Dori. God help him, no matter what she'd done, he could never turn her over to the authorities.

* * *

The smell of freshly brewed coffee seeped through Dori's sleepy haze. Opening her eyes, she found Jake sitting on the edge of the bed watching her. One of his hands rested on her bare shoulder, his touch flooding her with memories of the other, more intimate places he'd touched her last night and how she'd responded to him. "Time to get up," he said. "I ordered breakfast."

Dori raised herself on one elbow, then hesitated as her cheeks flooded with heat. This was the morning after, and she had no experience with mornings after. Every ounce of self-confidence drained from her. Pulling the comforter up to her chin, she stared at Jake, leaning over her, fully clothed. Paralyzed by embarrassment, nothing short of an earthquake could cause her to fling back the blanket and parade naked in front of him. No matter what they'd done last night.

Jake surprised her by grabbing a robe from the foot of the bed and holding it out for her. When she took the robe from his hand, he stood and turned his back while she slipped into it. "In case you've forgotten," he said, peaking over his shoulder, "I've already seen, touched, and tasted every square inch of you."

"In the dark." Cinching the terrycloth belt tightly at her waist, she slid off the bed, her toes sinking into the thick pile carpeting. "And you weren't dressed at the time."

He chuckled and turned back to face her. "Feeling at a disadvantage?"

"Definitely."

Jake stepped closer. The corners of his mouth twitched slightly as he reached for the robe lapels and drew them snuggly up to her chin. "Tonight, we leave the lights on." He planted a kiss on her forehead.

After all they'd done together last night, Dori wouldn't have thought it possible to go weak in the knees from such a platonic show of affection. But she did, circling his waist with her arms to steady herself. Apparently, she still had much to learn. "Is that a promise or a threat?"

"A little bit of both." He cupped her bottom with his hands and pulled her close against him. Through several layers of clothing, his growing need punctuated his words, but when Dori reached for him, Jake pulled away. "As much as I'd love to, we have an appointment in Orlando this morning, and we're still in Georgia."

"Suppose they'd miss us if we didn't show up?"

"What do you think?"

Dori sighed. Tonight seemed a million years away. She stared at the rumpled bed, so inviting, then glanced up at Jake. His face might mask his true feelings, but another part of his anatomy told her where he, too, would rather spend the rest of the day. "I guess I should go shower."

"Good idea. Don't take too long. Breakfast is getting cold."

Once in the bathroom, Dori slipped the robe from her shoulders and let it drop to the floor. As the room filled with steam from the shower, she studied the reflection of the stranger staring back at her from the full-length bathroom mirror. For years, beginning as a very young girl, she'd shouldered the responsibilities of a woman. Last night she'd finally become one. She lifted tentative fingers to her lips, still swollen from Jake's ministrations. As the mirror fogged, her gaze and her fingers focused on other parts of her body—a body she had paid little attention to before now. But last night changed all that. Changed her. Irrevocably and forever.

With her index finger, she etched a heart in the cloudy mirror on her reflection's chest. Then she dissected it with a jagged line, afraid her lies would eventually lead to heartbreak. Her heartbreak.

TWENTY-TWO

The first retail N.Y. McStore opened in Orlando three-and-a-half hours later to the accompaniment of a marching band and captured by local television crews. The festivities began with several long-winded welcoming speeches by various local dignitaries and a campaigning congressman. Dori followed with a short speech of her own, briefly touching on the McStore concept and praising Niles's innovative vision. Then, wielding an oversized pair of scissors, she cut through a wide red satin ribbon to officially mark the opening of the flagship superstore.

Thousands of Orlando residents, along with an equal number of tourists, crowded the roped-off area of the front parking lot which had been transformed into a miniature theme park. Employees, dressed up as cartoon characters, handed out balloons, baseball caps, T-shirts, and key chains—all emblazoned with the McStore logo. Food vendors distributed sodas, hot dogs, and ice cream—all free to the first day's customers. Under a blinding Florida sun, Dori mingled among the crowds, shaking hands, signing autographs, and inviting people inside to check out the store and do some shopping.

Niles hung back on the fringes with Jake, observing.

"I still don't get it," said Jake, keeping a close eye on Dori as a large group of Mexican tourists surrounded her. To his amazement he overheard her conversing with them in fluent Spanish. He shook his head. Was there no end to this woman's talents? But then he remembered some of her other talents, and his brows knit together in consternation. What the hell was he going to do about Dori Johnson?

"Get what?" asked Niles.

"You," said Jake. He waved his arm to encompass the sprawling discount store in front of them. "This is your baby, my friend, but here you are standing in the background while Dori Johnson basks in the limelight. You weren't even up on the podium, for crying out loud! She's receiving the accolades for your accomplishment, and you seem perfectly content with that."

"I am."

Jake stared at the smug expression on his friend's face. This was not like the Niles he had known for nearly two decades. Niles was anything but shy. He enjoyed being the center of attention. Hungered for it, even.

Niles York's picture had appeared numerous times on the covers of *Business Week* and *Forbes*. Countless articles had appeared about him and his various enterprises in *The Wall Street Journal* and the financial pages of *The New York Times*. And each one was expensively framed and hanging in his office. "Why? This isn't like you."

Niles turned to face Jake. "Look at me, Jake." He spread his arms akimbo. "I scream upper class establishment from every square inch of my body—from my custom-made shirts down to my hand-stitched Italian loafers."

He gestured behind him to the crowds. "Do you really think any of these people are going to identify with me? *Buy* from me to make *me* richer? Hell, no! They're jealous of me and my kind. But Dori's one of them. Look at her. They adore her, and because they adore her, they'll shop in *my* stores, order from *my* catalogs, and click on *my* website."

Jake glanced over at the front of the building where a larger-than-life Dori reclined within the *c* of the McStore logo. "Because they see it as Dori's store, Dori's catalog, and Dori's website."

Niles slapped him on the back. "Exactly. Now do you get it?"

Jake's vision drifted to the store entrance and the throngs of people leaving with armloads of packages and shopping carts filled with merchandise. He shook his head and chuckled. He got it. No doubt about it, Niles York was a marketing genius.

He turned his attention back to Dori. Although the sun beat down relentlessly on the crowd, wilting many, she looked as fresh and bubbly as she had an hour earlier when she kicked off the festivities. Still, he was looking forward to a repeat of last night. He had thought of little else since early that morning and didn't want an uncomfortable sunburn getting in their way. "Maybe we should bring Dori inside for a while," he said.

"Good idea. That will draw some of these people into the store."

Jake scowled at his friend. "Actually, Niles, I was more concerned with her turning into a lobster. It's hot as Hades out here."

Like Pavlov's dog, at the mention of the heat Niles reach into his breast pocket. Withdrawing an Egyptian cotton monogrammed handkerchief, he delicately patted dry the beads of perspiration that peppered his forehead. If Jake hadn't known Niles in college, he never would have guessed the man with the aristocratic mannerisms standing beside him had once played tight end for the Fighting Irish of Notre Dame. "Well, yes, of course," said Niles. "That, too."

After escorting Dori into the store, Niles ushered Jake off to a relatively quiet corner of the appliance department. "I understand you had a problem last night," he said.

Jake knew at once what Niles referred to, but he had no desire to discuss it. His nerves were still too raw from the experience and its incendiary aftermath. Of course, he had no intention of divulging any of the more personal aspects of the incident to Niles or anyone, but somehow relating any part of the episode seemed a breach of his and Dori's privacy. "The elevator?"

Niles nodded. "Dick Reichman called after you left the warehouse. Were you going to tell me?"

Jake shrugged. He scanned the shelves in front of him, holding row after endless row of every conceivable electric kitchen gadget and some that appeared inconceivable. He lifted one odd-looking device and turned it over in his hands, studying it from all angles.

"Eventually," he said. "It was no big deal. They were having problems with the cooling and heating system. A fuse blew or something. The power tripped. In an operation of that size you have to expect a few kinks the first few weeks, don't you? We weren't stuck for long."

Then, deliberately changing the subject, he held the item in his hand up to Niles. "What the hell is this?"

"Damned if I know." Niles grabbed the contraption out of Jake's hand and placing it back on the shelf. "Ask Dori. And don't change the subject."

"The subject is closed. There's nothing more to it."

"Dick disagrees. He said the malfunction was caused deliberately. Told me he knows who did it and fired the guy last night after you and Dori left."

Jake snorted. "He's sucking up to you, Niles. Reichman wanted to make sure he wasn't blamed, so he covered his ass by sacrificing a scapegoat."

A look of skepticism crossed Niles's face. "He seemed pretty convinced. Said the guy all but admitted it."

"For Pete's sake, Niles, how can you possibly believe someone rigged the elevator to injure me and Dori? That's ludicrous. Aside from the fact that we're only talking one floor, and the possibility of severe injure was slim to none, where's the motive?"

"It does sound pretty farfetched now that I think about it."

"Exactly. Maybe the ventilation guys are incompetent. Maybe one of them screwed up while trying to nail down the air problem, but it was hardly deliberate."

Since Niles had brought the subject up, Jake decided this was as good a time as any to voice his concerns about the plant manager. "You and I need to have a little talk about Dick Reichman. The guy's a loose cannon."

Niles shook his head. "I know he comes across as arrogant at times, but he has a reputation for running a tight ship and getting the job done. I spent a bundle to lure him away from FedEx, but he's worth every dollar. Look at the success he's had with the Atlanta hub—up and running on schedule and under budget."

"Oh, yes. He's very good at taking the credit for that. And

everything else. But he's equally quick to assign blame when things go wrong. Like with the elevator. He's a brown-nosing bastard, Niles. Spent most of yesterday kissing up to me, but he seems to take perverse pleasure in browbeating and belittling certain segments of the personnel. He even jumped all over Dori a few times."

"What do you mean?"

"He really tore into her after she gave that plug for the black suit."

"What? I thought her ad libbed sales pitch was great! I even told her so. I suggested we do weekly merchandise pitches for different products."

"I know, and that made Dick look like a big asshole. Dori tried to smooth things over afterwards, but he was really pissed that you supported her and not him."

"Well, that's just one isolated incident," said Niles. "Dick had a lot riding on last night's online chat. He was probably nervous as hell. I'm sure he didn't mean what he said."

"There's more. Besides the ventilation crew, who he has nothing but contempt for, he has a mile wide chip on his shoulder concerning the computer programmers—especially the ones monitoring the site. He thinks they're slackers and doesn't miss an opportunity to point it out every chance he gets."

"Fine. Just as long as they're not connected to the Russian-American mob." When Jake scowled, Niles quickly added, "It was a joke, Jake! I'll talk to him. You know I don't tolerate that kind of behavior in my companies. From anyone, no matter how good he is."

Jake grew thoughtful. There *was* always the possibility that the mob *had* infiltrated the Atlanta hub. Or elsewhere. But Niles had previously admitted none of his enterprises had experienced anything that might be attributed to mob retaliation. As he'd reminded Jake several weeks earlier, his problem with organized crime happened years ago. If they wanted revenge, they certainly would have struck by now. Besides, a minor glitch in the elevator hardly suggested sabotage.

Still...with so much at stake it didn't hurt to dig a little deeper. "Have any of the other plant managers reported unexplained problems or equipment malfunctions?"

"Not that I'm aware of." Niles eyed him suspiciously. "Are you saying you suddenly agree with Dick?"

"No. Just covering all the bases. Did you do a background check of personnel down in Atlanta?"

"On key people. Nothing unusual showed up."

Jake decided to call Charley and wheedle another favor out of her. She'd probably use him for target practice, but under the circumstances, a more thorough investigation of Niles's employees seemed warranted. "Have Dick keep his eyes open for anything else fishy or unusual. And have someone check with the other facilities managers. If nothing else occurs, we can chalk the elevator incident up to an isolated startup SNAFU."

TWENTY-THREE

He kept his distance, blending into the crowd but keeping his eyes on his prey. Miss High-and-Mighty was in for a big surprise. But not yet. He'd bide his time, plan his move when she least expected him to strike. And then she'd pay for what she'd done. He'd see to that. He sauntered over to the booth handing out free hot dogs and helped himself to three, consuming the first in two bites. The irony of the situation amused him. Usually, the condemned man received a last meal before the execution, not the executioner.

He polished off the remaining two hot dogs, tossing the paper wrappers on the ground. Then he grabbed a can of root beer and headed for his truck.

TWENTY-FOUR

After five hours Dori feared her face had frozen into a permanent smile and her right hand had developed a lasting crimp. Her voice had grown hoarse from answering endless questions. None of it bother her, though. She was genuinely enjoying herself. Still, it felt good to collapse into the back of the hired limousine and kick off her high heels.

Niles uncorked a chilled bottle of champagne and began pouring. "None for me," she said, waving off the flute he offered. "Not on an empty stomach. Especially since I still have to deal with the website tonight."

"Leave it for tomorrow," he said.

"Tomorrow, we have another opening, and I'll have twice as many messages waiting for me." She shook her head. "No. The e-mail gets done tonight before I go to bed."

Niles patted her hand. "See how dedicated my new

spokesperson is, Jake? I can't even convince her to play hooky for a few hours."

"How much e-mail?" asked Jake, ignoring Niles.

Dori shrugged. "I have no idea. Tonight will be the first time I access it. Could be a few dozen or even a few hundred. There really is no way to tell."

Jake studied her with those dark, brooding eyes of his. "A few hundred? You're not planning to answer them *all* tonight, are you?"

"That *is* part of my job, Jake." When his frown deepened, she added, "I'll get a jump on it as soon as we get back to the hotel. Before dinner."

He grunted. Dori smiled at him, suspecting he'd been planning a different pre-dinner activity. Well, he'd have to wait—as much as she'd like to partake in that particular pleasure herself.

She hoped the e-mail wasn't as time consuming as she led Jake to believe. She needed to surf the web for other reasons tonight, and it was best if Jake thought she was working.

Hopefully, she could forward most of the e-mail to the proper personnel and be done with it. Niles envisioned the *Ask Dori* feature on the site as a way for shoppers with unusual customer service inquiries and requests to receive white glove, individualized attention. Even if Dori really didn't personally handle each inquiry, he wanted his customers to come away with the perception that she had.

Once at the hotel, however, Dori discovered she'd need to employ an equal amount of creativity and cunning to find some time alone with her laptop. Niles had booked all of them into a three-bedroom penthouse suite!

On the ride back Niles had mentioned that the limousine

driver had delivered their luggage to the hotel after dropping the three of them off at the opening. Dori noticed her laptop sitting on the desk at one end of the large living room. She saw no other luggage. "My bags?" she asked Niles.

"Already unpacked." He indicated one of the bedrooms. "The suite comes with a butler."

"I'm going to take a shower before starting the e-mails." She reached for the computer.

Niles stopped her. "Leave the laptop. I'll order up some hors d'oeuvres. We can all change into some comfortable clothes and relax. Then we can check out the first batch of *Ask Dori* e-mails together before going out to dinner later."

Dori nodded and smiled, but a twinge of uneasiness crept through her. How was she going to track down Sammy Pak with Niles hovering over her shoulder?

* * *

Half an hour later Dori stared at the computer monitor and groaned as one-by-one the messages downloaded from the site into her mailbox.

"You've got mail," said Jake leaning over her shoulder and quickly brushing her lips with his while Niles had his back turned. He wasn't any happier than she about the endless stream of posts. And she knew he was hungry for something other than the canapés Niles had ordered. Then again, so was she.

Dori sighed, leaning back to brush her cheek against his. "I'll say."

"How many?" asked Niles.

"Three hundred sixty-two and still counting," said Dori.

Niles clapped his hands together. "Wonderful!"

"Yeah, great," muttered Jake.

"That's it," said Dori several minutes later. "Six hundred twenty-seven." She scrolled through the list. "Most of them right after the tour last night."

"This is exciting," said Niles, pulling up a chair next to her. "Let's get started. Open the first one."

"You'd think it was Christmas," said Jake.

"So go write a book or something," said Niles, tearing his gaze from the screen to glare at him. "You don't have to stay here while we're doing this."

"Wouldn't miss it for the world."

Dori clicked open the first message. Shirley from Cincinnati was having trouble deciding between a turtleneck and a blouse to go with a navy skirt and wanted Dori's opinion. Dori dispatched a quick reply, advising the woman to purchase both—giving herself both a casual and dressy outfit from one skirt. She then suggested a few accessories from the group offered on the site for Shirley to consider adding to her shopping cart.

"Good answer," said Niles.

Joline from Paintsville, Kentucky was another story, though. She wanted a suggestion for a birthday present for her five-year-old granddaughter who lived in Seattle. A seven-paragraph rambling diatribe described in excruciating detail how Joline's rotten son-in-law and ungrateful daughter had taken jobs on the other side of the country, depriving Joline and her husband of anything more than a short once-a-year visit with the child.

"God, I hope the other six hundred twenty-five aren't like this," said Dori, forwarding the message on to the customer service representative who specialized in toys.

"She didn't even bother to tell you anything about the kid," said Niles. "Does she like dolls or board games? Books or baseball?"

"I don't think it matters," said Dori."

"What do you mean?"

"Joline really doesn't want a gift suggestion. She wants a shoulder to cry on."

"And maybe some advice on how to get her daughter and son-in-law to move back to Kentucky," added Jake.

"That's not what *Ask Dori* is about," said Niles. "They were told that last night during the tour, and the website spells out quite clearly the types of questions Dori will answer."

"All the lonely people?" asked Dori, gazing up at Jake.

"All the lonely people," he agreed.

Click by click, Dori waded through one message after another. Many of the inquiries were about her—either complimentary comments about last night's tour or personal questions dealing with her background. For both she composed a standard reply—a thank-you note for the former and a diplomatic, polite none-of-your-business response to the latter. For posts better suited for a therapist she created a standard reply reminding senders of the type of questions she was qualified to answer.

By six o'clock Dori had dispatched over two-thirds of the e-mails. "Why don't we break for dinner?" suggested Jake, who had tired of the endless monotony after the first fifteen minutes and had stretched out on the couch with several magazines.

Instead of answering him, Niles yelled, "What the hell! Jake, get over here!"

Jake jumped to his feet and crossed the room in three long strides, coming up behind Dori and Niles who were both staring at the monitor. Jake leaned over the backs of their chairs and read the message on the screen.

Life is like an elevator, full of ups and downs. When I see your smiling face, the downs turn to ups, and my day is a little brighter. It was signed, *A. Friend.*

"Still think it was an accident?" asked Niles.

Dori twisted in her chair, switching her gaze from Niles to Jake. "What's he talking about?"

"Dick told Niles he thinks one of the ventilation crew deliberately rigged the elevator."

"But now it looks more like an outside job," said Niles. "There's your culprit. All we have to do is find out who sent that e-mail. Whoever it was hacked into our system and tampered with the elevator. And Lord knows what else."

"*A. Friend,*" said Dori. "That strange message last night was signed the same way."

"Yes," said Jake. He reached across her shoulder and hit the delete key.

"Why'd you do that?" yelled Niles. "Now we'll never catch him."

"Calm down, Niles."

"Calm down! This lunatic is out to destroy me!"

Dori shook her head. "I don't think so."

"My God, how can you say that? He nearly killed you last night!"

"Hardly. Besides, I think the reference to the elevator is a coincidence. *A. Friend* is just a lonely person. Probably someone without any friends. Maybe he suffers from bipolar disorder or some other mental problem."

"Exactly," said Jake. "You have a room full of brilliant computer technicians in Atlanta who would have noticed within a minute or two if someone hacked into the system."

"Besides," added Dori, "if someone on the outside wanted to

create problems for McStore, why tamper with an elevator? Why not crash the Internet site or sabotage the inventory system?" She hit a series of keys, retrieving the deleted post from the trash can.

"What are you doing?" asked Jake.

"He sounds so sad. Maybe I should write back to him."

"How do you know it's a he?"

Dori shrugged. "Just guessing."

"Don't encourage him," said Niles. "Even if he's not a hacker, he could be dangerous."

Dori turned to Jake. "Niles is right," he agreed. Once again, he reached over and trashed the message, but this time he also emptied the trash can.

Although she thought both Niles and Jake were overreacting, Dori dropped the subject. Too tired to argue, she exited from her e-mail and shut down the computer, but *A. Friend* remained in her thoughts throughout most of dinner.

Unlike either of the men, she understood loneliness all too well. Because of her family circumstances, she had grown up with few friends. Her life had revolved around school and caring for her brother and sister. It still did, except over the past six years, she'd also juggled a job. That left precious little time for cultivating friendships.

Sometimes Dori lay awake at night feeling cheated and sorry for herself—especially after viewing a family-oriented movie on television or watching some of the neighborhood children at play. She had only dim memories of playing with other children, mostly during school recesses.

After school and weekends always involved homework, housework, and caring for her siblings. Even before her mother had taken ill, many of the daily chores had fallen to Dori because her mother spent much of her time either working an outside job or catering to her demanding father.

Maybe *A. Friend* was stuck in a similar situation, but Dori had more pressing matters to consider and by dessert had forgot about the cryptic e-mailer. Her thoughts centered around finding Sammy Pak.

* * *

Later that evening, after she, Jake, and Niles retired to their respective bedrooms, Dori slipped out of bed and retrieved the laptop from the living room desk. Once back in her room, she quickly found the information she needed. Sammy had remained in Philadelphia, setting up a law practice with a partner in the Olney section of the city. She and Jake were scheduled to open a McStore superstore outside of Philadelphia at the beginning of the following week.

Dori jotted down the address and phone number, exited the program and turned off the computer. Slipping off the bed, she padded across the room. When she opened her bedroom door, she found Jake standing on the other side, about to knock. His gaze locked on the computer cradled in her arms, the corners of his mouth taking a rapid plunge downward. "What are you doing?"

Dori hugged the laptop closer to her chest and searched her mind for a plausible reason for taking the computer. Although she'd spent the last six years lying, the act wasn't easy for her in the best of circumstances, much less when caught cheating on her lover with a portable piece of computer hardware. "N...nothing," she stammered.

Jake raised one eyebrow as he lifted the computer from her arms. "Nothing? You weren't trying to find that post I deleted, were you?"

Dori released a loud sigh and offered him a sheepish smile. "Guess you caught me red-handed."

With her hand firmly clasped in his, Jake strode across the room and placed the computer back on the desk. Then he grasped her other hand and lifted them both to within inches of his face. "No crimson stains," he said. "Does that mean you were unsuccessful, or will I find a reply to that weirdo when I turn on the computer?"

"I couldn't access his message."

"You? The computer whiz?"

"I'm telling you the truth." she shrugged toward the laptop. "But go ahead and check for yourself if you don't believe me."

Instead of flipping open the laptop, Jake drew her closer to him. He wore only a pair of thin cotton boxers, and the moment their bodies met, Dori realized he'd come to her bedroom not for the computer but for her.

She tipped her head back and saw the same searing need in his eyes that she felt poking into her belly and igniting her womb. He lowered his head, capturing her mouth and swallowing the moan that forced its way from the back of her throat. Without taking his mouth from hers, he lifted her into his arms and carried her back to her bedroom.

"Niles," she whispered as Jake placed her in the center of the bed and lifted her nightgown over her head.

"He's not invited. This is a very private party."

Dori rolled to her side as Jake joined her on the bed. "He'll hear us," she managed to say before he dipped his tongue into her mouth and rolled on top of her.

Jake took his time with the kiss, his tongue exploring every moist corner of her mouth. "Not a chance," he murmured, moving to the hollow of her neck. "I roomed with him in college for four years. When Niles falls asleep, it takes a scud missile to wake him."

"What if he's not asleep yet?" she asked, gasping as he sucked on one of her nipples.

Jake lifted his head from her breast and chuckled. "I already checked. He's out cold.

TWENTY-FIVE

After the flagship opening in Orlando, Niles headed off to attend to other York Enterprises business while Dori and Jake continued to Kansas City for the next opening. Dori fell into a comfortable, although exhaustive, routine. Her days were filled with meeting and greeting throngs of curious shoppers as well as local dignitaries and politicians. In the late afternoon and early evening, she tended to her website duties. Since the initial deluge of mail after the cyber-tour, the hits to the *Ask Dori* site dwindled to a manageable few hundred a day.

The nights were reserved for Jake. She'd fallen in love with her work, and she'd fallen in love with the man who made love to her each night. The first revelation came as a welcome surprise, the second as a sucker punch to her solar plexus.

She didn't want to love Jake. Too many secrets lay within her, secrets that once exposed would drive them apart. Or worse. No, loving Jake was a bad move. A very bad move. But somehow her brain hadn't conveyed that message to her heart. Or if it had, her heart had refused to listen.

Dori lived with the constant fear that Jake would learn of her secrets before she had the opportunity to talk with Sammy Pak and figure a way out of the illegal mess she'd created. Only then would she feel truly free. Discovering Sammy's whereabouts had filled her with a renewed sense of hope. Sammy would know how to resolve her nightmare and keep her out of jail.

After all, the cases of forgery she'd read about and seen on the news all involved adults who'd acted out of greed. Those men and women deserved their jail sentences. She'd committed her crimes as a minor and out of desperation, not for profit. Surely, the government would understand she had no other choice at the time.

She had even begun to convince herself that Jake would understand, but she still feared he'd find out the truth before she found a solution. Knowing Jake, he'd jump right in and take over. She couldn't allow that. This was her problem, and she needed to solve it without involving anyone else—especially Jake. She'd already dragged her sister and brother down an illegal path. If Jake became involved, it might compromise his real job—whatever that job was.

But Jake kept pressing. He knew she was hiding something from him. Every so often, he asked a question about her past—a question which she sensed he already knew the answer to. Although on the surface his queries sounded innocent enough, Dori worried that he might have ulterior motives. After all, he did have government connections—connections he still refused to discuss. And he carried a gun.

Even though returning to Philadelphia filled her with anxiety, at the same time Dori counted down the days to their arrival with mounting anticipation—like a child awaiting Christmas morning. Going back to her hometown to meet with Sammy was her first step toward freedom. But part of her dreaded setting foot back in the City of Brotherly Love, a city which held reminders of very little love and far too much pain for her.

Compounding her anxiety, as the days approached, Dori felt as though she were running out of time, that she was racing against an unseen assailant who gained on her with each passing hour. By the time she and Jake arrived in Des Moines, her feelings of uneasiness bordered on paranoia, and she fought a constant battle to keep her fears from surfacing and consuming her. Most of all, she struggled to keep them hidden from Jake's observant eyes.

Someone was watching her. She became more and more convinced of it. Looking back over the past few days, she realized she first became aware of the feeling in Orlando but had shrugged it off as opening day jitters. And of course, someone *had* been watching her in Orlando. Two someones, in fact. Niles and Jake had kept a vigilant eye on her throughout the festivities.

But the feeling had persisted in Kansas City with Jake by her side and Niles back in Manhattan. On more than one occasion during the day she'd experienced a prickly sensation at the back of her neck—a psychic hint that someone close by had her in his sights. But each time, when she spun around, she found no one there.

"What's wrong?" asked Jake, drawing her aside after she'd greeted the mayor and various city dignitaries. "You're awfully jumpy this morning."

"I don't know." She offered him a weak smile. "Maybe I'm not getting enough sleep." She needed to keep her suspicions from him. If her feelings were correct, she'd have to reveal far too much. Right now, all she had was an ill-defined anxiety.

Scanning the crowd, she saw a sea of friendly faces, all anxious to meet her and be among the first to shop at N.Y. McStore. She saw no evidence of sinister demons or Russian mobsters lurking in the shadows or standing on the fringes of the crowd. But the feelings of paranoia continued, increasing by the hour.

This is Des Moines, she kept telling herself, fighting off the panic, *not Philadelphia. You have no ghosts lurking in Des Moines.*

That night she received yet another e-mail from *A. Friend.* Unfortunately, Jake came up behind her just as she clicked open the message. He proceeded to read it out loud. "*I thought you were different. I thought you cared, but you're just like all the others, aren't you?*"

He heaved an irate sigh. "I don't like the sound of that, Dori. This guy's got more than a few screws loose. Is this the first you've heard from him since that message last Monday?"

Dori hesitated.

"Dori?"

She shook her head. "No."

Annoyance spread across Jake's face and sounded in his voice. "You haven't answered him, have you?"

"I sent one of the standard replies."

"When?"

"Yesterday." She bit her lower lip and glanced up at him. "When he asked if I sleep on my stomach or on my back." She flinched when Jake let fly a stream of curses.

"Is that all?"

Dori took a deep breath. "And the day before that when he

asked if I prefer showers or baths." She wrinkled her nose and waited for another expletive assault.

Instead, Jake's frown deepened until large furrows covered his forehead and crease lines formed from the corners of his mouth down to his jaw. "He's sent a message every day?"

"Like clockwork."

"And you've sent the standard reply each time?"

Again she hesitated, this time refusing to meet his probing gaze.

Jake reached for her chin, lifted her head, and studied her intensely. "You answered him, didn't you?"

Dori stared into Jake's blue-black eyes, the irises nearly as dark as his pupils. They shone with anger. And something else that nearly made her gasp out loud—fear.

For the first time Dori began to wonder if Jake might not be right in his assessment of *A. Friend*. All her fears always centered around her past. When that prickly feeling occurred at the back of her neck, she thought in terms of Borka and his cronies, not an anonymous e-mailer. She hadn't thought Jake and Niles were justified in their reactions to the initial posts. Now she wasn't so sure.

A. Friend's questions had grown progressively stranger and more intrusive with each passing day. This last message read more like a veiled threat. "He sounded so lonely, Jake. I just didn't see any harm in answering him Tuesday when he asked about my favorite movie. I thought maybe he was interested in ordering a video."

"So you didn't answer any of his other questions?"

"None."

He dropped his hand from her face. "Maybe it's time to find

out just who *A. Friend* is." He hit the delete key. "Don't send him any more responses. Of any kind. I'll handle this from now on."

"You? I'm the one with the computer skills."

"And I'm the one with the connections."

Since she didn't necessarily want to know about those connections, she let the subject drop. "Fine. You take care of it."

Jake's face flushed with rage. He slammed the lid of the laptop down and dragged her off the chair, bringing his face to within inches of hers. "And how long were you going to wait until you told me about these messages, or weren't you going to tell me?"

Dori wiggled out of his grasp. "Stop overreacting. I was handling it, Jake! I can take care of myself. I've been doing it for a long time without any help from you or anyone else."

"Yes, but how well?"

She stared at him, her mouth hanging open, unable to find the words she needed for rebuttal. His question stung more than he could possibly imagine and far more than she wanted to admit. To him or to herself.

She lived with enough guilt over her past. She didn't need Jake heaping on more. Fighting back the tears that flooded her throat, Dori stormed off to her bedroom, slamming and locking the door behind her. If Jake Prentiss thought he was sharing her bed tonight, the man had another think coming.

* * *

Jake stared at the closed door and shook his head. He hadn't overreacted to the situation. Dori had. Although she refused to admit it, something was bothering her. She worked the openings like a pro, but in quiet moments he often found her distracted and preoccupied. Nervous and jittery.

He consistently found her darting quick glances over her

shoulder during the day as if expecting to see someone—someone she obviously didn't want to confront. Each day she grew more skittish, only truly relaxing once they were in bed at night where their lovemaking seemed to provide a release from whatever preyed upon her mind during the day.

Jake had a pretty good idea about what was causing Dori's heightened anxiety level. In a few days they arrived in Philadelphia. Knowing what he did of her past, that had to worry her. He wished she'd confide in him. He'd find some way to help her.

He already had Charley quietly working on the problem. So far nothing his former partner had uncovered revealed any connection between Dori and the mob other than her father's involvement with the elusive Boris Borka. Nothing pointed to any additional criminal activity on Dori's part.

Jake believed that Dori, Nikki, and Joey fled Philadelphia in fear for their lives. Somehow their disappearance was connected to their father's death, but what had Sergei's children seen or heard that had caused Dori to take such drastic measures? The answers could provide the key to exonerating her of all charges, but Jake wouldn't know *that* until she revealed the secrets she kept locked inside her.

Striding across the room, Jake rapped on the door. Silence greeted his knock. He rattled the locked doorknob. "Dori?" She refused to answer him. "Dori, please, sweetheart. I'm sorry."

"No you're not. You're just horny. Go away, Jake."

Yeah, that was certainly true, he thought, glancing down at the proof. But he doubted uttering such an admission at this moment would aid his case. "Can't we talk about this? I'm worried. That's all."

"Worry about yourself. I told you I can take care of myself! Now, leave me alone. I'm going to bed."

Jake threw his hands up in the air. Fine! Short of breaking down the door or picking the lock, he had no other option than to do as she requested. He glanced at his watch, then headed for the second bedroom on the opposite side of the living room. It was still early. He'd call Charley and have her track down *A. Friend* before the creep caused any more trouble to his love life.

* * *

Later that night Dori decided to forgive Jake. She *had* overreacted. Besides, if she started acting hostile, she'd have a more difficult time slipping away from him once they arrived in Philadelphia.

For days she'd stewed trying to find a way to see Sammy without having to tell Jake where she was going or trigger his suspicions. She couldn't use shopping as an excuse. Her wardrobe came from McStore. If she told him she needed to see a doctor, he'd start worrying and insist on accompanying her. Even if she just wanted to get some fresh air, he'd want to tag along. Jake hadn't let her out of his sight since they'd flown to Atlanta.

She also discovered after sharing a bed with him for nearly a week, that she couldn't fall asleep without him first inside her and then beside her. After tossing and turning for several hours, she finally gave up.

She found him sitting in the living room nursing a glass of something that in the muted moonlight looked suspiciously like milk. He wore a pair of silk boxers. Nothing else. He looked brooding and angry and sexy as hell, and she felt herself growing hot in all the right places at the sight of him.

She thought she saw a shadow of something she couldn't quite read settle over his face as she entered, but he said nothing.

She sat down on the sofa next to him. "I'm sorry."

"No, you're not. You're just horny."

She started to sputter in indignation but stopped herself before she managed to utter a coherent word. Jake eyed her with the lust of a man too long shipwrecked on a deserted island. She shivered in response.

"Cold?" He thrust the glass mug into her hand. "Have a sip."

She took a mouthful of the drink, nearly choking as the stinging liquid coursed down her throat.

"I said a sip!" He grabbed the cup out of her hands and patted her back.

"What was that?"

"A white Russian."

"I thought it was warm milk."

Jake laughed. "Warm milk? Do I look like a warm milk kind of guy?"

"I couldn't sleep. I thought maybe you were having the same problem."

"I know a solution." He stood and offered her his hand.

Dori stared at his outstretched palm. When Jake made love to her, she forgot about the world and all her troubles. Nothing else existed besides the two of them, entwined as one. She needed that escape—needed it more with each passing day. She slipped her hand into his and allowed him to draw her off the sofa.

* * *

Although Niles had located the Philadelphia area McStore in a suburb directly north of the city, Dori and Jake were booked into a downtown hotel—the area known to the locals as Center City.

"Better restaurants," said Jake when she questioned the location. "Besides, you know Niles. First class all the way. His travel planner wouldn't think to stick us in some second-rate suburban motel."

Dori fought to contain her excitement. She still hadn't devised a plan to slip away from Jake for a few hours, but at least now she had a subway at her front door.

Several hours later Jake presented her with the perfect opportunity. "I'm running downstairs to the barbershop," he said as she opened her e-mail. He paused as she scanned through the list of posts. "Nothing from our friend?"

"Not since the other night. What did you do?"

"Me? What makes you think *I* did anything?"

Dori smirked. "You're the one with the connections, remember?"

"Maybe he just got bored." He gave her a quick kiss. "I won't be long."

"Take your time. I have about an hour's worth of work here."

As soon as Jake left the suite, Dori glanced at her watch, then reached for the hotel phone. Five minutes later, dressed in jeans and a wool blazer, her head covered by a navy Pashmina scarf and her eyes hidden behind dark glasses, she grabbed her purse and headed for the elevator.

* * *

Jake entered the barbershop located in the hotel's lobby. Two customers already occupied the chairs of the barbers on duty, but there were no other men in the waiting area.

One of the barbers, a dapper looking gentleman who reminded Jake of an English manservant straight out of a Merchant-Ivory period film, welcomed him. "I'll be with you momentarily, sir. Would you care for some coffee or tea while you wait?" He motioned to a corner of the shop where a small counter held a double brewer and accoutrements.

Jake helped himself to a cup of coffee, then settled into one of the chairs in front of the large plate glass window that overlooked the hotel lobby. A moment later he saw Dori hurry across the marble floor toward the exit.

Every one of Jake's finally honed investigative skills, as well as all his previous suspicions, kicked into action. *What the hell was she up to?* Jumping to his feet, he hurried after her, maintaining enough distance to keep from being detected but not enough to lose sight of her.

When she descended the steps to the Broad Street subway, he kept to the shadows, placing himself behind a large group of uniform clad, backpack toting teenagers. Jake waited until Dori stepped into one of the crowded train cars, then entered the car directly behind hers, finding a spot near the connecting door where he could keep an eye on her through the windows.

She remained on the car for several stops, exiting in the Olney section of the city. Once back on the street she crossed the busy intersection and headed north, entering a storefront office three blocks from the subway. Jake took up a position on the opposite corner. He gritted his teeth and watched with growing anger as a tall man with dark hair rose from his desk and embraced her.

Betrayal overwhelming him, Jake tore his vision from the painful scene and focused on the sign painted in large black letters above the front window. *Puchenko and Pak. Attorneys at Law*, the words repeated underneath in both Russian and Korean.

* * *

A soft bell above the door heralded Dori's arrival. She quickly glanced around at the small room that she suspected served as the reception area. She recognized Sammy at once. He hadn't changed much since she last saw him over six years ago. A latticework of tiny lines had etched their way into the corners of his eyes and mouth, and he now wore glasses and carried a few additional pounds. Other than that, he looked the same.

Sammy sat alone in the office, behind a battered wooden desk that faced the front door, his thick head of blue-black hair nearly hidden behind several stacks of books. Floor to ceiling bookcases, crammed with alphabetized law volumes, covered the walls on either side of him. A doorway in the center of the back wall opened onto a narrow hallway with a closed door on either side and a third at the end of the hallway marked *Restroom*. As she closed the front door behind her, he waved an acknowledgement of her presence. "I'll be right with you. Have a seat," he said without raising his head from the paperwork in front of him.

A row of cheap plastic chairs lined the front of the reception area, their backs toward the window. Instead of taking one of them, Dori perched on the edge of the one chair at the side of the desk and studied Sammy as he skimmed a page in a thick legal tome, then copied some information onto the yellow pad in front of him. "Sorry for the delay, Miss..." He glanced at the date book on one corner of the desk. "...Miss Johnson. My secretary is out sick, and my partner is in court. I'm pulling triple duty today. I won't be much longer."

"You always had your nose in a book," she said. "Your poor mother used to worry that you weren't getting enough fresh air."

Sammy's pen stopped mid-word. He raised his head, removed his glasses, and stared at her, a look of bewilderment playing across his face. "Do I know you?"

Dori pulled the scarf from her head and removed her sunglasses. "It's me, Sammy. Dasha."

Sammy blinked. "Dasha? Little Dasha Ivanichek?"

She nodded. A moment later she found herself engulfed in a warm embrace. Tears sprang to her eyes. Sammy's hug overwhelmed her, bringing back the few pleasant memories she possessed of growing up in Northeast Philadelphia.

The Paks had lived next door to the Ivanicheks. As a child, Dori had worshipped Sammy, five years older than she, as both a surrogate big brother and a fantasy boyfriend. Sammy had taught her how to ride a bike and how to use a computer. He introduced her to Shakespeare and Dylan—both Bob and Thomas. He even secretly taught her how to drive the summer before she ran away with Nikki and Joey.

"You know you broke mamma's heart when you left for California without so much as a good-bye," he said, holding her at arm's length and studying her from head to toe.

"California?"

"Or was it Colorado? Wherever Sergei sent the three of you to live with your aunt."

So that was the story her father spread to cover their disappearance! She took a deep breath. "I have no aunt, Sammy, and I didn't go to California or Colorado."

His brow furrowed in puzzlement. Dori continued. "Is it true that if I tell you something, you have to keep it in confidence? You can't tell anyone if I ask you not to?"

The furrows deepened, and the fine lines around his mouth grew more pronounced. "This isn't a social visit, is it, Dasha?"

She shook her head. Sammy dropped his hands. Stepping around her, he headed for the front door. He flipped over the open/closed sign, locked the deadbolt, and pulled down the blinds on both the glass door and the large window. Then he slowly walked back to his desk. "Do you have a dollar?" he asked, taking his seat and indicating that Dori should do likewise.

"Yes," she said, sitting down.

"Give it to me."

Dori fumbled in her purse for her wallet. Pulling out a worn bill, she handed it over to Sammy.

"You've just paid me a retainer to represent you. We are now bound by lawyer/client confidentiality."

He cleared a space on the cluttered desk and removed a fresh legal pad from one of the drawers. With his pen poised over a blank sheet, he turned to her and asked, "How can I help you, Dasha?"

For the next hour Dori poured her soul out to Sammy, explaining how she had run off with Nikki and Joey six years earlier and why. And how she'd gotten away with it by creating new lives for the three of them. "I never could have done it if you hadn't taught me so much about computers. I used the money I took from my father to pay the deposit and first month's rent on a small furnished apartment and buy the computer equipment."

Sammy paused in his note taking and turned to her. "You forged birth certificates yourself?"

"Birth certificates, school and medical records, and Social Security cards for the three of us."

He placed the pen on the tablet and lowered his head into his hands. "Dasha, why didn't you seek help? Go to the authorities for protection?"

"The authorities? Who was going to help me, Sammy? The police? Borka used to brag that half of them were on his payroll."

"You could have gotten a restraining order against him."

"A restraining order? I read the newspapers, Sammy. I watch

the evening news. Restraining orders aren't worth the paper they're printed on. Countless abused women throughout the country can attest to that—at least the ones that are lucky enough to still be alive."

She sighed. "Besides, I was a minor. Who was going to believe me? I couldn't take the chance."

"You could have gone to child welfare."

Dori laughed. "Child welfare? In Philadelphia? By the time they got around to investigating, I would have been pregnant with my third child!"

"So you took Anika and Yusif with you and ran?"

"I had no choice. I had to protect them as well. Borka was going to put Joey—Yusif—to work in the mob. And God knows what they planned for my sister eventually. I couldn't run off and leave them."

"Look, I know what I did was wrong, but I've read up on the criminal codes, and since I really didn't use the forged papers to commit any crimes, I'm sure you can straighten things out and get me off with a reprimand or probation or something."

She took a deep breath. "I'll even pay a fine, Sammy—no matter how steep. I'm making good money now. I may not be able to pay it all at once, though. I can't live with this hanging over me anymore, but I can't turn myself in unless I can be assured I won't go to jail. Nikki and Joey need me."

The room filled with an awkward silence. Dori waited for Sammy to say something. Anything. He leaned back in his chair, took a deep breath, then slowly exhaled. Raising his glasses with one hand, he massaged the bridge of his nose with the thumb and forefinger of his other hand. "A little knowledge is a dangerous thing, Dasha."

He rose from his chair and grabbed a book off the shelf. "You may have read the criminal codes concerning fraud, but unfortunately, you haven't correctly interpreted them. I'm afraid you're in far greater trouble than you realize."

TWENTY-SIX

"You can't be serious!" cried Dori, staring at Sammy in disbelief. Law degree or not, his explanation of the federal criminal codes seemed flawed. "How can I be in bigger trouble for creating the papers myself than if I'd bought them from a criminal? That makes no sense!"

"The law often doesn't make sense, Dasha, but it's still the law. And you've broken some major ones. The Feds don't look very kindly on this sort of thing. I know white collar criminals who are serving longer sentences for nonviolent crimes than rapists and murderers."

"But surely they'd understand that I had no choice, Sammy."

He shook his head. "Don't make the mistake of thinking of Uncle Sam as a benevolent relative. Most federal prosecutors don't look at the various shades of gray in an issue. It's either black or white. Right or wrong. They could throw the book at you, Dasha.

You might be facing up to fifteen years. And that's just for the forgery charges."

"Fifteen years?" The shock of his statement was unlike anything she'd ever experienced. She'd read in the criminal codes that fifteen years was the maximum sentence for forgery, but she'd assumed the maximum applied to hardened criminals who profited from their crimes. In her worst nightmares she'd never expected the law to treat her so harshly.

She'd been a kid—a kid trying to escape from the clutches of organized crime, trying to save her brother and sister from a similar fate. Everything was going terribly wrong. Sammy was supposed to help her, not make things worse. She choked back a sob.

"Fifteen years for starters," he continued. "Then there are the kidnapping charges."

"Kidnapping? What kidnapping?"

"The government can charge you with abducting Anika and Yusif."

Dori buried her head in her hands. She hadn't thought it possible for the nightmare to get any worse. *Kidnapping?* If she weren't so terrified, she'd laugh at the absurd charge. How could anyone think she'd kidnapped Nikki and Joey?

"I didn't take them against their will or coerce them into coming with me." She raised her head and stared at him through watery eyes. "They came willingly. They were just as much at risk as I was! You have to believe me!"

Sammy reached out and clasped her hands in his. "I do believe you, and I'll do everything in my power to help you, Dasha, but I wouldn't be doing my job if I didn't explain what we're going to be up against. And keep in mind, I don't have much experience in this sort of thing."

"I can't risk trusting anyone else, Sammy. Besides, I don't know any other attorneys."

He released her hands and picked up his pen. "I wish you did, Dasha. You deserve someone better than a novice used to dealing with petty criminals. I could try to find someone else for you."

"No, please help me, Sammy."

He tapped his pen against the legal pad and stared off into the distance for several long seconds before answering her. "All right, Dasha. We'll figure something out. What I laid out for you is the worst-case scenario. Maybe we can come up with something to use as a bargaining tool with the prosecutor."

Dori took a ragged breath, clinging to the small ray of hope Sammy offered. "What do you mean."

"Borka's a slime bag. We both know that, but he's managed to stay more than a step ahead of the law all his life. He spent a good deal of time in your home. Sergei was one of his enforcers. Think back, Dasha. Surely, you overheard things—things the Feds would love to know."

Dori had heard plenty over the years. Vodka had a way of loosening tongues, and plenty of Stoli had been poured at the kitchen table in the Ivanichek row house on Fanshawe Street.

But Dori didn't have to dredge through dim memories. For most of her teen years she'd kept a journal. In it she'd recorded her unhappiness and her dreams for the future. She'd also written about the fears that plagued her from eavesdropping on her father's late-night conversations with Borka and his cronies. "You mean like evidence they could use to convict him of some crime?"

"Exactly. We're going to play *Let's Make a Deal* with the boys in the suits."

Borka derived most of his income through extortion. His reach extended throughout the Russian immigrant community in the greater Philadelphia area, into south Jersey and down through Delaware.

He offered businesses protection. If the owners refused to pay for that protection, Sergei and his fellow enforcers convinced them otherwise. Borka's men enjoyed bragging to each other about their assignments, and Dori had recorded much of it.

"I have proof." She told Sammy of the diaries she had taken with her when she ran from her father's home.

"Too bad we can't get Sergei to corroborate any of this. But maybe some of Borka's victims will."

"My father would never turn on Borka to help me. No matter what the prosecutor offered him."

Sammy gave her an odd look, one she couldn't interpret. "Dead men don't tell tales. Your father's hardly in a position to help you now."

"What do you mean?"

In a split-second Sammy's expression changed from one of bewilderment to one of awareness, then the full impact of his words hit her as his eyes reflected the shock coursing through her body. "My God, Dasha. You didn't know?"

Know? How could she have known? "Dead? Sergei? My father's dead?" She whispered the words that rang hollow in her ears. A deafening roar filled her head. "When?"

"A month or so after you left. At first, we thought he'd gone to visit you. Then several months later some teenagers found his remains in Pennypack Woods. I remember mamma saying how she couldn't believe you hadn't come back for the funeral. Especially under the circumstances."

A chill ran up Dori's spine. "What circumstances?"

"He was murdered, Dasha. Execution style. A bullet to the back of his head."

Like a knife-edged boomerang, Dori's anguished cry reverberated off the walls of the tiny room, ricocheting back to stab at her heart. Clasping her hands over her mouth, she sprang to her feet. The chair tipped backwards, her purse fell from her lap, spilling its contents across the linoleum floor. In a blur of tears, her stomach churning bile that threatened to back up into her throat, she ran for the door at the end of the hallway.

Borka had ordered her father killed! It was the only logical assumption. Knowing Sergei, he'd taken the dowry and most likely gambled it away, conveniently forgetting to tell Borka that his children had disappeared. Until it was too late. And her father had paid for his greed and deceit with his life.

Sergei Ivanichek was a hard drinking liar and a thief. He had beaten his wife and neglected his children. He took pleasure in bullying his victims and had broken more than a few kneecaps. For all Dori knew, he'd probably committed his own share of murders as well. But for all his faults, he'd been her father, and she was responsible for his death.

"The apple sure didn't fall far from the tree, did it?" she asked Sammy after she'd composed herself enough to return to the outer office. Her hand shaking, she dabbed at her damp face with a rough brown paper towel. "Look what I've done. He's dead because of me."

"This isn't your fault, Dasha. The police found no evidence to connect Borka with the murder."

"Of course not. They're all on his payroll, remember?"

Sammy shook his head. "I think you're jumping to

conclusions. Not every cop in Philadelphia is corrupt. If you want to quote dumb proverbs, how about the one about lying down with dogs and waking up with fleas? Sergei chose his life, and he paid for it—with his life."

"I have to leave," she said, reaching for the purse Sammy had retrieved and repacked after she raced into the restroom.

"Let me drive you back to your hotel." He pushed back his desk chair and stood. "You've had a terrible shock. You're in no shape to get back on your own."

She declined his offer. "No. Thank you, but I really want to be alone right now. I need time to think." She raised herself onto her toes and kissed his cheek. "I'll be in touch."

"Leave me a number where I can reach you, Dasha."

Dori shook her head. She didn't dare divulge the number of the cell phone Niles had given her. She had no idea if Jake or someone else monitored her calls. "I'll only be in town until tomorrow, then I'm off to Boston for another opening. I'll call you in a few days. I promise."

Sammy walked her to the door. He unbolted the lock, then embraced her once more before opening the door. "Take care of yourself."

Nodding, Dori choked back a sob and hurried out into the rush hour crowds.

* * *

From his vantage point across the street, Jake watched as Dori left the law office and hurried toward the subway entrance. He noticed the change in her demeanor immediately. She'd exited the hotel with an air of self-confidence. Her posture erect, her head held high, she'd walked with the determined gait of a woman on a mission.

A different Dori departed the attorney's office, her body language now showing signs of extreme distress. Hugging her chest with both arms, her head bent, she darted around the knots of pedestrians as if fleeing a pursuer.

He hurried after her.

When Dori reached the subway entrance, she was swallowed up by a sea of commuters. As they descended the steps, Jake lost sight of her.

The sidewalk beneath his feet vibrated, heralding the arrival of a train rumbling into the subterranean station. Jake quickened his pace, pushing past a throng of people. Fighting his way down the stairs, he raced to keep from losing her, jumping into the nearest car as the doors closed behind him.

Squeezing past dozens of straphangers clutching shopping bags, briefcases, and squirming toddlers, Jake searched for Dori within the packed train. After passing through three cars, he found her toward the back of the fourth. She sat sandwiched between a teenage boy with an oversized boom box on his lap and an elderly nun fingering her rosary beads. Her torso twisted toward the window, she gazed out into the darkness as the train raced through the tunnel.

Jake positioned himself directly in front of her, the creases of his Dockers brushing against her jean clad knees. He studied her reflection in the window—her eyes devoid of life, her jaw quivering slightly. She held her hands laced firmly in her lap, the knuckles white with tension. The color had drained from her face, and he could see the tracks of dried tears on her cheeks.

When she noticed his image in the dirt-streaked window, she slowly turned to face him. All Jake's pent-up anger dissolved in an instant. The defeat and hopelessness reflected in her troubled eyes nearly destroyed him.

Dori said nothing. Her face blank of emotion, she dropped her gaze to her lap and sat in silence as the train headed down Broad Street. Part of Jake wanted to sweep her up in his arms and protect her from whatever demons chased her. Another part of him wanted to shake some sense into her stubborn head. He did neither. When the train pulled into the Walnut Street Station, he grasped her firmly by the wrist and led her back to the hotel.

Once inside the suite, he confronted her, blocking her path to the bedroom. With his arms folded across his chest and his legs spread apart, he fought to keep his voice from echoing the anger inside him. He was certain this little side trip of hers was connected to her jumpiness of the past few days. They were in Philadelphia, and she had just come from the offices of a Russian lawyer. Jake didn't need any investigative skills to figure out the events were tied to her past.

"What the hell is going on, Dori? Who is Puchenko, and why were you meeting with him?"

TWENTY-SEVEN

"Puchenko?" Her eyes glazed over with confusion. She reached for her temples and began to massage them. "I don't know anyone named Puchenko."

"Victor Puchenko, attorney-at-law. Damn it, Dori! Don't play dumb. You just spent over an hour with him!"

A shadow of fear crossed her face. "You don't know what you're talking about." She tried to push around him, but he refused to budge. "I don't feel well, Jake. I want some aspirin. Then I'm going to bed."

"Not until you tell me why you went to see a Russian lawyer."

Dori moaned. She sighed in resignation, her shoulders drooping further. "Not that it's any of your business, but I went to visit an old friend. Sammy Pak. And he's Korean, not Russian. We lived next door to each other years ago." She gripped the back of her neck and kneaded the muscles. Her face contorted with pain.

"Why didn't you tell me you were going out?"

"Why? Are you my jailer?" When he refused to answer her, she continued, "Please, Jake. My head is splitting."

He stepped aside and let her enter the bedroom. "This isn't over, Dori."

"It never is," she whispered as she headed toward the bathroom.

Jake exhaled forcefully and headed for the mini bar. The woman had wormed her way under his skin—the thick impenetrable layer he'd grown after extricating himself from Gwynne. Despite his initial resolve not to get involved with Dori, he was in over his head—and he'd managed to drag his heart into the fray. Now he had to figure out a way to save her from herself. He yanked open the refrigerator, removed a bottle of Sam Adams, and collapsed onto the sofa. As he nursed the beer, he weighed his options.

Dori was in deeper trouble than he suspected she realized. If the Feds got wind of her and decided to press charges, she faced some stiff jail time. He could help her, but she had to trust him first. From what he knew of Dori, she hadn't trusted anyone in a long time, and he doubted she would confide in him—or anyone. She was too used to going it alone. The only time she dropped her defenses was in bed.

Jake thought about coming out and confronting her with what he knew about her past, but he ran the risk of having her panic and flee. If she felt cornered and thought she had no other option, she might. However, unlike six years ago, Dori wouldn't find it as easy to disappear and start a new life—not with her face displayed from coast to coast.

He drained the beer and helped himself to another. After

placing an order for room service, he called Charley.

"I want to know everything there is to know about a Sammy Pak," he said when his former partner answered. "He's an attorney in Philadelphia."

"This have anything to do with Mata Hari?" she asked, referring to the code name she'd given Dori.

"You tell me."

She sighed through the phone line. "Hold on while I punch up some files." In the background he heard the click of a keyboard. "You know, if you came back to work, you could do this yourself."

Jake chuckled. "Not a chance, Davis. I'm enjoying the writer's life too much."

"Oh? When was the last time you wrote anything, hotshot? Looks to me like you're spending all your time babysitting. *And* walking a very thin line."

"Don't remind me."

"It's my duty to remind you—especially since you've dragged my ass onto that line along with yours. Hold on. I've got something." She paused for a moment. "Samuel Henry Pak. Broad Street?"

"That's the one."

"Hmm. Penn State grad. Got his law degree from Temple University four years ago. Handles mostly criminal law cases within the Korean community. So far, I don't see any red flags, other than he's a defense attorney, and you know how they make their living. What's the connection?"

"A Russian law partner."

"Victor Puchenko. I see that."

"Mata Hari spent an hour with Pak today. Afterwards she looked like someone had just told her she only had an hour to live."

Charley clucked her tongue. "Not good. Wait a minute. Here's something."

"What?"

"I'm doing a background check on his family. Pak is part Russian. You'll never guess his maternal grandmother's maiden name."

Jake rubbed his jaw. "Don't tell me. Puchenko?"

"Bingo. Victor Puchenko is her brother—Sammy's great-uncle." Charley whistled under her breath. "You're not going to like this."

"What?"

"Victor Puchenko's niece was Boris Borka's first wife."

Jake cursed under his breath.

"Jake?"

"Hmm?"

"You're falling for her, aren't you?"

Silence filled the air between the phone lines. "Hard and fast."

"Be careful, partner."

Too late, he thought as he hung up.

* * *

Twenty minutes later a waiter arrived with the dinner Jake had ordered for himself and Dori. Leaving the dishes covered on the cart in the living room, he poured a cup of tea and brought it into the bedroom. He found Dori curled up on the bed in a tight ball, a pillow clutched to her chest, her back turned to him. "I brought you some tea." He placed the cup and saucer on the nightstand. "I ordered dinner if you're hungry."

She shook her head. "I'm not."

Jake sat down on the edge of the bed and ran his fingers

through her hair. "Talk to me, Dori. Maybe I can help."

Again she shook her head. "You can't."

"How do you know?"

"Because no one can change the past," she whispered.

Jake decided not to press her. At least she'd volunteered some clue to her distress. As he surmised, whatever happened inside Pak's office had something to do with her prior life in Philadelphia. "Still have a headache?" He began massaging her scalp.

She nodded.

He lowered his fingers to her neck, kneading the tight muscles on either side. At first her body fought his ministrations, but gradually he felt the tension loosening its hold on her. Her breathing grew less ragged, her limbs slackened as he moved on to the knots in her shoulders and then her back. By the time he reached the base of her spine, her jaw had relaxed, and the lines creasing her mouth and eyes had disappeared.

Within minutes she was sound asleep.

* * *

Dori woke the next morning to find herself curled up in Jake's arms, her stomach sounding a none-too-gentle reminder that she hadn't eaten anything since lunch the previous day. Glancing over Jake's shoulder, she saw an untouched cup of tea on the nightstand and her clothes in a heap on the carpet. She had no recollection of either, only a frightening memory of her visit to Sammy's office.

Beside her, Jake stirred. His dark lashes fluttered open. "Feeling better?" He drew her closer and placing a soft kiss against her temple.

Dori doubted she'd ever feel *better* again, but if she didn't force a smile and offer Jake some explanation for her behavior yesterday, she'd have to contend with another grilling.

She was so tired of dancing around the truth, of sidestepping his questions. When she discovered he'd followed her to Sammy's, her first instinct was to come clean. Tell him everything. Lying to Jake bothered her more than she wanted to admit. But when she'd told Sammy about Jake, including his unspecific government connection, he warned her not to say anything.

"I'm sorry. I guess I was in a state of shock yesterday."

Jake levered himself up on one elbow. With his free hand he brushed a lock of hair from her face. "Want to talk about it now?"

Rolling to her side, she snuggled against him and drew a deep breath. She didn't want to talk. She wanted him to make love to her, to do those things that forced all the horrible thoughts and worries from her head and for a brief few minutes offered her peace.

But Jake wanted an answer, and she knew he wouldn't rest until he had one. "Someone who was once part of my life died a few years ago. I never knew. Not until Sammy mentioned it yesterday."

She paused, collecting her thoughts. "There were things I would have liked to say. I always thought someday I'd have the chance, but now I won't." When he didn't say anything, she caressed one of his nipples with her fingers and continued. "I should have told you. I was just feeling very vulnerable at the time. And sorry for myself."

She shifted her weight, rubbing against his groin, and felt him grow large with need. "Make love to me, Jake. Please."

He rolled her onto her back and slipped inside her.

Dori sighed. "Make it all go away," she whispered.

* * *

Jake didn't understand what *it* was, but at the moment, he wasn't about to analyze her plea. There was a desperation to the way she responded to his lovemaking, as though she were imprinting every touch, every sensation on her brain.

From the first night their lovemaking had rocked him like nothing he'd ever experienced. With anyone. Now, though, the intensity of their coupling blew his mind. Neither of them could get enough of the other. He grew hard within her seconds after reaching climax. She shattered over and over and still begged for more.

Make it all go away. Her words echoed in his head, haunting him. Even in the throes of passion, he saw the sadness and resignation in her eyes and knew this time, no matter how heated their lovemaking, he wasn't succeeding in making *it* all go away. Jake didn't believe a word she told him earlier. Something happened to her at that law office—something that had her terrified, and Jake couldn't make it all go away. Not unless she told him the truth.

* * *

Several hours later, a transformed Dori stepped into her role as McStore spokesperson. Somehow, she'd managed to exorcise all traces of yesterday from her face. Only it wasn't her face. Jake was all too aware of the tightly secured mask she wore over her emotions, no matter what she showed to the outside world.

Smiling and exuding a false confidence, Dori stood flanked by the seven members of the Cheltenham Township Board of Commissioners as she gave a short speech extolling her employer and his newest business venture. She spoke of the jobs Niles brought to the area and the value, quality, and convenience shoppers would find at McStore.

"Remember," she told the crowd, "this is Not-your-Mother's-Chain-Store. It's yours. Welcome." Then, as photographers snapped her picture, she cut the huge satin ribbon draped across the front of the superstore.

The crowd quickly dispersed, some heading for the store entrance, others wandering the parking lot in search of free food and souvenirs. Dori stayed to answer some reporters' questions, then began mingling with the various groups, chatting and signing autographs for those waiting in hot dog, cotton candy, and T-shirt lines.

Jake glued himself close to her side, a growing sense of foreboding heightening every nerve in his body. The sooner they finished up in the Philadelphia area and got on the plane for Boston, the better. He suspected Dori felt the same. Although outwardly she showed no signs of distress, her eyes couldn't hide from him the worry that her smile masked.

As if sensing his mood, the weather suddenly turned raw. Storm clouds crept in and hung over the horizon, blotting out the warmth of the autumn sun. A chill wind whipped through the parking lot. Jake suggested they enter the store. "After all, Niles is paying us to get these people to spend money, not pig out on freebies, then go on their way."

"Haven't you heard me urging everyone to check out the store?" she asked.

"Yes, but you're drawing crowds out here, Miss Big-time Celebrity. If you go inside, they'll follow." *And I'll feel more comfortable.* Jake sensed trouble—from what, he didn't know—but he felt he could better protect Dori in closed quarters.

She didn't protest, but as she headed for the entrance, she shook her head and chuckled softly. "Me, a celebrity. I still can't get used to that. It's not like I'm Julia Roberts—or even Vanna White."

"You are now," said Jake. "Just as recognizable. Maybe more so. Julia and Vanna aren't featured on shopping bags, and they don't get their picture splashed across buses and billboards as frequently as you. That recognition is what makes you a celebrity in the public's eye."

Her step faltered. A cloud of uncertainty passed across her face, and Jake immediately regretted his words. He reached for her hand. "Let's go inside."

Like the Pied Piper, Dori and Jake were followed by a stream of prospective customers, children in tow. All chattered effusively, tossing questions at her in a steady stream. Many munched on assorted junk food and sipped sodas. The youngsters, their bellies sated, their faces smeared with mustard and ice cream, held fast to their parents with one hand and to helium filled balloons with the other.

"See what I mean?" said Jake as they entered the store.

"Do you ever tire of being right?"

He squeezed her hand. "Never. Maybe you should remember that."

Dori frowned. "I need to use the restroom," she whispered, nodding to a back corner of the store. "Do you think you can keep these people from following me into a stall?"

Jake led her in the direction of the restrooms. Along the way Dori maintained a continuous monologue for the benefit of the people following her, pointing out various departments they passed and suggesting items they might want to purchase. When they reached their destination, she thanked her entourage for their attention, then excused herself, slipping through a doorway marked *Employees Only.*

To Jake's relief after three or four minutes the crowd grew bored of waiting and dispersed. Five minutes later Dori had still failed to return.

Something wasn't right. A prickle of fear played at the back of Jake's neck as he rushed down a long corridor toward the employees' restrooms. Pounding on the door marked *Ladies*, he didn't wait for a response before barging in and shouting her name. The bathroom was empty.

Jake checked the men's room, then each of the offices that lined the hallway on either side, hoping Dori had stopped to chat with one of the office staff.

"I saw her talking to Elmer Fudd a few minutes ago," said one of the accountants. "Did you check the parking lot? Maybe she went back outside with him."

Waving a quick thanks, Jake headed for the employees' door at the end of the corridor. He didn't want to think that Dori had given him the slip twice in two days. Fear turned to anger, then back to fear. The two emotions see-sawed inside him, his adrenaline pumping.

The parking lot surrounding the store was thick with people. Dori could be within several feet of him, and still be hidden from his sight. Jake scanned over the heads of the crowd, searching for a larger-than-life Elmer Fudd, thankful that Dori had left with a cartoon character from his own childhood and not one of the hundreds of newer creations he wouldn't recognize.

The costumed entertainers stood out amid the boisterous gathering, towering over all but the tallest in the sea of faces. Straight ahead he found Sylvester the Cat, Tweety Bird, and Porky Pig. Daffy Duck was entertaining a group of children off to his right. On his left he saw the Tasmanian Devil and several other characters he couldn't identify but no Elmer Fudd.

Cursing under his breath, he fought his way through the crowds on the side of the store. Ducking under a roped off section that kept people from filtering into the shipping and receiving area, he rounded the corner of the building.

He finally saw them at the far end of the employee parking lot.

Elmer Fudd and Dori were walking arm-in-arm, hurrying at a quick pace through the rows of parked vehicles. Jake sprinted toward them, cupping his hands over his mouth and shouting her name as he ran. When she tried to turn toward him, Elmer yanked on her arm, dragging her forward.

That's when Jake saw the unmistakable glint of a gun pressed against her side.

TWENTY-EIGHT

From somewhere behind her Dori heard Jake call her name. Twisting her head, she tried to find him, but the man who'd followed her into the restroom and forced her outside, jabbed the gun further into her ribs. She winced.

"Keep moving," he warned her. Although the thick padding of the cartoon head muffled his words, the menacing tone came through clearly enough.

He dragged her through several more rows, zigzagging his way between cars until he reached a black Ford pickup at the back of the lot. He tossed her up against the side of the truck hard enough to knock the wind out of her, then yanked open the driver's side door. "Get in." He forced her up the running board and across the bench seat.

He hadn't quite thought out his escape plan, though. As big as the truck was, Elmer Fudd was bigger. When he tried to jump in beside her, he became momentarily wedged in the opening. As he fought to free himself, he dropped the gun. Seizing the opportunity, Dori flung open the passenger side door and jumped out.

Behind her she heard Elmer curse as he slammed his door and started the engine. Dori stole a glance backwards in time to see him tear out of the space, slamming into the car parked a row behind him. Gunning the engine, he shifted into drive, and headed straight for her.

"Look out," yelled Jake, catching up to her. Grabbing her arm, he yanked her between two parked cars. Elmer missed them by inches. Rounding the parking lot on two tires, he headed for the exit.

"Sonofabitch," muttered Jake, reaching for his cell phone. Then he turned to her. "Are you all right?"

"I think so." She rubbed her arm where Elmer Fudd had gripped her.

Jake punched in three numbers on the keypad. A moment later, he gave an abbreviated account of the incident. "You can't miss him. He's dressed as Elmer Fudd." He paused for a moment, then yelled into the phone. "Of course, the cartoon character! You know any other Elmer Fudd? He's driving a late model black Ford pickup with rear end damage. No plates. Heading west out of the rear entrance of N.Y. McStore." After another brief pause he continued. "No, we don't need an ambulance." He gave his name and cell phone number, then ended the call.

"Who was he? Do you have any idea? Did he say anything?" he asked her.

Dori couldn't identify her assailant, but she had a good idea who sent him. Borka had finally found her. And that meant...Dori stifled an anguished cry. "Nikki and Joey," she said. "They'll be after Nikki and Joey!"

"Who? Borka?"

Dori froze at the name. She stared at Jake, her mouth hanging open. Time stood still; the world closed in around her. She slumped against the car behind her. Her legs gave way beneath her and slid to the blacktop. "You know."

Jake kneeled beside her. Placing his palm against her cheek, he spoke in a soothing tone. "From the very beginning, Dasha."

Dori cringed at the sound of her real name on his lips. If he knew her true identity and knew about Borka, he had to know she was a criminal. "And Niles?" she asked.

He nodded. "As soon as I knew. That's why he asked me to keep an eye on you."

"He still wanted me as his spokesperson knowing what I had done?"

Jake nodded, but his mouth had curved into a tight grimace.

"You didn't want him to."

"Not at first. No. Niles had his own run-ins with the Russian-American mob. Years ago, when he first started out, the mob tried to muscle their way in and gain control. He set them up for a sting. They vowed revenge. I warned him you could be a plant, but he overrode my objections."

"I'm not."

"I know, sweetheart."

Dori gazed into his eyes—eyes that she once thought brooding, eyes whose penetrating stare once frightened her with their intensity. Now she saw only compassion in his midnight blue eyes.

"I can help you, Dori, but you have to trust me enough to tell me everything."

"Nikki and Joey are in danger."

"I have people watching them. They're safe. You don't have to worry."

"No!" She jumped to her feet and hurried toward their rental car. "I have to go to them. You thought I was safe with you and look what just happened. Borka is ruthless. He killed my father after I ran away. He hasn't forgotten. I was a fool to listen to Joey. I never should have accepted Niles's offer. I exposed myself. Borka wants me, and he'll do anything to get me back. I know that now."

Jake grabbed her arm, forcing her to stop mid-stride. "All right. We'll drive up the turnpike and check on Nikki and Joey. On one condition."

She stared at him in trepidation. Was he going to insist she turn herself in? "What condition?"

"On the way, you have to promise to answer every one of my questions. Truthfully."

For several long seconds they stood toe-to-toe in the middle of the parking lot, locked in a standstill. Finally, Dori broke the tense silence. "Will you agree to answer one of mine?"

He nodded.

She sighed in resignation. "All right. I'll tell you whatever you want to know, but I have a feeling you already know everything."

"Then humor me." Clasping her hand in his, he guided her through the parking lot.

* * *

Once they were settled inside the rental car, Jake placed a call to the McStore manager, explaining that Dori had taken ill, and they were returning to the hotel. Then he started the engine and pulled out of the lot. He said nothing. Up ahead the storm clouds had thickened, darkening the sky. He could hear the distant rumbling of thunder and see an occasional bright flash of lightning. Dori stared out the window, and Jake could only imagine the storm of emotion roiling through her.

Ten minutes later he exited onto the access ramp for the Pennsylvania Turnpike and pulled into line at the toll booth. "Start at the beginning," he said after taking a ticket and merging onto the ramp heading east. "Don't leave anything out."

She jumped at the sound of his words, taking a deep breath before turning fearful eyes toward him. Jake gripped the steering wheel, a heavy staccato beat filling his ears. For a moment he imagined the sound, the first heavy drops of rain splashing against the windshield, as the rapid beating of Dori's heart. His own heart wrenched at the sight of the pain and uncertainty shadowing her face.

"You promised to answer one of my questions first," she reminded him.

He relaxed his grip on the steering wheel and watched as the color returned to his knuckles. "I don't remember saying anything about first, but go ahead. Ask your question."

"Are you an FBI agent?"

"No."

"CIA?"

Jake glanced over at her. "That's another question. I only agreed to one." Her eyes filled with desperation. He'd hoped a bit of humor might alleviate some of her tension, but his attempt at comic relief backfired. He reached across the seat and clasped his hand over hers. He was asking her to trust him enough to confess everything to him. It was only fair that she know who she was dealing with. "Up until nearly two years ago, I worked for a special branch of the Navy. One you've never heard of. As an investigator of sorts."

"What kind of investigator?"

"I was an intelligence operative."

"You're a spy? You mean like James Bond?"

Jake chuckled. He'd risked his life on more than one occasion for his country, but his career had been far from the glamorous fantasies depicted by Hollywood. Intelligence work was ninety-five percent paperwork, four percent legwork, and one percent excitement. "Not quite. He's always had better luck with women."

The color rose in Dori's cheeks. She stared down into her lap at their joined hands. "So all your conquests aren't as easy as I was?"

He lifted her hand to his lips. "None of the others were worth the effort." He planted a gentle kiss across her palm.

Dori raised her head and turned to face him. "What's going to happen to me, Jake? Sammy said I could go to prison for a long time for what I did."

Jake stared out at the blur of traffic in front of him and switched the wipers to high. "Did you know your friend Sammy is connected to Borka?"

With a strangled whimper, Dori recoiled, pulling her hand from his. "I don't believe you! Sammy's my friend. He hates Borka!"

"So tell me how Borka all of a sudden found you after six years?"

Uncertainty clouded her eyes and wrinkled her brow. The corners of her mouth dipped. "Maybe Elmer Fudd wasn't sent by Borka. Maybe he's the e-mailer. *A. Friend*? He could have flipped out when I didn't answer him."

Jake inhaled deeply, letting the air escape his lungs in a slow, steady stream. "I had your e-mail buddy checked out." There's no way *A. Friend* was inside that Elmer Fudd costume."

"You can't know that for sure."

But he did. Jake glanced over at her. Dori's eyes filled with pleading desperation. She nervously kneaded her hands and chewed on her lower lip. Unwilling to accept Pak's treachery, she grasped for the only other obvious straw, a straw which Jake was about to crush. "Yes, I can." He reached for her hand once more. "Her name is Anita Friend. She's a fifty-two-year-old borderline schizophrenic confined to a wheelchair. She lives in a group home in South Bend, Indiana."

Confusion knit her brows together. For several long seconds she stared out the window, shaking her head and worrying her bottom lip with her teeth. "How? Why?"

"A well-meaning benefactor donated several computers to the home. Turns out Anita wasn't the only resident misusing the Internet. One of them is quite skilled at creating viruses. After a visit from a less-than-friendly government official, the social worker cancelled their hookup."

Dori's hands trembled under his. Shaking her head, she sucked in a ragged breath and once more pleaded Pak's case. "It can't be Sammy. He would never do anything to hurt me, Jake. I know he wouldn't."

Jake connected the dots for her. "Pak's mother's first cousin was Borka's first wife. Don't you think it's more than a little coincidental that Borka struck after all these years the day after you met with your good friend Sammy? Pak knew why you were in Philadelphia and exactly where you would be this morning."

Jake studied Dori as his words penetrated. Pain flooded across her features. "He betrayed me," she whispered, pulling her hands out from under his and covering her mouth.

"It sure as hell looks that way."

* * *

For the remainder of the ride Dori sat quietly staring out at the rain drenched landscape that mirrored the desolation consuming her. She only spoke when she answered Jake's many questions. He told her what he already knew. She supplied the one missing puzzle piece—the reason she'd fled Philadelphia. Jake even knew about her father's murder. He just hadn't realized she didn't know until last night.

The shrill ring of his cell phone broke into her thoughts. Jake reached into his jacket pocket. Holding the phone to his ear, he pressed one of the buttons. "Prentiss," he said, breaking the ensuing pauses of silence with an occasional "Hmm" or "Uh-huh."

"Let me know if you find out anything else," he told the caller, then disconnected the line and placed the phone back in his pocket. "They found the pickup," he said without turning to her.

Dori stared at his profile, his words echoed the grim set of his jaw. "Where?"

"Abandoned along with the costume about a mile from the parking lot. The truck was hot. No surprise."

"Borka wouldn't send just one man. His enforcers always worked in pairs or groups. Someone was probably waiting where he ditched the car."

She darted a quick glance out the passenger window, then twisted her torso to check the cars behind them. Traffic was heavy, the rain heavier. She couldn't tell if they were being followed. "They could be anywhere. What if someone else was in the parking lot and saw us get into this car? What if we're being followed, Jake? We're leading them right to Nikki and Joey!"

"Do you want me to turn back?"

"Yes. No." She buried her head in her hands. "I don't know what to do!"

Jake wrapped his arm around her shoulders and drew her as close to him as her seatbelt and the gear shift console allowed. "Trust me, sweetheart."

She shook her head. "You don't understand. Borka won't give up. Not until he has what he wants." She threw her head against the seat. "I was such a fool. Why didn't I leave well enough alone?"

Jake's voice grew as soft as the caress his fingers were giving her neck. "Everything's going to work out. I promise. I won't let him get you. Or Nikki and Joey. I promise. You just have to trust me, Dori."

I promise. Dori focused on the rapid to-and-fro of the wipers until her vision began to blur. The swooshing sound mocked her, repeating the words over and over. *I promise. I promise. I promise.* Sammy had promised. And now things were worse than ever.

I promise. I promise. I promise. Her life was an unending chain of broken promises from people she'd learned not to trust. *He won't hurt you, Dori. I promise.* How often had her mother made that promise as she locked her children in the bedroom closet?

Then she'd died, and Dori had learned a hard lesson. Trust no one. But like a fool destined to repeat the same mistake, she'd forgotten that lesson and trusted Sammy, only to have him stab her in the back. Dori could trust only one person to free her from Borka—the only person she'd ever been able to count on. Herself.

* * *

Two hours after they pulled out of the McStore parking lot, Jake slid the rental car into an empty spot in front of her rundown

Jersey City apartment building. The rain had tapered off to a steady drizzle. Dori glanced warily up toward her front double windows, awash with the dim blue glow of the living room television. "Someone's home," she said.

"See that car across the street?" Jake asked, drawing her attention from the windows.

Dori turned in the direction Jake pointed. "The dark blue one with the man sitting in it?"

"He's a private detective keeping an eye on Nikki and Joey."

Dori frowned. "Great! There's only one of him and two of them. What does he do when they go off in different directions?"

With a heavy sigh Jake set the emergency brake and yanked the key from the ignition. "Damn it, Dori! He's not the only one. Give me some credit, will you?" He opened his door. "Sit here for a minute."

Before Dori could ask why, Jake bounded across the street, darting around traffic and puddles. Through the curtain of rain, she watched as he carried on a brief conversation with the man, then crossed back and opened her door. "There hasn't been even an inkling of anything suspicious. Nikki and Joey are both upstairs. They've been home for several hours, and no strangers have entered the building."

Dori released her breath—the one she'd figuratively held since leaving the Philadelphia McStore—and stepped from the car. If anything had happened to her brother and sister, she wouldn't have been able to forgive herself. Her life was spinning out of control. For the first time in six years, she fully understood the consequences of her actions and the danger she'd placed both herself and her siblings in—not only from Borka but from the law.

She lifted her chin until her eyes met Jake's. "I'm sorry. I know

I'm acting irrationally, but—"

He placed a rain drenched finger against her lips, preventing her from finishing her sentence. "Shh. Let's go upstairs."

After lacing his fingers through hers, he slammed the car door shut and led her toward the apartment building. "I don't think you should tell Nikki and Joey what happened," he said as they made their way up the first flight of stairs. "It will only worry them."

Dori stopped on the landing and turned to confront him. "But they have to know. How else will they be able to watch out for themselves?"

"The detectives are watching out for them. Trust me, Dori. We don't want them panicking and doing something foolish."

Trust me. There it was again. Trust. She averted her eyes, glancing down at the worn linoleum covering the steps of the dimly lit staircase.

"Dori?" Jake cupped her chin, lifting her head until their eyes met. His voice took on that menacing, no-nonsense timber that had originally sent shivers of fear through her. The shivers had returned. "I'm serious about this. We do it my way. I want your promise."

"All right," she said, compounding her lack of faith in him with a whopper of a lie that she hoped he couldn't detect in her eyes. "I promise."

"We tell them we had a scheduling change and decided to surprise them with a short visit. We'll head back to Philly after dinner."

She couldn't do that. If her plan was to work, she needed a night away from Jake. Dori thought for a moment, then shook her head. "No. I want to spend the night here. I don't want to go back to Philadelphia."

"We have to check out of the hotel."

She squeezed his hand. "I'm scared, Jake. Please! You can drive back down to pack up our things, can't you? We can fly up to Boston after you return tomorrow morning. I need more than a few hours with Nikki and Joey."

Jake's gaze bore into her as if he were reading her mind. Dori held her breath, hoping the guilt roiling inside her didn't show on her face. Finally, he nodded. "All right, but you're not to leave the apartment tonight. Understood?"

She bit down on her lower lip and nodded.

* * *

As Dori suspected, Jake invited himself to stay for dinner, offering to call out for pizzas, but Joey and Nikki stopped him. "You've got to see this," said Nikki, grabbing his hand and dragging him into the kitchen. Dori and Joey followed. Nikki swung open the refrigerator door and pulled a huge baking dish off the shelf.

"Lasagna," she said, setting the pan on the counter and turning on the oven. "Compliments of Mrs. Menotti."

"Every day she brings over enough food to feed half the apartment building," said Joey. He opened the freezer door to display row after row of plastic containers filled with leftovers, each marked and dated. "One dish would last us a week, but she comes with more every night."

"I should thank her," said Dori, seizing on the opportunity to institute the first step of her plan. She grabbed a cucumber from the crisper and tossed it at Jake. "Peel and slice," she said, not wanting him to follow her next door. "Nikki will show you where to find the cutting board and utensils."

* * *

Ten minutes later Dori returned with a set of car keys in her pocket and a platter of fresh-baked brownies in her hands. "Mrs. Menotti baked dessert," she said, placing the brownies on the counter.

TWENTY-NINE

Damn it! He should have taken care of her in the bathroom. Slit her throat and been done with it. But she never would have known why. She wouldn't have suffered, and he wanted to make her suffer. He wanted her death to be slow and excruciatingly painful. He wanted to hear her beg for mercy. Then he'd laugh in her face and hurt her more. Hurt her until she begged him to finish her off.

He wanted her to know she'd screwed with the wrong man, and she wasn't going to get away with it. No. Ending it in the bathroom would have given him little pleasure. And she owed him a hell of a lot of pleasure after what she'd done to him.

There'd be another time. Another place. Then he'd make her suffer even more for having made him fail the first time.

THIRTY

After Jake left her apartment, Dori sat down at the kitchen table with her brother and sister and told them everything that had happened. "Jake didn't want you to know," she said, fiddling with the cup of cold tea sitting in front of her.

"This concerns us," said Joey. "We have a right to know what's going on."

Dori met Joey's gaze and nodded in agreement. "That was my feeling. Besides, we can't depend on some private detectives sitting in a car outside the apartment to keep Borka's men away. He had our father killed. He's capable of anything."

"Do you think he'd kill us?" asked Nikki.

Dori reached over and wrapped her arm around her little sister's shoulders. Nikki shuddered beneath her touch. Her lower lip trembled. "He's not going to get the chance," said Dori. "I'm going to see to that."

"What are you planning?" asked Joey. He leaned forward, resting his elbows on the table. His eyes narrowed with suspicion. Worry tinged his words.

Taking a deep breath, Dori braced herself for the outburst she expected from her brother and sister. "I'm going to pay Borka a visit. He leaves us alone, or I turn my journals over to the federal prosecutors."

Joey and Nikki gasped in unison.

"Are you crazy? That is the dumbest idea you've ever had!" yelled Joey. He pounded the table with both fists, then jumped to his feet, sending his chair crashing backwards onto the linoleum.

Dori glared at her brother, but before she could defend her plan, Nikki grabbed her arm. "Let Jake handle it, Dori. Please!"

Dori shook her head. "No. I can't trust Jake. I can't trust anyone but myself. Look what happened when I confided in Sammy."

"I can't believe Sammy ratted you out," muttered Joey, righting the chair. He began pacing across the small kitchen. His fists clenched and unclenched as he reached the doorway leading into the living room, then pivoted to repeat the few long strides that carried him to the opposite end of the kitchen. "He always treated you like a little sister."

"Sammy's treachery taught me a hard lesson. One I knew but stupidly chose to ignore." She trapped first her brother, then her sister with her gaze. "Never, *ever* trust anyone," she told them, emphasizing her words with a slap to the table. "All men have their own agenda. You...me...none of us means anything. Unless they can use us. And if stabbing us in the back gets them what they want, they won't think twice about plunging the knife. Don't ever forget that."

"Not Jake," Nikki protested. "He wouldn't do anything to hurt you. Or us. We can trust him, Dori. Please! He loves you."

Dori brushed a stray tear from Nikki's cheek. "I know you'd like to believe that, baby."

"He does!" Nikki insisted. "I can tell."

Dori shook her head. Nikki still lived in a world of fairy tales. She saw Jake as the knight in shining armor who galloping to their rescue on his white charger, even if that white charger happened to be a black BMW.

Nikki yearned for a normal family life, not just for herself, but for all of them. Dori had no doubt that Nikki's dreams included her older sister marrying Jake and living happily ever after in a house in the suburbs with a white picket fence and a passel of nieces and nephews for Aunt Nikki to spoil.

It was a lovely dream but one that would never come true, not for her and Jake. When Dori dared to gaze into the future, she now saw prison bars, not a picket fence. Besides, men sworn to uphold the law didn't marry felons. Even if she managed to cut a deal with the government and stay out of jail, she was still a criminal, and nothing would ever erase that.

"Jake doesn't love me," she told her sister. Jake made love to her and made her feel alive, but he had never once said the three words she longed to hear from him. She now knew she never would. Jake had known of her past from the beginning, and lawmen didn't fall in love with criminals.

She didn't believe he'd used her. She couldn't believe that of him. In his own way she knew he cared for her, and she believed he genuinely wanted to help her, even if it placed him in a compromising position.

But Dori had been so badly burned that she couldn't trust even

Jake. She couldn't believe he or anyone would take that last leap of faith for her. Besides, this was her battle, and she had no right to drag Jake or anyone else into it. It was bad enough her brother and sister were involved.

"Borka forced me to break the law," she said to Nikki. "He tried to destroy our lives, and he's still doing it. To escape him and protect you and Joey, I committed some very serious crimes. Jake is sworn to uphold the law. I can't allow him to compromise himself to help me."

"But Borka's a killer," said Nikki. "You said he killed our father because we ran. What if he tries to kill you, Dori? You can't go there alone."

"He killed Sergei because he spent the dowry," said Joey, "not because we ran away."

Dori turned her gaze to her brother. Joey had stopped his pacing and stood leaning against the kitchen counter, his hands crossed over his chest, his face contorted in a scowl.

"We don't know that," she said. "Although it's certainly in keeping with the way Sergei led his life. All we know is our father was executed soon after we left. Who else would have him killed if not Borka? And for what other reason than a double-cross?"

"Then I'm going with you," said Joey. "You're not confronting that bastard alone."

Nikki nodded in agreement. "Yes. We'll all go. This is as much our battle as yours, Dori."

Dori turned back to Nikki and placed a kiss on her cheek. "No. You're both staying here. I'll be safe. Borka has never dirtied his own hands, and he won't have any of his thugs around when I confront him."

Nikki started to protest, but Dori stopped her. "Please try to understand. I can't keep living like this, and I want more for you and Joey. I want you both to be able to lead normal lives. We can't keep hiding from the world to hide from Borka. I'm tired of letting him wield this control over us."

Nikki nodded in understanding, but her eyes mirrored her fear. "Be careful, Dori."

"I will."

THIRTY-ONE

For hours he sat hidden behind a large potted fern in the hotel lobby, eyeing the front entrance through the curtain of fronds. She never returned. Shortly before nine the man who always accompanied her finally entered the hotel—alone—and headed for the bank of elevators. Twenty minutes later he reappeared with a bellman, luggage cart in tow.

He slipped out of the hotel, careful to avoid being seen by the man, and hurried to his own car, parked in a metered spot on the street. When the man pulled away from the hotel, he followed. He had expected him to head for the private airport where they'd flown in on one of York's corporate jets. Instead, the man surprised him by heading up the New Jersey Turnpike.

He knew their itinerary. They were due in Boston tomorrow, but he couldn't believe they planned to drive that distance this late at night. And where'd he leave the bitch? Only one place sprang to mind. Her apartment. He reached into his pocket for his cell phone and punched in the number he'd memorized.

The phone rang three times before someone answered. "Hello?"

Bingo! He ended the call without saying a word.

THIRTY-TWO

At one in the morning, under the cover of a starless and moonless night, Dori stood on the roof of her apartment building. The rain had tapered off to a fine mist that settled on her face and hair and sent chills through her.

Dressed in a pair of black jeans and a black turtleneck sweater, her purse and a canvas bag slung over her shoulder, she carefully climbed over one slippery firewall after another, making her way across the buildings until she found one with an unlocked roof door. Tiptoeing down several flights of stairs, she exited half a block from her own building, flipping the flimsy catch on the front door before quietly closing it behind her.

Dori pulled a travel umbrella from her tote and popped it open. With a purposeful stride but holding her breath, she walked along the opposite side of the street from the dark blue sedan with the detective.

As she approached from the rear, she could make out his silhouette in the dim glow of an overhead streetlamp. Adjusting the umbrella to block her face from his view, she continued down the street, hazarding a quick glance as she drew parallel to the driver's side window. Sipping from a thermos, he paid no attention to her.

Dori crossed the street after passing two cars beyond the detective. Unlocking the door of the third vehicle, Mrs. Menotti's fourteen-year-old white Geo Prism, she tossed in her purse and the canvas tote carrying her journals and slipped behind the wheel.

The interior smelled of garlic. A set of rosary beads hung from the rearview mirror. A plastic statue of St. Christopher stared at her from the dashboard. "I know," Dori whispered to the dethroned saint. "I'm breaking another law. You don't have to remind me that I don't have a driver's license."

Dori had never been overly religious. Her family had ceased attending church after her mother's death. Sergei had decided it was a waste of time. But a desperate need for divine intervention suddenly rose inside her, and Dori reached for the statue.

Holding St. Chris against her heart, she murmured a short prayer before placing him on the seat beside her. "You can ride shotgun," she said as she started the engine. "I need all the help I can get."

Then as an afterthought, she grimaced at the statue and added, "You wouldn't happen to know if Mrs. Menotti keeps a statue of St. Jude in the glove compartment, would you? I won't turn down your help, but what I really need is your buddy, the patron saint of desperate causes."

When the statue didn't respond, Dori sighed and issued another silent prayer, hoping she remembered all that Sammy had taught her about driving. She hadn't been behind the wheel of a car on six years. Then she slowly inched her way out of the tight parking space and down the street.

At the corner she stopped for a red light and glanced into the rearview mirror. No one followed her. She could still see the detective's car parked down the block. Dori took a deep breath and pressed down on the gas pedal as the light changed to green.

Ten minutes later she pulled into the parking lot of a twenty-four-hour copy center.

After her conversation with her brother and sister, she'd spent hours poring over her journals, earmarking pages of evidence that could be used against Borka. She spent the next hour copying those pages.

Shortly after two in the morning, she parked Mrs. Menotti's car around the corner from her apartment building and retraced her steps, leaving the journals and a letter for Jake in an envelope on the coffee table. She gave one last hug to a tearful Nikki and a grimacing Joey, then once again made her way up to the roof.

* * *

Jake decided against spending the night at the hotel in Philadelphia. Instead, he made the nearly four-hour roundtrip after leaving Dori's apartment shortly after dinner. By seven the next morning he stood ringing the buzzer outside her building.

After being buzzed through, he climbed the four flights and found Nikki and Joey waiting for him at the entrance to the apartment. Both were dressed in the clothes they'd worn the previous night. Neither looked like they'd gotten any sleep. Nikki's eyes were rimmed with red. Joey's sullen.

A wave of apprehension crept up Jake's spine. He stepped into the apartment, scanning the living room and the kitchen beyond.

"Where's your sister."

"She's not here," said Nikki, exchanging a worried glance with her brother.

Jake slammed his hand against the door jamb and let fly a string of expletives. Damn her! He should have known she was up to something. Fearing he already knew the answer before he asked the question, he zeroed in on Joey and demanded, "Where is she?"

"She went to make Borka stop."

A million thoughts raced through Jake's brain, none of them good, but he pushed them aside and forced himself to continue his questioning. "And just how was she planning to do that?"

Nikki walked over to the coffee table and picked up a large, padded envelope. "With this. There's a letter inside for you."

Jake crossed the room in two long strides and grabbed the package out of Nikki's hand. He reached inside, pulling out several dog-eared, spiral-bound notebooks and one sealed white business envelope with his name written on it.

Dumping the notebooks and padded envelope on the coffee table, he tore open the envelope. It contained one sheet of loose-leaf paper with a short note.

Dear Jake,

I don't expect you to understand why I have to do this on my own, but I do. The choices I made six years ago were forced on me. I never wanted to break the law. In fleeing Borka, I ran headfirst into the very life I was trying to escape, but I saw no other way.

I want it to end, but Borka has to pay for what he's done to me and my family—even to my father. Sergei had his faults. He belonged in jail for his crimes, but he didn't deserve to die the way he did because I ran from an arranged marriage.

The notebooks in this package are my journals from the four years before we left Philadelphia. In them you should find enough evidence to put Borka away for a long time. I recorded everything I heard each night as I lay in bed and listened to him and his men brag while they played cards and got drunk in our kitchen. You'll find names, dates, places—of his victims, the perpetrators, and various state and local officials who were on his payroll.

After I complete my task, I will turn myself over to the authorities. But first I have to confront Borka on my own. I need to see the look on his face when he learns that he destroyed one life too many, and that "little Dasha," the child he tried to corrupt, will be his downfall.

I need that revenge, Jake. I have carried around too much anger for too long. I will never know peace until I cleanse myself of that anger and the past. Only I can do that. Please try to understand.

I'm sorry I couldn't trust you. I know that must hurt. You have given me so much, but I am an albatross you don't need hanging around your neck, and we both know we have no future together. You're the law, and I'm a criminal.

Please tell Niles how sorry I am. I may not get the chance to do so in person. I've hurt so many people, and I never meant anyone any harm. I'll understand if you don't believe me, since I've given you little reason to believe anything at this point, but I do love you.

Dori

Jake whipped out his cell phone and called her. The phone rang five times, then went to voicemail. A generic voice told him the caller wasn't available. Leave a message.

"Damn!" He crumbled the paper in his fist. He wanted to throttle her, but he might never get the chance—not if Borka got to her first. He turned to Joey and Nikki. "When did she leave?"

"Shortly after two this morning," said Joey. "She promised to be back before you got here, but just in case something went wrong..." he nodded to the letter, his voice trailing off.

Nikki began crying. "Something *has* gone wrong. I know it! I told her not to do it, Jake, but she wouldn't listen to me."

"Or me," muttered Jake, glancing at his watch. Dori had a five hour lead on him. There was no telling what kind of trouble she'd gotten herself into with Borka, and from the reference in her letter, he couldn't trust placing a call to the authorities in Philadelphia. He was on his own. "How was she planning to get to Philly?"

"She borrowed Mrs. Menotti's car."

After getting a description of the vehicle, Jake jotted down his cell phone number on the back of Dori's envelope and handed it to Joey. "You call me the moment you hear from her, understand?"

Joey nodded.

Jake headed for the door.

"Jake?" Nikki grabbed for his sleeve. Big fat tears streamed down her face.

He placed a hand on her cheek. "I'll find her, Nikki. I promise." Then he raced out of the apartment and down the stairs.

* * *

Dori was startled awake by a sharp rapping behind her head. Blinking her eyes, she stared in confusion at her surroundings, the interior of a small car. Slowly, the repeating noise swept the cobwebs from her brain, and reality came flooding back into her consciousness. Rubbing her eyes into focus, she twisted around. On the other side of the raised window, she discovered her reflection gaping back at her from the mirrored glasses of a uniformed state trooper. Panic wound its fingers around her throat.

"You all right, miss?"

Dori managed a tight nod. When the officer continued to stare at her, she rolled down the window no more than an inch or two and forced a nonchalance into her voice. If he asked for her license, she was doomed. "Yes, officer. Thank you. I was feeling tired and pulled over for a short rest. I guess I dozed off."

"You did the smart thing. Too many accidents are caused by overtired drivers falling asleep behind the wheel. Only next time make sure you lock your doors." He motioned to the raised button and gave her a stern frown.

"Yes, of course. That wasn't too bright of me."

"There's a rest stop about five miles down the road where you can get some coffee and breakfast. I'll follow you to make sure you're okay."

"Thank you." She started the engine, hoping he'd already eaten and wasn't planning to join her in the restaurant. Making small talk with a state trooper wasn't high on her list of morning activities today.

She smiled and waved as she pulled into traffic, then glanced down at the dashboard clock and groaned. So much for her plan to surprise Borka in the middle of the night. Halfway to Philadelphia, she'd found herself beginning to fall asleep from the hypnotic stretch of turnpike. Neither rolling down the windows nor blasting the radio at full volume had helped. When her eyes began to flutter closed, she pulled off the road for a ten-minute rest. That was nearly four hours ago.

Now she'd lose more time ordering a breakfast her stomach would rebel against. She glanced up at the rearview mirror. The trooper was still behind her. She clicked on her turn signal and switched into the access lane for the rest area. He followed, parking his patrol car next to the Geo.

Dori hopped from the car and flashed him another bright smile. "So what do you recommend?"

"The breakfast sandwich is pretty good." He stared at her for a moment before continuing. "Aren't you the girl from that new store? Dori?"

Dori tried not to think about the acid churning in her stomach or the huge desire to flee consuming her. Instead, she shrugged her shoulders and chuckled. "I've been getting that a lot lately." She turned on her heels and headed for the restaurant. "Breakfast sandwich, you said?" she called over her shoulder.

"With sausage," he answered, climbing back into the patrol car.

Not a chance, thought Dori, breathing a huge sigh of relief as he backed out of the space and drove toward the exit ramp.

She entered the building and made her way to the area marked *Women*. After using the facilities and splashing cold water on her face, she left the building, ignoring the trooper's recommendation of breakfast. Five minutes after pulling into the rest area she was back on the turnpike heading for Philadelphia.

She arrived in front of Borka's unassuming brick row house on Bowler Street shortly before eight o'clock and parked the car in a spot directly across the street. "We're here," she told St. Christopher as she reached for the figurine. Turning it over and over in her hands, she sat for several minutes staring at the house and working up the courage to proceed with her plan.

Dori closed her eyes and inhaled deeply, slowly releasing the air. She repeated the calming breath several times, with each one reminding herself of how Borka had hurt her and her family, of the road he had forced her to travel. After the fourth breath her nervousness abated, and her resolve returned. She pulled the key from the ignition, grabbed the copies of her journal pages, and stepped from the car.

Borka's home looked like every other house on the street, only the colors of the doors and shutters distinguishing one from the others. A stone retaining wall supported a postage stamp-sized lawn. A set of four concrete steps, bisecting the lawn, led from the sidewalk to a cement walkway. Two chrysanthemum filled clay urns stood sentry on either side of the steps atop the corners of the retaining wall. Neatly trimmed yews and azaleas lined the front of the house.

Unlike some of his counterparts, Borka kept a low profile, preferring the middle-class neighborhood to an iron-gated enclave. As she walked down the path leading to the front door, Dori remembered hearing Borka brag that most of his neighbors believed he was a retired auto worker. Those who knew the truth, knew to keep quiet.

Dori stood in front of Borka's dark red front door and stared at a straw wreath decorated with brown and gold silk leaves. Not exactly Borka's style. A wave of panic seized her. Maybe he'd moved. Then what? How would she find him? There was only one way to find out. She took a last deep breath, then placed a shaky index finger against the doorbell.

A moment later the front door swung open, and Dori was assaulted by the heavy odors of frying bacon, stale tobacco, and dirty diapers.

THIRTY-THREE

"May I help you?"

Dori stared at the young woman standing in front of her. A thick braid of wheat-colored hair fell across her right shoulder. A thicker Russian accent colored her words. She held an infant, furiously sucking on a bottle, balanced on her left hip. Behind her, a wide-eyed toddler, his thumb firmly planted in his mouth, peaked out from behind the folds of her long, brightly patterned floral robe.

"I'm sorry." Dori took a step backwards in search of some much-needed fresh air. "I was looking for Boris Borka. I must have the wrong address."

"Papa," said the little boy at the mention of Borka's name.

From inside the house, a deep voice, one that sent shivers of memory coursing up Dori's spine, called out. "Who's at the door, Natasha?"

The woman answered back over her shoulder. "A woman to see you." She stepped to the side and ushered Dori in. "My husband is in the kitchen. This way."

Husband? Puzzled, Dori followed Natasha through a well-furnished but cluttered living room and dining room, stepping around enough toys to fill a floor of F.A.O. Schwartz. Natasha looked nearly young enough to still be playing with some of the toys herself, yet she already had two children. Dori stole a glance at the girl's figure as she rounded a corner and suspected another baby was already on the way.

Apparently, Borka hadn't wasted much time finding himself a new wife after Dori's disappearance. So why was he still after her?

Natasha crossed a small hallway into the kitchen. Dori stopped at the entrance and watched as she lowered the infant into a highchair at one end of a long wooden table. Then she lifted the toddler onto a booster seat and handed him several pieces of dry cereal which he immediately stuffed into his mouth alongside his thumb.

Two other children, a year or two older than the toddler, were already seated at the table, gorging themselves with fistfuls of the same pink and yellow sugary cereal while they carried on an animated conversation between themselves. The toddler joined in, adding his gibberish to the mix. The baby accompanied them with loud sucking noises from his bottle. In the background an all-news radio station blared traffic updates.

The man she had come to see stood at the stove, frying bacon. The heavy odor of the sizzling bacon, along with the other strong smells in the house, wreaked havoc with Dori's stomach. She fought to hold both her queasiness and her nerves at bay.

After adjusting the flame, Borka glanced at her, then turned his attention back to the frying pan. One by one he lifted the strips of bacon from the fat and placed them onto a paper towel-covered plate. "Yes?" he asked, draining most of the fat into a metal can sitting on the back of the stove. "You wish to see me about something?"

In her wildest imagination, Dori could not have envisioned meeting Borka under such domestic circumstances. She stared at the portly man, his middle covered by a dark red striped dishtowel tucked into his belt.

In six years, his belly had grown a little larger, his hair a little grayer, the lines in his face a little deeper. Other than that, he looked as he had the night she fled Philadelphia. But the Borka she remembered would never have cooked breakfast—for himself or anyone else. The Borka she remembered expected to be waited on hand and foot.

As if in defiance of her memories, Borka handed his wife the platter of bacon. While Natasha divided the strips between five plates lining the countertop, he poured a bowl of egg batter into the frying pan. The mixture sputtered. Smoke rose.

"*Govno*," he muttered, flipping on the overhead exhaust and lowering the flame.

Out of the corner of her eye Dori noticed Natasha wince at the sound of the Russian vulgarity and quickly steal a glance toward her older children. "You don't recognize me?" asked Dori, turning her attention back to Borka.

He tossed her another curious look before turning his attention back to the pan. "Should I?"

Dori swallowed hard. "I'm Dasha Ivanichek." She braced for his reaction.

As if the admission meant nothing to him, Borka turned off

the flame under the pan and set about dividing the eggs onto the plates. Natasha, who had ignored Dori since ushering her into the house, added a slice of buttered toast to each plate before placing one in front of each of the three older children. Then she helped herself to the fourth plate and took a seat between the baby in the highchair and the toddler on the booster seat.

Borka carried the remaining plate to the head of the table and sat down. "So," he said, shoveling a forkful of egg into his mouth and talking around the food. "The prodigal daughter finally comes home. Why after so many years, Dasha?"

He looked up from his plate, spearing her with those beady blue eyes she remembered all too well. "You never even came home for your poor father's funeral."

"My poor father's funeral?" Not believing her ears, Dasha repeated his words, shaking her head at his audacity. "Interesting choice of words coming from the man who sent him to his grave."

"How dare you!" Borka slammed his fork onto the table and jumped to his feet. A deep red flush swept from his neck up to his face. "I loved your father like a brother. I was there when they laid him to rest. I shed tears into his grave that day and have missed him every day since. Where were you and your brother and sister, Dasha? How many tears did the three of you cry for Sergei?"

Borka's phony histrionics buoyed Dori's confidence. She crossed her arms over her chest and leveled her threat in a calm, steady voice. "Your crocodile tears pull no weight with me, Borka. I know what you did to my father. I know everything, and if you don't call off your thugs and leave me alone, so will the federal prosecutors. I have all the proof they'll need."

Borka's face darkened from deep red to purple, his eyes narrowing into tiny slits, his mouth thinning into a tight line. But instead of the furious explosion Dori expected, he took a deep breath, waved his hand dismissively, and sat back down, the anger fading from his face as quickly as it had appeared.

"I don't know what you're talking about. You were a crazy, stupid child, and you've grown into a crazy, stupid *sooka*. You know nothing. Go back to wherever you came from before you raise my blood pressure further with your wild ravings."

Dasha stared in amazement as Borka went back to his breakfast. After a moment of watching him feed his face, she quietly asked, "Does your wife know what you do for a living, Borka?"

He raised his head. His voice grew low and menacing. "My wife is with child. I'm warning you, Dasha, do not say *anything* that will upset her."

"Or you'll do what?" Dori glanced at Natasha. The woman shifted her attention from her husband to Dori, then back to Borka. Her head swung to and fro like a spectator at a tennis match, confusion covering her face.

The children had ceased their chatter, and they, too, were eyeing her and their father. Dori broke the pregnant silence that filled the room. "You and I need to talk, Borka. Either we do it in front of your family or in private. It's up to you."

"Fine." He grabbed his cup of coffee and took a loud slurp. "Someone needs to set you straight before you make any other wild accusations." He turned to his wife. "Take the children upstairs, Natasha."

Without a word of protest Borka's young wife gathered up her brood and hurried from the room. "That's the life you and Sergei would have forced on me," said Dori, her gaze following Natasha, her voice nearly a whisper. "That's why I left." She turned back to

Borka. "And for that you took your revenge and had my father killed."

"Who filled your head with such garbage?"

"It doesn't matter. I know the truth."

"You know lies!" Borka slammed his coffee cup on the table. Dark brown liquid erupted like a volcano, spewing in droplets across the red and white checkered vinyl cloth. He reached for his napkin and blotted up the puddle. Then he heaved a heavy sigh and waved toward the chair Natasha had vacated. "Sit down, Dasha. I will tell you what happened to your father."

Dori hesitated.

"Sit down, girl. You're wearing my patience."

Dori sat on the edge of the wooden chair, clutching her purse and canvas tote like a shield. Borka pushed his empty plate aside and poured himself another cup of coffee from the carafe on the table. After stirring in two heaping spoonfuls of sugar, he took a long draught before speaking again. "I don't know where you come by these wild accusations, Dasha. I did *not* kill your father or have him killed. I *avenged* his murder."

Dori's mouth gaped open.

"Surprised?"

"You're lying. You had Sergei killed because he spent the dowry after I ran away."

Borka shook his head. "I never paid the dowry, stupid girl. Why would I pay for something your father couldn't produce? And why would I want such a troublesome wife? When you ran off, I changed my mind. Sergei wanted me to send some men after you, but I refused. You were more trouble than you were worth."

"But you killed him anyway."

Borka slammed his hands on the table and leaned forward.

"Haven't you been listening to a word I've said? I didn't kill Sergei. Your father was killed by some punks from South Philly who were trying to horn in on my territory." He leaned back and smiled in satisfaction. "Those *mudaks* won't be sticking their *khuis* where they don't belong anymore."

"You had them killed?"

Borka crossed his arms over his chest and leaned back in his chair. He grinned, showing two rows of stained, crooked teeth. "They got what they deserved. It was slow and painful, and I enjoyed watching every moment of it."

Dori shuddered. Slowly the truth dawned on her. Sammy had told her Sergei's murder had gone unsolved. But Borka knew who killed her father and had dispatched his own form of justice. A man with those kinds of connections wouldn't have any trouble finding her six years ago—had he wanted to. But if all Borka said were true, why had he tried to have her kidnapped? "Then why are you still after me?"

"Your nonsense tries my patience, Dasha. I haven't given you a second thought since you ran off."

"Someone tried to kidnap me."

"And you think I had something to do with it?" Borka stood. "Look around you, Dasha. I have a young, gorgeous wife who warms my bed at night without complaint and bears me beautiful children. Why would I want to bother with a troublemaker like you?"

Dori no longer knew what to believe. Or whom. She studied Borka's face intently, searching for a sign of deceit, but she saw no evidence of lies hidden within the jowls and creases of his arrogant expression. Strange as it seemed, she began to suspect he was telling the truth. The revelation threw her off balance, upsetting all she had come to believe. She rose and turned toward the doorway. "Tell your wife I'm sorry. For everything."

"Dasha."

Dori stopped but didn't turn back toward him.

"I would have made you a good husband. I would have taken care of you."

At what price? She had sacrificed plenty to escape Borka's antiquated idea of marriage, but the alternative still left a foul taste in her mouth. He may have changed enough in six years to cook breakfast for his family, but inside he was the same ruthless bastard.

"You would have used me as you use Natasha and everyone else."

He said nothing more.

Dori hurried from the house. The need to place as much distance as possible between herself and the row house on Bowler Street consumed her. Drawing in large lungfuls of fresh air, she raced down the path and across the street to Mrs. Menotti's car. Nothing made sense. All the evidence had pointed to Borka. Jake had eliminated *A. Friend* as a suspect. If not Borka, if not *A. Friend*, then who was stalking her? Who had tried to kidnap her? And why?

With trembling hands, she inserted the key into the ignition and started the car. Clutching the steering wheel with a white-knuckled grip, she jerked the Geo out of the parking space and lurched several yards down the street before regaining control of the car.

At the traffic light she turned onto The Boulevard, the main thoroughfare that led to the turnpike entrance. The road was crowded with morning commuters. All around her, horns honked, and brakes screeched.

As she waited in a line of snarled traffic, Dori lowered her window and took several deep breaths. The exhaust filled air only added to her queasiness. Between Borka's revelations and her limited driving experience, she felt ill-equipped to navigate the maze of congestion confronting her, but she had no choice. She inhaled once more before raising the window and squeezing into the line of traffic inching its way toward the turnpike.

* * *

Jake's cell phone rang as he crossed the bridge over the Delaware River connecting the New Jersey and Pennsylvania Turnpikes. "Prentiss."

"Jake. It's Joey. Dori just called. She's okay. She's on her way back."

"I'm on my way. Make sure she stays in the apartment. Sit on her if you have to."

As he hit the button to end the call, Jake felt a surge of relief sweep through him. For nearly two hours he'd fought back image after image of every worst-case scenario his mind could conjured up. Every fifteen minutes he'd placed a call to her. Each unanswered call ratcheted up the level of horror in his mind. And something else. With each passing minute, he came closer and closer to admitting his true feelings for Dori, realizing she meant more to him than anything.

At the end of the bridge, he made a U-turn through the tollbooths and headed back across the river. All he wanted was to get her into his arms, to know she was truly safe.

Then he'd wring her neck for such a stupid stunt.

And then he'd make love to her.

After his devastating marriage to Gwynne, Jake had sworn off all but the most casual of relationships. He'd settled into a comfortable, if solitary existence, but that was what he'd wanted. No demands. No attachments.

Self-doubt became his only companion, and that had given rise to a far bigger mistake. He could no longer trust himself to make the right decisions in either his personal or his professional life. Experience taught him he didn't have what it took. His high maintenance wife and his stress-filled career burned him out, leaving nothing but a scattering of cold ashes in their wake.

The moment Jake set eyes on Dori Johnson, he knew he was in trouble. The electricity generated between them could have powered a city, but the warning sirens in his head had blared at a piercing decibel. His first instinct was to get the hell out of Niles's office and never look back. He didn't want another woman having that kind of power over him. Been there; done that. Never again.

But he couldn't deny Niles. He owed his friend too much. Niles came to his rescue once, borrowing against his trust fund to help Jake finish college. If it weren't for his friend's generosity, he'd probably have wound up selling used cars. Or worse. His career may not have turned out as he'd hoped, but that was his fault. He'd never turned his back on Niles, and he never would.

Now he was glad he hadn't. Because of Niles he had Dori. And now he owed his friend one more debt.

All his life Jake had seen the world through a lens of pure black and white. Good and evil. Right and wrong. Shades of gray only existed in photographs, not life. He believed extenuating circumstances were nothing more than excuses used by weak people to justify their actions or inactions.

He'd walked away from his career because he refused to accept the extenuating circumstances defense his boss offered him. An innocent man died because Jake made a mistake, and no extenuating circumstances in the world would bring Calvin Bigelow back to life. There was right, and there was wrong. Black and white. Life and death. Nothing in-between.

Then Dori barged into his well-ordered world and shattered the walls separating right from wrong, good from evil, black from white. Guilty Dori. Innocent Dori. She forced him to question the rigid beliefs that had controlled his life. She opened his eyes to the shades of gray and made him realize that not everything in life could be cubby-holed into two diametrically opposed boxes.

Until Dori, Jake never understood the true meaning of life. Or love. Now he only hoped he hadn't learned the lesson too late to save them both.

THIRTY-FOUR

Dori arrived back on her street after ten-thirty in the morning. She had spent much of the drive from Philadelphia trying to make sense of the last few days, but her higher reasoning functions had stalled from lack of sleep and food. For most of the two-hour trip she kept awake by listening to the grumbling of her empty stomach and the ringing of her cell phone.

Like clockwork, every fifteen minutes Jake called, but she refused to answer. She was too afraid to use the phone while driving for fear of being pulled over by a state trooper. Not mention her fear of Jake at this point. He probably wanted to kill her himself.

Nothing made sense to her. Now that she had time to reflect on her conversation with Borka, she began to doubt whether he'd told her the truth. When had Borka ever prided himself on honesty? He had a reputation for revenge. Forgetting about her wasn't in keeping with the man she knew.

Borka never forgot. And he never forgave. Her journals contained plenty of evidence to support that contention. Marriage or no marriage. Children or no children. A sixty-six-year-old leopard didn't change his spots.

Throughout her journey back to Jersey City, her gaze kept darting to the rearview mirror. A sense of foreboding churned in her stomach like a swarm of trapped moths. She couldn't shake the feeling that someone was following her. And that someone had to be Borka.

Dori circled her block once. She saw neither Jake's car nor the rental from Philadelphia. The dark blue car with the detective was gone. In its place sat a dark green four-by-four with a man seated behind the wheel—probably the next detective shift keeping an eye on Nikki and Joey.

Jake had done that for her. Knowing her background, he'd made certain her brother and sister were safe while she traveled throughout the country, and she'd repaid him with distrust. Dori slipped into the empty parking space in front of the detective and sighed as she pulled up the emergency break.

Jake. She owed him much more than the brief explanation she left him in that letter—so much more, but would he even listen to her at this point? Why should he? She hadn't listened to him. She hadn't trusted him. She hadn't even answered the phone when he called.

She placed Saint Chris back on the dashboard. As she reached for the ignition key, her door swung open, and a large, gloved hand reached in and clamped over her mouth, stifling her scream.

"Payback time, baby doll."

A glint of metal flashed before her eyes. Then everything went black.

THIRTY-FIVE

Jake rounded the corner onto Dori's street in time to see the white Geo pulling out into traffic. He caught up with her on the turnpike but kept a discreet distance, not wanting to panic her. Several blocks from her street he lost her when a garbage truck cut in front of him and kept him from making a traffic light. Still, there was no way Dori had arrived more than a minute or two before him. No way could she have made her way up to the apartment, then come back down to the car. So what was going on, and where the hell was she headed?

Jake stepped on the gas, but before he could catch up with the Geo, a gray Honda turned onto the street, cutting between him and Dori. It then slowed to a crawl.

A block ahead the light turned red, but instead of stopping for it, Dori raced through the intersection, nearly broad siding a panel truck approaching from the left. The truck swerved at the last minute, winding up on the sidewalk within inches of several pedestrians.

Damn her! Something had her scared beyond reason, but if she weren't careful, she'd get herself killed and take a dozen innocent people with her. Jake pounded the steering wheel and leaned on the horn, cursing at the top of his lungs. The driver in the Honda glanced into his rearview mirror and raised his hand, telling Jake with one finger what he thought of his impatient outburst.

A moment later the Geo rounded the next corner on two wheels. Jake watched helplessly, still stuck at the traffic light behind the Honda. "But not for long," he muttered, his eyes darting left and right. No vehicles approached from either direction. He swung his BMW around the Honda and sped through the intersection after Dori, finally catching up to the Geo three blocks later.

That's when his heart leaped into his throat. Dori wasn't behind the wheel of the Geo—not unless she'd grown a foot, gained at least seventy-five pounds, and gotten a buzz cut since last night.

* * *

Dori's head throbbed. She couldn't move. Her body was folded in on itself, her arms pinned under her. The room swayed beneath her as if she were on a boat in a violent storm, but she heard no waves, only the muffled sounds of a man ranting about getting fired from his job.

She forced her eyes open, but everything remained dark. And stifling. Something heavy covered her head. It weighed down her upper body and tangled around her legs, trapping her. Blocking all light and air. Suffocating her.

She tried to fill her lungs. Panic and the covering squeezed her throat closed. Bile churned in her stomach. She lurched first one way then the next, her feet, the only part of her body free of the snare. She struggled to ease her arm from under her torso and push herself to a sitting position, but the room and her head both kept spinning.

"Oh no you don't!"

Someone knocked her back down, punching repeatedly at her head and shoulders. The room spun. Tires squealed, and she remembered she was in a car, not a room or a boat. Mrs. Menotti's car. Her body reeled to one side. The man cursed. Then she pitched back. He stopped beating her. His hand clamped down over her head, forcing the covering tight against her mouth and nose.

"You're not escaping this time. I've got you, and you're going to pay for getting me fired, you little bitch."

The man grew more agitated, raising his voice to a fevered pitch that even the tarp failed to muffle. "You think you can control people's lives. All of you big shots with your money and power. Well, I've had enough." He emphasized his words with another blow to her head.

Dori gasped from the sharp pain.

"I didn't mess with that elevator," he continued. "No matter what you and Reichman think, but he wouldn't listen to me. Said it didn't matter. Said his hands were tied. Said you wanted me fired, so he had to fire me. Like you're some goddamn Queen of Hearts sitting up on your throne saying, 'Off with his head.' Like in that cartoon my kid watches all the time. Well, no more. No one messes with me and gets away with it. I'm going to hurt you for what you did to me. You're going to be sorry you ever messed with Moe Rossnauer.

"I ain't got nothing more to lose. Because of you my wife up and left me and took my kid. Said she'd had it with me not being able to keep a job. Said I was nothing but a drunken loser. But it wasn't my fault. Not this time." He pummeled her head with his fist. "Not this fucking time, damn it!"

Dori's lungs burned. She felt herself slipping into a dark void and fought to keep the blackness from overwhelming her, but the pain sucked her deeper into its depths. She found it hard to concentrate on the man's words. Nothing he said made sense. She hadn't gotten anyone fired.

"No," she tried to tell him, but the word died in her throat. She clawed at the tarp, struggling to shield herself from his blows. He responded by forcing her head deeper into the seat, his hand clamped over her nose and mouth.

His words faded, blocked by a hollow roaring in her ears. Life drained from her body. With her last vestige of consciousness, she saw her brother and sister and Jake. Too late she realized how much her mistrust had cost her. Cost all of them.

I don't want to die! As the world slipped away from her, she mustered on last ounce of strength and fought back.

* * *

The man driving the Geo bobbed his head in a frenzy of animation, apparently singing along to something on the radio. With one arm he maneuvered the steering wheel. The other repeatedly waved around like a frenetic conductor pounding out a rhythm on the passenger seat. As he sped down the thoroughfare, his driving grew more erratic. After nearly sideswiping a car, he came to his senses and ceased his arm gestures, but once he regained control of the car, he returned to his thumping.

The man gave no indication that he suspected he was being followed. Jake hadn't noticed him glance into his rearview mirror once. The Geo was no match for Jake's imported sports car. As soon as the road widened into four lanes, he pulled alongside the car and hazarded a quick glance over at the passenger window.

Then his heart stopped.

A large canvas tarp covered something lying across the passenger seat—something that undulated slightly under the thick covering. The man held it firmly in place with his right hand, leaning his weight into it and shouting with such rage that his face had gone purple.

A face that Jake recognized.

A face that recognized Jake.

The man released his hold on the tarp and grabbed for something lying between his legs.

Jake saw the unmistakable outline of the gun. As the man raised his arm to fire at him, the tarp moved. Dori's legs shot up and to the left, kicking wildly. She made contact with first the gun, then the steering wheel.

The man fought back, swinging viciously with both hands. The Geo sped out of control. Jake floored his gas pedal, pulling out ahead of the Geo, then cut the wheels, swerving in front of the runaway auto.

* * *

The impact threw Dori to the floor, loosening the tarp from around her head and creating a pocket of air. She gulped hungrily, filling her lungs with life. From under the tarp, she heard shouting and screaming, sirens, shrieking tires. Something that felt and sounded like hailstones pelted the canvas.

A woman screamed, "He's got a gun!"

Then everything grew eerily silent.

Dori found a corner of the canvas and pulled, trying to free her head.

"Dori! Don't move!"

She froze. "Jake?"

"Stay perfectly still. He's pointing a gun at you."

"No. Let her see the face of the man she destroyed. I want my face to be the last thing she sees before I send her to hell."

Dori recognized the voice as that of the man who had captured her. Moe something. He had claimed she got him fired. "Please," she said. "I didn't get you fired. Tell him, Jake."

Moe snickered. "Sure. You'll say anything now. Well, it won't work, bitch. It's too late. Take off the tarp."

"Don't do it, Dori."

"Jake?" She wished she could see where he was, what he was doing.

"Remember the bus," he said. "Trust me."

The bus. The two thugs. Jake's gun. *I shoot to kill, and I never miss.* Dori held her breath, not moving a muscle.

"I said take it off!"

She felt Moe grab for the tarp and yank at it. Dori held fast. A shot exploded near her head. A heavy weight collapsed on top of her, and once again she fought for air.

"It's all right, sweetheart. Stay put. I'll have you out of there in a minute."

The weight lifted from her body. A moment later, Jake removed the tarp and pulled her from the car. He leaned up against the side of what was left of Mrs. Menotti's Geo and cradled her in his arms. She clung to him, burying herself in his chest.

Neither one of them spoke for the longest time. And then they both spoke at once—only three words, but three words that said everything.

"I love you."

THIRTY-SIX

Trust me. Jake's words echoed inside Dori. For years she trusted no one. Before she'd grown to adulthood, she shouldered the burdens of an adult, trusting in no one to help her, Joey, and Nikki. She broke the law to do right by her brother and sister. To protect them. To protect herself. The time had come to own up to her mistakes and accept responsibility for her actions.

She sat at a long polished cherry conference table, her hands firmly clasped in front of her, her eyes staring blankly at the closed door at the opposite end of the mahogany paneled room. Jake sat beside her. Niles paced back and forth in front of the door. He had nearly as much at stake in the outcome of the meeting in the next room as Dori.

Dori sucked in a ragged breath. The air smelled musty and slightly mildewed from the shelves of law and reference books lining the walls. Jake reached over from the seat beside her and covered her hands with both of his. But he held so much more. Her heart. Her fate. *Trust me.* She had placed her destiny and Nikki's and Joey's in Jake's hands. Because she loved him, and she had learned that there can be no love without trust.

And now she waited as a large Regulator clock mounted on the far wall ticked off the minutes, a countdown to her fate. In the next room a group of men she barely knew were deciding her future. She had placed her trust in Jake, and he in turn had placed it in the hands of those men—his connections, Niles's attorneys—men who now pleaded her case before a federal prosecutor.

She had done all she could to help her own cause. The attorneys had assured her it was enough. The Feds wanted Borka, not her. She had supplied them with enough evidence to get him locked away for the rest of his life. Now it was up to the attorneys to convince the prosecutor it was enough to keep Dori out of jail.

She had other allies, as well. Jake had been wrong about Sammy. Neither he nor his partner and great-uncle, Victor Puchenko, held Borka in high esteem. For years Puchenko had suspected foul play in the death of his niece, Borka's first wife. Fear and intimidation had kept him silent. No longer.

After Dori confessed to Sammy, he and Victor had come to her defense by producing Victor's evidence against Borka. Dori had every right to fear for her life when she fled Philadelphia. The suspicious death of the first Mrs. Boris Borka proved as much.

Borka deserved his fate, but when Dori closed her eyes, she saw pregnant Natasha and her brood of little ones, and the vision consumed her with guilt. In bringing down Borka, Dori added to his list of innocent victims. "What will happen to Natasha and her children?"

Niles ceased his pacing. "Those men in there are trying to keep you out of jail, and you're worried about that degenerate bastard's wife and kids?"

Dori turned to Jake. "They don't deserve to suffer because of Borka. Natasha's my age—maybe even younger. I'm sure she was forced into marrying him. She barely speaks English, and she's got four kids already with another on the way. How will she support them?"

Jake squeezed her hand, then glanced up at Niles. For several long seconds the two men stared expressionless at each other until Niles finally threw his hands up in the air and sighed. "All right. I'll make sure they don't wind up out on the street, but tell me something, Dori."

She held her breath. "What?"

"Do you *ever* think of yourself?"

Dori smiled at her boss. For all his bluster, the grizzly was really a teddy bear in disguise. "I suppose not."

"Hmmph!" Niles crossed his arms over his chest and shifted his attention to Jake. "And you thought she was another Gwynne."

Before Dori could ask who Gwynne was, the door leading to the prosecutor's office opened. She clutched Jake's hand. Her pounding heart quickened its pace, overtaking the ticking clock. She forced herself to look up as the six men entered the room.

She locked gazes with the lead attorney. Time froze. Then he smiled. "The prosecutor has agreed not to press charges against you."

Niles bombarded the lawyers with questions, but all Dori heard was a background din. Without knowing how it happened, she found herself in Jake's arms, his lips capturing hers. Tears streamed down her cheeks.

"It's over," he said, breaking the kiss and brushing away the moisture. "No more tears."

"No more tears," she agreed, fighting back a fresh onslaught.

Niles came up behind her and clasped his arms around both of them. "Well, all's well that ends well. Let's go celebrate."

"Who's Gwynne?" asked Dori as Niles led them from the room.

Niles's expression grew smug. "Let's just say I always knew Jake needed an emerald-eyed strawberry blonde in his life. I just had to find him the right one."

Jake stopped dead in his tracks. "Are you saying what I think you're saying, old buddy?"

A sheepish expression covered Niles's face. "Someone had to keep you from fading into oblivion. You were wallowing in self-pity. When I saw Dori—"

"You set me up!" cried Jake, finishing his sentence. "You set the whole goddamn thing up, didn't you, Niles?"

"It worked, didn't it?"

Jake shook his head, but he couldn't help laughing. "Niles, you are the biggest manipulator I've ever met." He draped his arm around Dori's shoulders and drew her close against his body. "And you were right. Not all green-eyed, redheads are cut from the same cloth. Dori is certainly no Gwynne."

Dori stepped out of Jake's embrace and turned to face him and Niles. "There's something you should know." She dipped her head into her hands and popped out her contact lenses. Raising her head, she revealed the crystal blue eyes she'd hidden from the world for the past six years. "The strawberry blonde isn't natural, either."

Jake roared with laughter. "There goes your theory, Niles. Oh, and by the way," continued Jake. "You owe me a week in St. Thomas."

Niles winked at Dori. "Consider it your wedding present."

ABOUT THE AUTHOR

USA Today and Amazon bestselling and award-winning author Lois Winston writes mystery, romance, romantic suspense, chick lit, women's fiction, children's chapter books, and nonfiction. *Kirkus Reviews* dubbed her critically acclaimed Anastasia Pollack Crafting Mystery series, "North Jersey's more mature answer to Stephanie Plum." In addition, Lois is an award-winning craft and needlework designer who often draws much of her source material for both her characters and plots from her experiences in the crafts industry.

Connect with Lois at her website, www.loiswinston.com, where you can learn more about her and her books, sign up for her newsletter, and find links to follow her on social media.